Least We Forget

ISBN: 978-1-63950-100-7   [Paperback Edition]
         978-1-63950-101-4   [eBook Edition]

Printed and bound in The United States of America.

Writers Apex

Gateway Towards Success

1309 Coffeen Avenue
STE 1200, Sheridan,
Wyoming, 82801 USA
+13179780258
www.writersapex.com

LEAST WE FORGET

*High School Coaching Legends
from the Panhandle/Plains Region*

R O N   M A Y B E R R Y

Note:

WHEN I STARTED THIS BOOK, my intention was to bring notice to the high school coaches that made a difference with young athletes in high schools from the Texas Panhandle/Plains region. My thinking was to bring attention to high school coaches that stayed the course [Didn't Jump ship and start coaching on the college level], made a huge difference in the sport they were coaching, and made an impact on student athletes.

However, when I got into the writing part and the research part, I understood that there are legends at every school that exists in the Panhandle/Plains region. Soon, I realized that my desire to write this book was over my head because I didn't want to leave anyone out nor did I want to leave any sport out. I quit twice during the writing of this book because for me it was an impossible task. Also, during that time period my wife became serious ill and after several months she passed away.

Finally, I got enough courage to continue and started making decisions about which direction to go and so forth. One of the changes I made after stating over was to research each sport in relationship to each UIL state championships. After doing just that, I decided to provide the information to you only to make a positive statement for the Panhandle/Plains coaches. Also, during this period, I had two mini strokes leaving me void of memory recall. After three long years, this book is finished but I have made many mistakes. To put it another way, I'm a used to be person. I used to be able to handle many tasks with a steady hand. I am no longer that person but wanted to finish what I started. After all, is that not what we teach and coach?

So, what I am saying is in every school a coach makes a difference in students and because of that, every coach/school is a legend to someone. That is why coaches need to understand their responsibility that is involved in coaching. You do make a difference in all respects to all kinds of students, not just athletes. Because I feel so much passion for coaching, a passion that has paved the way for my coaching career, totally God given I continued this book until I couldn't do much more but finish what I started.

I hope you enjoy this information as much as I enjoyed researching it. Choices were made by the available information that I could obtain. The information came from 80 different resources listed at the back of this book.

Thanks for obtaining this book.

Ron Mayberry
220 E. Llano Ave
Lubbock, Texas 79407

Introduction

LEAST WE FORGET – HIGH SCHOOL COACHING LEGENDS OF TEXAS UIL HIGH SCHOOLS IN THE PANHANDLE/PLAINS REGION

THE MAJOR PURPOSE OF THIS book is to give recognition to the legendary high school coaches that made a huge difference in the sport they were coaching from the Texas Panhandle/Plains region.

This book is dedicated to those coaches that have coached in the public schools coaching a UIL sport, then somewhere along your lifelong path of growth, some coach made a difference in your life. That is what coaching is about and that is why there are so many legends in the coaching world. It is impossible to mention all the legends in the coaching world, so we must limit some of the good ones because they weren't nominated by their peers. Winning state championships, district championships or creating a winning attitude at certain schools is what makes legends. That is why there are so many legends in coaching particularly to the normal person that is not associated within the school itself. The opinion of the people involved within the arena are the ones that know the real legends of any sport and that is why it was decided that they had to be nominated by their peers. For sure a legend is one that makes a difference in all respects to the school and the community they represent. Most important, they had to be a legend that represented the Panhandle/Plains region.

Everyone has a definition of a legend, most are close to the same, but all see it a little different. To get names for this book I sent out e-mails to every AD in the Panhandle/Plains region. I wanted nominations from high school coaches in every sport and I asked AD's to pass the information to their coaches. Of course, the objective was to gather information that I could use in this book. However, my response was not very good, so I did the same with e-mails to every coach in the Panhandle/Plains region, concentrating on the schools that were classified 3A-6A. This time, the response was good, so that gave me a start.

Next, I contacted several coaching legends on my own in every sport and ask them to help me nominate coaches that they thought were high school coaching legends of the past.

Last, I went to the record books and studied the winning records of coaches in all sports and studied the Hall of Fame coaches in the Panhandle/Plains region. Then I studied the State Champions in each sport and reported those results in this book to illustrate which schools and towns were involved with state championship attitudes.

The rules to be nominated were:

1. Had to be a high coach that made a difference in schools that were in the Panhandle/Plains region, a coach that stayed in high school and by doing so, made a huge difference in athletes over a long period of time.
2. Had to be a high school coach, not a college coach. Often, the high school coach takes a college/university coaching position and that coach becomes a legend at the university they are coaching. If the college coach received recognition and rewards as a college coach, then we would mention the name but would concentrate on other high school coaches.
3. Each coach had to be nominated by someone that was a coach in the Panhandle/Plains region.
4. Had to be a coach that is not active in coaching and removed from the arena of coaching for at least one year.
5. There was no limit on the number of coaches you could nominate and you could nominate any coach in any sport.

Panhandle Plains

A small copy of a map of the Texas Panhandle/Plains Region.

Sport fans often identify schools or cities with high school sports. The following are reasons that influence that mind set in the Panhandle/Plains region.

Football	Wins	Boys Basketball		Girls Basketball		Baseball	
Amarillo	783	Dimmitt	17/4	Canyon	26/18	L. Monterey	14/4
Abilene	694	Nazareth	16/6	Nazareth	25/24	A. Wylie	9/2
Albany	692	Morton	13/6	Sudan	11/6	Snyder	8/2
Sweetwater	686	Pampa	12/5	A Wylie	11/5	Abilene	4/2
Wichita Falls	668	Lamesa	11/3	Claude	10/5		
Stamford	668	Seminole	10/2	Plainview	8/4		
Littlefield	654		^			^	
Childress	650	[# of state tournament appearances]		[# of state tournament championships]			

Softball		Boys Cross Country		Boys Cross Country		Volleyball	
				[Number of Texas State Champions]			
Coahoma	11/1	Sundown	10	Canyon	8	Windthorst	22/14
				Sundown	5	Amarillo	17/10
				Nazareth	5	Plains	15/9
				Gruver	5	Bronte	14/6

Boys Track Field		Girls Track Field		Boys Golf		Girls Golf	
		[Number of Texas State Champions]					
Munday	7	Canyon	5	Robert Lee	7	Andrews	14
Andrews	6	Munday	4	Andrews	6	Booker	12
Abilene	6			Baird	5	Baird	11
Rule	5					Snyder	5
L. Estacado	4					Memphis	5

Team Tennis		Boys Wrestling		Girls Wrestling		Girls Soccer	
Wichita Falls	21/5	Canyon Randall	7/2	A. Caprock	15/13	Wichita Rider	7/2
A. Cooper	8/3			A. Palo Duro	4/1		
A. Wylie	5/3			A. Tascosa	3/1		
L. Coronado	4/1						

(# of state tournament appearances] / [# of state championships]

Swimming/Diving [No state champs]

Without information concerning each legendary coach/school this book couldn't be produced. **The resources** that I used in my research **are listed at the end of this book as required**. The research was awesome and required many hours of re-writing. The information that I am transferring to you is my responsibly and it is being used for information only. One of my objectives was to educate the sports fan and coaches in the Panhandle/Plains region about how this region compares to other Texas regions in all UIL sports. Also, I wanted to give some positive recognition to the coaches that stayed in the high school coaching circles, made a huge difference in the schools and the community. If mistakes are made, it is not the fault of my resource but because of my lack of ability to read and write at the same time.

Table of Contents

Football

1920-2017 - **96 YEARS OF high school football.** Coaching legends are not born but developed by their environment that brings out the talent they have. True, some are a natural, but all learn from each other. All coaches benefit when coaching at a school with a winning tradition and talented athletes. The question is which came first, the tradition, the athletes or the coach? Either way, legends are developed within this type of atmosphere.

This book is about the High School coaching legends of the past in the Panhandle/Plains region and the first section is about the eleven-man high school football legends in that region. **Least We Forget – High School Coaching Legends of the Panhandle/Plains Region** is about remembering all the good that comes from each legend in their own environment. No one should be left out and that is the one of the purposes of this book because being a high school football coaching legend is a special title. That title is an awesome name and brings the thinking that a high school legend is one that made a huge difference in the lives of everyone on all levels. One thing is for sure the proof is usually in the pudding.

The following are cities and schools, not coaches that we all recognized as winners in football in the Texas Panhandle/Plains region. If you have ever been involved with a football state championship city or school, you will never forget that experience. The experience is awesome for everyone involved and for sure those that win the championship. You witness cities that stop everything supporting their team, sometimes leaving only a handful of people left in the city. You will experience long

1

lines to get tickets, long lines of cars and buses with the hopes of a state championship. Pep rallies are spontaneous from the young to the old and it never gets old. Buses get police escorts out of town and coming back into town from the arena of the battle. The local coffee shops everywhere are full of talk about the team along with every other shop where people gather to shop. Everyone attends including all children because they want their children to remember this huge event for our town, our city, our school and our family. If you are lucky enough to be having dinner at a café when the team drops by to eat a meal, you witness what the team means to the everyone because of the huge long-lasting ovation, standing room only event. The truth of the matter it is an awesome experience.

All teams in Texas that play high school football witness this to some extent but those that make the runs into the playoffs are the real winners of this experience. Not everyone makes it to the final championship because Texas is very competitive, and most teams are good. Texas high school football coaches have been above the norm for many years in my opinion. I personally learned more about coaching from football coaches than anyone. I thought that was ironic since my special coaching field was basketball. Sometimes advancing in the playoffs in high school football luck plays a role in the outcome but most of the time it is the talent of the young athletes and the preparation of the coach that decides the outcome. This is usually where legends are born but not always because there are always coaches that do an awesome job of coaching that never gets the opportunity to play for the state championship.

For Image
???

High School football teams located in the Panhandle/Plains region that played for the State Football Championship starting in the decade of 1920 to the decade of the 2010.

THE FIRST TWENTY YEARS 1922-1942.

Below are the results of appearances in the State Championship games of the UIL Format [Name of the School-W-champs-R-Runner up-the year they participated]

If mistakes are made, I am the one that made them. Most of this Information came from the UIL website and Dave Campbell football magazine.

Abilene- R-22-23, Abilene-W-23-24, Abilene-W-28-29, Abilene-W-31-32
Amarillo-R-30-31, Amarillo-W-34-35, Amarillo-W-35-36, Amarillo-W36-37,
Amarillo-W-40-41 Lubbock-R-38-39, Lubbock-W-39-40

The dominate football teams in the first twenty years of the UIL was Amarillo with 4 state championships and one runner up. Abilene was second with 3 state championships and one runner up. Lubbock was third with one state championship and one runner up.

THE SECOND TWENTY YEARS 1943-1963

Abilene Woodson-R-53-54, Abilene-W-54-55, Abilene-W-55-56,
Abilene-W-56-57 Albany-R-54-55, Albany-W-60-61, Albany-W-61-62
Amarillo-R-48-49, Amarillo Carver-W-52-53 Ballinger-R-53-54
Big Spring-R-53-54 Borger-R-62-63 Denver City-W-60-61
Dumas-W-61-62, Dumas-W-62-63
Kermitt-W-50-51 Littlefield-W-49-50
Lubbock-W-51-52, Lubbock, W-53-53, Lubbock Dunbar-R-62-63
Monahans-W-48-49
Phillips-W-54-55 San Angelo-W-43-44
San Angelo Blackshear-W-50-51
Stamford-W-55-56, Stamford-W-56-57, Stamford-W-58-59,
Stamford-W-59-60 Stinnett-R-55-56
Sundown-R-59-60 Sweetwater-R-57-58 Rotan-W-62-63
Vernon Washington-R-57-58 White Deer-W-58-59
Wink-W-52-53

The dominate football teams in the second twenty years of the UIL was Stamford with 4 state championships. Abilene was second with 3 state championships and Albany was third with two state championships and one runner up. Dumas won 2 state championships and Lubbock High won 2 state championships.

THE THIRD TWENTY YEARS -1964-1984

Abilene Cooper-R-67-68
Childress-R-75-76, Childress-R-76-77
Clarendon-R-72-73
Cotton Center-R-78-79, Cotton Center-R-79-80 Eastland-W-82-83
Follett-R-75-76 Groom-R-75-76 Petersburg-W-63-64 Littlefield-R-82-83
Lubbock Dunbar-W-1963-64, Lubbock Estacado-W-68-69, Lubbock
Estacado-R-83-84 Mullin-R-81-82, Mullin-R-82-83
Wheeler-W-77-78, Wheeler-R-78-79, Wheeler-W-79-80
Whitharral-W-81-82
White Deer-R-65-66
Wylie-W-77-78, Wylie-R-78-79
Rankin-R-80-81 Roscoe-R-82-83
San Angelo Central-W-66-67 Seagraves-R-77-78
Vega-R-73-74

Wheeler was the dominate football team in the third twenty years of the UIL with two state championships and one runner- up championship. Estacado and Wylie tied with one state championship and one runner up. Next was Childress, Cotton Center, Mullin all tied with two runner up trophies.

THE FOURTH TWENTY YEARS – 1985 – 2005

Abilene Cooper-R-96-97 Albany-R-91-92
Amherst-W-94-95, Amherst-W-95-96 Borden County-W-97-98
Cisco-R-2002-03
Hereford-R-99-2000 Groom-R-99-2000
Iraan-W-96-97
Jayton-W-84-85, Jayton-W-85-86 Memphis-W-91-92
Munday-W-84-85, Munday-R-90-91 Panhandle-R-84-85
Roscoe Collegiate-R-95-96 Sanderson-R-2002-03 Sweetwater-W-85-86
Sudan-R-89-90, Sudan-R-92-93, Sudan-W-93-94
Stratford-W-2000-01, Stratford-R-2004-05 Turkey Valley-R-2004-05
Wellman-R-87-88 Wheeler-W-87-88
Whitharral-R-96-97, Whitharral-W-2001-02 White Deer-W-88-89
Wylie-R-2000-01, Wylie-W-2004-05
Vernon-R-89-90, Vernon-W-90-91

Sudan won two state championships and one runner up to finish first in this era. Amherst and Jayton each won two state championships to finished second. Stratford, Munday, Whitharral, Wylie, and Vernon were close with one state championship and one runner up trophy.

RESULTS UP TO 2018-19

Abilene-W-09-2010
Albany-R-09-2010, Albany-R-2015-16 Big Sandy-R-2005-06
Bushland-R-09-2010
Borden County-W-08-09, Borden County-R-09-2010, Borden
County-R-2011-12, Borden County-W-2016- 17, Borden County-W-2018
Canadian-W-2007-08, Canadian-W-08-09, Canadian-W-2014-15,
Canadian-W-2015-16, Canadian-R-2019 Cisco-R-2006-07, Cisco-R-08-09,
Cisco-R-2011-12, Cisco-R-2013-14
Crowell-W-2013-14, Crowell-W-2014-15, Crowell-R-2015-16 Gruver-R-2019
Follett-R-08-09, R-2019
Garden City-W-09-2010, Garden City-W-2010-11 Graham-R-09-2010

Grandfalls-Royalty-W-2013-14 Groom-R-2014-15
Idalou-W-2010-11 Iraan-R-2016-17
Jayton-R-2006-07 Littlefield-R-2006-07 Seymour-R-2007-08
Stamford-R-2011-12, Stamford-W-2012-13, Stamford-W-2013-14
Sweetwater-R-2016-17
McCamey-R-2006-07
McLean-W-2019
Motley County-W-2007-08, Motley County-R-2011-12 Muleshoe-W-2008-09
Munday-R-2007-08, Munday-R-2011-12, Munday-W-2012-13 New
Deal-R-2019
Stratford-W-2005-06, Stratford-W-2008-09 Turkey Valley-R-2005-06
Wall-R-2013-14
Wellington-W-2013-14
Wylie-R-2009-2010, Wylie-R-2016-17
Vernon Northside-W-2006-07

Canadian won 4 state championships and one runner up to take the top honors in this era but very close behind was Borden County with 3 state championships and 2 runner up trophies. Cisco with 4 runner up championships was next. Not to be outdone, Stamford and Crowell had 2 state championships and 1 runner up. Close behind were Munday with 1 state championship and 2 runner-ups. Keeping their great football traditions, Stratford had 1 championship and 1 runner up along with Wylie and Albany with 2 runner ups. Not to forget that two cities started a strong football tradition, Garden City won 2 state championships and Motley County won 1 and a runner up championship.

Follett had two runner up trophies in this era.

Results of schools that played for the state championship in the Texas Panhandle/Plains region that covers 97 years.

It's one thing to get to the top but totally a different thing to stay at the top. Every coach that has experienced this can relate to that statement. When you have a team that competes on a yearly basis then you have a football program developed by a legend somewhere and maintained by everyone. It takes a family to keep a tradition at the top and in Texas we have several of those cities, schools and followers. The following schools have been at the top for a long time. Here is some of their history compared to others in the last 97 years.

Abilene played for the state championship 8 times winning 7 championships
Stamford played for the state championship 7 times winning 6 championships
Amarillo played for the state championship 6 times winning 4 championships
Albany played for the state championship 6 times winning 2 championships
Wylie played for the state championships 6 times winning 2 championships
Canadian played for the state championship 5 time winning 4 championships
Lubbock played for the state championship 4 times winning 3 championships
Stratford played for the state championship 4 times winning 3 championships
Wheeler played for the state championship 4 times winning 3 championships
Borden County played for the state championship 5 times winning 3 championships
Cisco played for the state championship 4 times and was runner up 4 times
Crowell played for the state championship 3 times winning 2 championships
Sudan played for the state championship 3 times winning 1 championship
Munday played for the state championship 3 times winning 1 championship

To put **winning in perspective let's look at how difficult it is to make the state championship game in the two highest classifications** 4AAAA and 5AAAAA from the Panhandle/Plains region. That includes the latest edition of the UIL to expand the classification system to 6AAAAAA which was needed in my opinion. So, with that change the two highest classifications would be 6AAAAAA and 5AAAAA. Regardless since 1970, only two schools from the highest classifications in Texas have played for the State Championship. **Abilene** won the championship in 2009-10 and **Abilene Cooper** finished as runner up in 1996-97. However, **Sweetwater** won the State Championship in 1985-86 in the second highest classification then **Hereford** was runner up 1999-2000, along with **Lubbock Estacado** in 1983-84. So, to put that in a summary, in the highest classification coaching football in the Texas Panhandle/Plains region only two schools have played for the state championship in the last 47 years. In the second highest classification, only three schools have played for the state championship in the Texas Panhandle/Plains region.

However, in the last 47 years, the three lower classifications in the Texas UIL have played for 109 state championships. Most all high school football coaches understand this concept because there is a huge difference coaching a school that has 1500 student enrollment and a school that has 3500 enrollments. Not only that, there is a huge difference coaching a team from large cities such as Houston, Dallas, San Antonio, Ft Worth, and El Paso. That is where jobs are located and that is where people find work and stay. Also working against the Panhandle, Plains area is the weather and some people are just not suited to live in that area.

This doesn't mean that the large schools in the Panhandle/Plains region didn't have play-off teams, but it does illustrate how hard it was to make it to the final game for the State Championship. But the Panhandle/Plains region can be proud of the fact that they don't have to make any excuses for wins in a season nor play-off performances.

INDIVIDUAL COACHES THAT COACHED IN THE PANHANDLE/ PLAINS REGION THAT HAD TREMENDOUS WINNING SUCCESS

Charlie Johnston	Childress	35 years	315 wins	94 losses
Denny Faith *	Albany	31 years	290 wins	95 losses
Hugh Sandifier *	Abilene Wylie	32 years	283 wins	109 losses
Larry Dippel	Amarillo	35 years	253 wins	134 losses
Bobby Davis	Wolfforth Frenship	38 years	247 wins	163 losses
H. Elmer [Pete] Shotwell	Abilene	33 years	243 wins	83 losses
Mel Maxfield *	Amarillo	31 years	239wins	113 losses
Louis Kelley	Lubbock Estacado	31 years	232 wins	104 losses
A.D. Shaver	Seagraves	35 years	209 wins	152 losses
Tom Ritchey	Sweetwater	25 years	207 wins	67 losses
L.G. Wilson	Floydada	30 years	207 wins	102 losses
Leo D. Brittain	Vernon	28 years	207 wins	107 losses
Glenn [Red] Frazier	Andrews	32 years	206 wins	115 losses
Harold C. [Chesty] Walker	Phillips	23 years	197 wins	41 losses
Butch Henderson *	Lubbock Coronado	32 years	196 wins	153 losses
Joe Bob Tyler	Wichita Falls	36 years	193 wins	158 losses
David Bourquin	Mineral Wells	31 years	189 wins	141 losses
Kenny Davidson*	Graham	28 years	187 wins	117 losses
Johnny Taylor	Idalou	22 years	188 wins	36 losses
Steve Warren	Abilene	23 years	186 wins	88 losses
David Wood*	Muleshoe	31 years	185 wins	78 losses
Jimmie Keeling	San Angelo Central	30 years	183 wins	124 losses
Brent West*	Cisco	17 years	183 wins	39 losses
Wade Williams*	Wellington	22 years	183 wins	79 losses

Active coaches*

SCHOOLS WITH THE MOST WINS LOCATED IN THE PANHANDLE/ PLAINS REGION

SCHOOLS	WINS	RANK IN THE STATE OF TEXAS
Amarillo High School	783	2
Abilene High School	694	14
Albany High School	692	15
Sweetwater High School	686	16
Stamford High School	668	21

Wichita Falls	668	21
Littlefield High School	654	24
Childress	650	26
Breckenridge	646	28
Vernon High School	641	29
Ballinger High School	632	36
San Angelo Central	616	42
Canadian	600	54
Graham	590	63
Iraan	589	65
Wellington	582	74
Cisco	576	83
Perryton	570	90
Floydada	567	94
Roscoe	566	95

SCHOOLS WITH THE MOST PLAY-OFF SEASONS IN THE PANHANDLE/ PLAINS REGION

Amarillo High School	57
Abilene	50
Breckenridge	47
Albany	45
Littlefield	43
Wichita Falls	43
Wink	41
Childress	41
Seagraves	40
Ballinger	40
Denver City	39
Stamford	39
Iraan	39
Wheeler	39
Idalou	38
Perryton	38

To name a few football coaches that are legends in the high school coaching world is impossible even if the region is isolated to the

Panhandle/Plains region. Look at the numbers above and you have many legends of high school football and to name just a couple would be very difficult. Add the many coaches that have done an outstanding job of coaching football in this region that are not on the list above and it is totally impossible to name just a few. I worked for Larry Wartes, Larry Dippel, Mark Cotton, Joey Fernandez, John Wilkens, Dee Windsor, Mal Fowler, and Steve Taylor and I can honestly say I was the lucky one to even be associated with those guys. They were outstanding and my coaching career was blessed because of their guidance and wisdom. Also, I personally knew Brian Huseman, Greg Sherwood, Leo Brittain, Bobby Davis and Butch Henderson and my association with those outstanding football coaches was excellent. I have worked with other coaches that were associated with Denny Faith, Mel Maxfield, Louis Kelley, A.D. Shaver, Tom Ritchey, L.G. Wilson, Johnny Taylor, Harold C. [Chesty Walker], Pete Shotwell, and David Wood. Everything I heard about those coaches was outstanding.

So, for us to name the Football Legends of the Panhandle/Plains region we all find it impossible to just name one or two. Simply put, there are too many great coaches to list or mention. So, we decided to name the most outstanding legends in certain categories. The categories are:

1. The football coach with the most wins [small school]
2. The football coach with the most wins [large school]
3. The football coach/coaches that sustained a successful football program year after year for the longest period. [Small School and Large School]
4. The fourth category is the football coach that had an outstanding football career and an outstanding Athletic Directors career.
5. Others [Football coaches that are legends – must have been nominated by someone]
6. A legendary athletic program that should never be forgotten but who remembers?
7. A legendary assistant coach whom everyone respected

THE FIRST CATEGORY IS THE COACH WITH THE MOST WINS [SMALL SCHOOL]
CHARLIE JOHNSTON-CHILDRESS HIGH SCHOOL

Charlie Johnston clearly has more wins as a football coach than any other football coach in the Panhandle/Plains region. He was in the coaching business for 35 years gathering 315 wins and 94 losses. That is a 77% winning tradition for 35 years which is awesome. 34 of those years was at Childress and at one time in the decade of the 1970's he compiled a won lost record of 113-17-3 [86.9 %] Not only that Childress advanced to the state finals or semifinals five consecutive seasons [1975-79]. He still holds the state record for most wins at one school.

Charlie grew up in Paducah, Texas, played high school football, basketball and baseball. He was an outstanding quarterback at Paducah. He was coached by two former Abilene coaches, Raymond Troutman and John Higdon along with Coleman Nichols of Baird. Charlie continued his athletic career at Southeastern Oklahoma State where he played football, basketball and baseball. He credits Ken West and his wife Carol instrumental in getting him a partial scholarship to Southwestern Oklahoma State University. Charlie said that the experienced he had at Southeastern Oklahoma gave him the foundation for coaching. He played football for Melvin Brown and Bob Thomas. His basketball and baseball coach were Bloomer Sullivan. Charlie's comment about playing football at Southeastern Oklahoma was "He always admired his coaches at Southeastern." They somehow got the job done with one assistant coach. The players had to do a lot of drills on their own. He continued "I wasn't a great athlete by any stretch of the imagination, but they drove me to get the most of my ability." Coach Thomas recalled Johnston as a small quarterback who was a winner. At Southeastern he was a player that all the coaches admired because of his positive attitude about school, winning, coaches and teammates. He was selected All-Conference in 1963.

Coach Johnston married Jeanene Riddrell in 1961. They were married 40 years and she died due to cancer after a long hard battle. He admitted that a little of him died when she passed away. They had two children [Jeana and Boyd] who now live in Amarillo. He has 3 grandchildren to keep him busy. His first coaching position was at Alamogordo, New Mexico from 1964-67 where he was a varsity assistant football coach. In 1967, he moved to Childress because he wanted his children to know their grandparents well. It didn't hurt that it was close to Paducah, his home where he was raised, and his mother lived. His comment about moving to Childress was that God blessed us with a beautiful home and a great church family giving us plenty of opportunities to spend time with family and loved ones. He said that he has always been thankful for his teachers, coaches, and classmates for sowing seeds in his life.

Dave Campbell of Waco, founder of Dave Campbell's Texas Football Magazine made this comment about Charlie. "One thing makes Charlie stand out more than anything else. Usually when you win a lot of game, a lot of people don't like you." He continues, "But that's not the case with Charlie. He did everything with class. He won with a lot of class and it's a credit to him that so many people genuinely like him." Charlie was so respected that the Texas High School Hall of Fame made him it first recipient of the "Tom Landry Award" for coaching excellence in 1991. As stated in an article, Charlie was in true to form because he was more excited about meeting Landry than receiving the award.

Charlie retired from coaching in 2001 as the third–winningest high school football coach in Texas. He is now 8th in Texas and 1st in the Panhandle/Plains region. In 35 years of coaching at Childress, they had 24 district championships, five trips to the state quarterfinals, four semifinals battles and two trips to the state championship game. All this is good, but the winning is not really what separated him from other coaches. Charlie remains and always has been humble to his success and always gives credit to others before himself. It is almost impossible to find someone that is negative about his success which tells you what kind of character he had. When he was selected to the High School Hall of Fame in 2004, Greg Sherwood said, "That is a no brainer". Everyone has tried at one time or another to hire Charlie away from Childress. Celina coach G.A Moore, the state's all-time winningest coach with 426 wins stated, "He is truly one of the legends in coaching, not just in the Panhandle but all over the state. What he has done in a small town like Childress is truly significant because he stayed with it through all the ups and downs you have in a small town. His impact on coaching can't be underestimated. Greg Sherwood, former athletic director for the Lubbock ISD, and former president of the Texas High School Coaches Association who was a very successful high school coach coaching in five different high schools said this about Charlie. "I can't think of a single negative thing to say about Charlie". "He was such a positive individual and a straight-shooter". Another comment that stuck with this author is "He is just a great example for coaches." When Charlie went to Childress, they had a football record of 4-33 in a four-year period. In his first year as a head football coach his team went 0-10, but then ended up being the all- time winningest coaches in history. But I don't think his won-loss record compares to what he's done for the coaching profession. He's such a professional. He does things the right way and is a great model for young coaches to follow." Lubbock Coronado High basketball coach Randy Dean, one of four brothers who played cornerback and wingback for Johnston in 1979-80 and was Childress' boys' basketball coach and assistant football coach from 1987-93 made this statement about Charlie. "The first thing you notice about Charlie is that he really cares a lot about the kids and especially in Childress". "He just feels a special feeling for Childress because he loves Childress and the community loves him also". "It really makes for a great fit for him". Former Texas Longhorn head coach Mack Brown said this of Johnston. "When I was just starting out as a young coach in the early 1970's, I learned quickly to respect the reputation of High School football in Texas." He continued saying, "When I came to Childress and met Charlie Johnston, I understood why nobody did it better than he did during the decade of the 70's."

A very humble man, he doesn't even like taking about his coaching record. With him it was always about the people, the players and the game of football. Charlie made the game simple, he said, "You see, football is about two things; blocking and tackling. If you can block and tackle, everything else falls into place. Although he made it to the big dance twice in his career, a state championship eluded Johnston, but looking back, it wasn't his biggest regret of his time on the sidelines. His biggest regret was not about wins or losses. I was about not having enough time to get to know each kid personally. He said, "As a head coach, I often had to be the bad guy and I didn't get to spend as much time as I wanted with the kids." Another comment he stated about coaching, he said "When I hired coaches at Childress, I always looked for people who came from small schools. I wanted to make sure my coaches had been exposed to all the sports because you have to be able to work with other programs." When asked which award he was most proud of, he said, "I guess I'm most proud of the Tom Landry Award." It was the first award that came out. "He [Landry] was my hero. I guess it was what he stood for. I got to meet him once and I read everything about him." Another highlight for him was serving as president of the state coaches association in 1985 -1987. When asked what was special since he retired about living in Childress, he said, "Since I retired, I really enjoy looking around and seeing the kids that I used to coach actually running this town and doing it pretty well. I've got former players who are judges and doctors and police. They are doing a pretty good job of keeping this town going." Finally, Johnston said this about being selected to the Texas High School Football Coaches Hall of Fame, "When they put you in something like this, you don't get there by yourself. You always have your family, the guys you coached with and your players that helped you. You never do something like this without a lot of help."

If it is not clear to you now, it should be. Charlie Johnston was selected because of his winning ways but also his character and his leadership in this great profession called coaching.

THE SECOND CATEGORY IS THE COACH WITH THE MOST WINS [LARGE SCHOOL] LARRY DIPPEL [AMARILLO HIGH SCHOOL]

Larry Dippel ended his football career with 253 wins and 143 losses. Larry played his high school football at Stamford. Little did he know that he was being coached by two hall of fame coaches [Gordon Woods/ Larry Wartes], and he would follow them into the coaching Hall of Fame. During Larry Dippel's high school football playing time, Stamford won one state championship then when Larry came back to Stamford to coach as an assistant coach, Stamford won two more state championships under the head coaching of Larry Wartes. When Larry Wartes took the Athletic Director/Head Football coach at Hereford, Larry Dippel followed him as an assistant football coach at Hereford. Larry Dippel first year as the head football coach at Hereford found his team playing for the state championship in the highest classification in Texas called 4AAAA. Then in 1985 Larry Dippel became the Head Football coach at Amarillo High School. Thirty-one years later in 2005 he resigned his position at Amarillo high school. So, in summary, Larry Dippel started his coaching career at Stamford High School and finished at Amarillo High School. Stamford and Amarillo High School combined won 10 of 13 state football championships. Both of those school's football tradition is awesome. Larry played for Gordon Wood and was mentored by Larry Wartes. He received the best football education known to Texas high school football coaches. -off performances.

Larry Dippel was the Head Football coach for 31 years at Amarillo High School which says so much about his character, his ability to communicate and relate to all concerned at Amarillo High School. His 31 years at Amarillo High is the longest stay any coach has ever had at Amarillo High School regardless of the sport they coached at Amarillo High School which happens to be one of the strongest football traditions in Texas, much less the Panhandle/Plains region. David Bornstein, an assistant football coach at Hereford when Dippel took his first head coaching position made this statement about Larry Dippel when he left to pursue his own football career. Any coach that works under Larry Dippel will win if they follow his lead and use him as a mentor. Coach Dippel is one of a kind and only time will let everyone know it. No truer statement has ever been made about Coach Dippel. He is a rock at whatever he does, and coaching football is his thing.

Larry was born in Old Glory, Texas, went to the first grade in Sagerton, and then spent the rest of his young life starting in the second grade in Stamford, Texas. Larry had 3 sisters and 1 brother, Gaynelle Florence of Hawley, Texas, Carolyn Baird of Hamlin, Texas, Charlene Bray of San Antonio, Texas and David Dippel of Stamford, Texas. He married his high school girlfriend Sandras Davis in 1962 and they had two children, Carrie Dippel Brown and Jason Dippel. Carrie lives in Amarillo and she is a curriculum specialist for Amarillo ISD. Jason is coaching football at Reagan High School [San Antonio] as an offensive line coach.

In high school at Stamford, Larry was a guard/tackle on offense and a defensive tackle on defense. He also participated in basketball, track, and baseball. His success wasn't just football although three state football championships [1955/56/58] overshadows most accomplishments but he did participate in the Regional Basketball tournament and the Regional Track competition his senior year.

He attended Hardin Simmons University on a football scholarship. Sammy Baugh was the coach in 1960, Howard McChessney was the coach in 1961-62, and Jack Thomas coached in 1963. Coach Dippel made this statement about his college football playing days. The game is more than winning although winning is very important, but the game is bigger than that. Long term relationships that are developed from competing, winning and losing are a huge factor in the development of a coach. As a coach you must be able to provide the leadership in dealing with winning and losing. Keep the game in prospective to life and the lessons of life we all learn from playing athletics.

Larry was lucky [from a coaching standpoint] in the fact that he graduated at Stamford then finished his coaching career at Amarillo. Coach Dippel started his career in coaching at Corpus Christi Carroll high school working for Cotton Ashton, who was the Head Football Coach. Coach Larry Wartes was responsible for hiring Coach Dippel at Stamford and from that point on, Larry Dippel developed into one of the State of Texas finest football coaches. Coach Dippel gives Larry Wartes, and Cotton Ashton plenty of credit for his beginning and knowledge of football. But he says that Bill Anderson who was an assistant football coach at Stamford influenced him in the coaching world and in his personal life as much as anyone.

My first encounter with Larry Dippel was when I was coaching at Albany and we had a football scrimmage with Stamford. Larry Wartes was the head coach and Larry Dippel was the assistant coach. I was an assistant coach coaching the two techniques on defense and during the scrimmage, our twos were getting beat on a regular basis. Finally, I had enough of those guys getting beat so I stopped the scrimmage and attempted to explain why we were getting beat. I know my voice carried over to the next city but from that point on, our twos didn't get beat again. After the scrimmage, Larry Dippel asked me if I would come over to Stamford once a week and coach their two's. Of course, he and Larry Wartes were smiling at my expense, but it broke the ice and we all became instant friends from that point on.

The one thing that I want to point out to all coaches is when I was exposed to that scrimmage, Albany vs. Stamford I learned something from Larry Dippel that made a huge impact on my coaching career. I was just learning and those coaches at Stamford really impressed me, particularly Larry Dippel. There was something different about them and I couldn't figure it out, but I liked what I witnessed. I didn't know what it was at the time, but I knew I wanted to be like them. Later I learned that what I witness was a coaching staff that understood team and understood what it meant to be a team. They were together and the players were on the same page with the coaches leading to everyone supporting each other. There was no individualism anywhere on that team including the coaching staff. I loved it and I started my coaching career trying to create an atmosphere just like they had.

Spike Dykes, the legend of all legends said this about Coach Dippel after his Midland Lee High School football team played Dippel's Amarillo High School team in the play-offs, "I'll tell you what, Amarillo is stouter than 30 acres of onions." Also, "that Dippel can coach the spots off a leopard." In the 1930's Amarillo High School had a true dynasty under Blaire Cherry, but the Sandie's had not made the play-offs since 1959. Dippel turned around the program, leading the Sandie's to 222 wins and 23 playoff appearances until his retirement in 2005. Throughout his career his teams have won 14 district Championships and 20 play-off appearances. He has been named "District Coach of the Year" 12 times and "Panhandle Coach of the Year 4 times." In 1993, he was selected for the "Tom Landry Award" and the High School Extra, "Coach Who Made a Difference" award. He is a member of the "Texas High School Football Hall of Honor", the "Hardin Simmons Hall of Fame", "the Big Country Athletic Hall of Fame", the "Texas Panhandle Hall of Fame", and is the past president of the Texas High School Coaches Association. In 2000, he was chosen as one of the top 100 sports legends of the 20th century. Then he was the inaugural winner of the national "Power of Influence" award given by the American Football Coaches Association.

Larry Dippel demonstrated great influence on everyone that he was surrounded by during his coaching career. I coached 53 years and I can clearly say that Larry Dippel influenced my coaching career more than anyone in my lifetime. Larry was a winner that stood out over time and his influence stood out big over everyone that was lucky to be associated with him regardless of what they did for a living or who they were. When asked what advice he would give young coaches coming up, he made this statement. <u>Understand what it means to be professional. Loyalty to the school, to the people you work with and the students you are coaching. Be prepared to invest your time in the intelligent pursuit of the game and individual progression of teaching the fundamentals of the skills required to play the game. Be accountable for your coaching and have a passion to be the best coach you can be. You are coaching kids through the vehicle of the sport of football.</u>

The third category is the coaches that maintained the longest winning tradition in a high school [winning means competing for the championship year after year with little or no drop-off]

The Littlefield Connection [Jerry Blakely, Lewis Boomer, and Brian Huseman] [Small School] From 1971-2017 Littlefield football challenged opponents for the state championship year after year without a drop off for 46 years. Jerry Blakely coached at Littlefield for fifteen years, Lewis Boomer coached for fifteen years, and Brian Huseman coached sixteen years.

Keeping a winning tradition in football is very difficult and I salute those guys and particularly the administration at Littlefield during those years. It is sad but very true; it is very difficult to keep a winning tradition over a long period of time because of **change**. Change is something that lives in our life's day by day and often it is not always good for keeping a winning tradition in football. First off, change occurs when a head coach decides to give up coaching football at a school. When this happens many things occur, and depends on the attitude of the administration, community, players returning, players coming up, student body, teachers, coaches returning, and the new coach being hired. At any point in time with all concerned, something negative can happen and tradition can change. To be honest keeping a tradition following one coach to another is almost impossible. A school that has a rich tradition of winning football games is expected to change when one coach leaves and another is hired. Just look at all the schools that win a state championship then fall on hard times.

For forty-six years Littlefield football was in the thick of the battle in the high school football arena. During this time, Littlefield went through three coaches and that is what makes them so special because Littlefield stayed strong when change occurred.

Coach Blakely arrived in Littlefield after coaching in Clovis, New Mexico and Olton, Texas. He started at Marshall Junior High School, Clovis, New Mexico then the next year he went to Clovis High School where he was the head track coach and assistant football coach. From there he became the athletic director, head football coach at Olton. In April of 1971, Jerry Blakely became the head football coach and athletic director at Littlefield. He didn't step into a program that was winning because Littlefield had only won seven games in three years. Coach Blakely made an immediate impact by winning the district championship his first three years. In the end, Coach Blakely had 9 district championships, 7 bi-district championships, 3 area championships and 4 regional championships. In 1982 his team played Refugio for the State Championship losing 21-20. Over all-he coached in 26 play-off games and was selected "Coach of the Year" six times by the Lubbock Avalanche Journal. In 1986, Coach Blakely became the Superintendent of Littlefield with a football record of 127-40-6. His over- all record was 142-45-7.

Coach Blakely was inducted into the "Top of Texas Football Hall of Fame" in 1983 and The Texas High School Coaches Association "Hall of Honor" in 2001. He served as the Superintendent for the next 28 years.

Jerry Blakely loved Littlefield and they loved him in return. But what he did that most people don't understand is help maintain the football tradition he started by becoming the Superintendent. He was an excellent Superintendent doing the same type of job in administration as he did in coaching. He was responsible for many renovations and additions to LISD facilities and was committed to improving LISD fiscal and academic performances.

Next came Coach Lewis Boomer who was hired to replace Coach Blakely in 1986 was no newcomer to the Littlefield tradition. He served as an assistant coach for fifteen years under Coach Blakely. Coach Boomer was accustomed to winning football games and when he took over the head coaching position, that is exactly what he continued doing. His teams went 31-5 in his first three seasons winning three straight District Championships. During his stint as head football Coach of the Wildcats they won eight district championships, five Bi-District Championships, and one Regional Co-Championship. Coach Boomer career record all in Littlefield was 120-41-4. In 1997 he was inducted into the "Top of Texas Football Hall of Fame". Coach Boomer retired in 2000 and still lives in Littlefield.

Next up to the plate is Bryan Huseman who is no stranger to Littlefield. Bryan served as the Head Boys' basketball coach for the first ten years he coached at Littlefield. Then he was selected to become the Athletic Director and Head Football coach when Coach Boomer retired in 2000. Coach Huseman started his 32-year coaching career in Memphis in 1985. He then coached at Idalou where he had 3 Regional Tournament girl's teams. Bryan spent one-year coaching in Snyder before being named the Head Boy's coach at Littlefield. Coach Huseman certainly left his mark in basketball, taking three teams to the regional tournaments and his 1994 basketball team made it all the way to the Class 3AAA Championship game. He finished his basketball career with a record of 320-158.

In football his teams qualified for the State Play-offs 14 out of 16 years. During this time his Wildcats won 6 District Championships, 11 Bi-District Championships, 2 Area Championships, 3 Regional Championships, 2 Quarterfinals Championships, and 2 Semi-Finalist. His 2006 team played for the Class 2A State Championship. Coaching a team to the State Championship in both football and basketball is an accomplishment that is unheard of in our present day in time. His ability to win in both sports reflects his winning attitude and his positive attitude toward his family, his coaching and entire life dealing with everyone concerned.

Coach Huseman finished his football career in Littlefield as the winningest football coach in program history. He finished with a record of 132-61. Bryan Huseman certainly had a strong influence in the coaching world and his contribution the world of sports will not be forgotten soon.

Putting it all together, Coach Blakely, Coach Boomer and Coach Huseman had a career football record at Littlefield of 379-142. This included 23 District Championships, 23 Bi-District Championships, 8 Regional Championships, 3 Semi-Final Championships, and 2 State Finals Championships. Their record is outstanding, but nothing compares to the positive influence they had on the community of Littlefield and the Panhandle/Plains region of the State of Texas.

THE ABILENE CONNECTION [P.E. "PETE SHOTWELL, DEWEY MAYHEM, CHUCK MOSSER, AND STEVE WARREN] [LARGE SCHOOL]

The Abilene connection is most likely the greatest accumulation of high school football coaching **legends** in the Panhandle/Plains region that can't be challenged. Seven state championships are involved and so much success that it is a no brainer not to mention the legends of the Abilene Eagles football program. Pete Shotwell started the movement in his third year at Abilene by taking his team to the semi-finals two straight years and then to the finals in 1922. Then in 1923 he hit the jackpot winning the state football championship going undefeated.

After trying the college football scene, Pete jumped back into the high school ranks coaching at Breckenridge winning another state championship in 1929, then jumped to East Texas at Longview high school and won another state championship in 1937. He was the first one to win a state championship in football at three different schools, Abilene, Breckenridge, and Longview. Pete returned to Abilene in 1946 and retired in 1952 with a coaching record is 243-83. The "Public Schools Stadium" in Abilene was renamed "Shotwell Stadium" in his honor.

One would think there would be a huge drop-off, but it just didn't happen. Dewey Mayhem followed Pete and quickly followed suit by taking the Eagles to the state finals in 1927 and a state championship in 1928. The Abilene Eagles couldn't be stopped until Dewey gave the job up in 1946. Coach Mayhem's record at Abilene was 97-36. Pete came back to Abilene then the glory days of Abilene took a short nosedive, but they did make the play-offs once. Pete retired from Abilene high school in 1952.

In the Texas Panhandle when a storm approaches, everyone pays attention because storms in the Panhandle can be very dangerous. Most of the time, if a storm approaches everyone gets quiet and still, it is scary because you know for sure something big is fixing to happen. Well, that is exactly what happened with the Abilene Eagles. A guy by the name of Chuck Moser stepped up to the plate and took the head football coaching position at Abilene High School in 1953. History was made and very few football fans will forget it. Many fans in the Abilene area consider Coach Moser in the same line as Vince Lombardi or Bear Bryant. He was almost God to them in the football world. Why not, he took an undefeated "B" team that he inherited and in seven years as the head football coach at Abilene High School he compiled a 78-7 record. His three straight state championship with 49 consecutive wins from 1954-57 will never be forgotten. Then in 1957 his team was in the semi-finals vs. Highland Park and they tired Highland Park 20-20 but lose on penetrations to end the unbeaten record. Not only that, the next two years Abilene advanced to the quarterfinals twice after the winning record of 49 consecutive wins.

Church Moser was a person that changed the way football coaches coached the game of football. He was intense, organized, tough disciplinarian [ahead of his time] producing new thoughts about football such as:

- Organized strong off-season training
- Eligibility Reports-Every week players had to get teachers to sign off on their grades and attitudes in the classroom. If they weren't passing, they didn't play the next week. If they were a problem in the classroom, they had to pay with tough discipline exercises.
- "No Pass-No Play"-if they didn't pass, they didn't play-his rule
- Sophisticated scouting reports that the players had to pass an exam in order to play Statistic play book-using the material for half-time adjustments
- Game film-Every week the players walk game film and coaches would instruct them on what they did right and what they did wrong

During that spell of state championships and winning records, Abilene was called by the Dallas Morning News "The football team of the century" but what went unnoticed was that the Eagles won the state championship in baseball in 1956/1957, then won the state championship in track/field in 1954, 1959, 1960 and 1961. In 1959 Chuck Moser became the Athletic Director at Abilene Public Schools with an over-all coaching record of 141-29.

In 1960, Abilene Cooper high school was developed and for the first time, Abilene high school was split. After that everything football wise came back to a normal life, but Abilene Cooper did rise to the occasion and exactly eleven years after the Abilene High football 1956 state championship, Abilene was in another state championship game, but it was Abilene Cooper, not Abilene High.

Then in 1996, Steve Warren was selected as the Head Football coach at Abilene High School after being an assistant coach under Gary Gaines. Abilene High had suffered through eight consecutive losing seasons with a 12-65 record. The Eagles had not qualified for the play-offs since the 1959 season.

Isn't it ironic where Abilene High went from a period where no one that they could lose to a period where no one thought they could win? In 1999 the Eagles reached the state quarterfinals and started a winning pattern of their own winning 14 consecutive playoff games that included at least a share of nine district championships. After four straight regional losses, the Eagles finally advanced to the semifinal state championship game. Then in 2009 Warren's Abilene High School won their seventh state football championship. Then the Eagles made another run but ended their season in the quarterfinals in 2011. Warren became the Eagles winningest football coach win a 172-61 record when he retired from his football duties at Abilene High School.

THE NEXT CATEGORY IS THE FOOTBALL COACH THAT HAD AN OUTSTANDING FOOTBALL CAREER AND AN OUTSTANDING ATHLETIC DIRECTOR'S CAREER.

GREG SHERWOOD/FOOTBALL COACH AND ATHLETIC DIRECTOR

For me personally, I will never forget my first association with Greg Sherwood. I was the Athletic Director/Head Men's basketball coach at Wayland Baptist University. We were working out for basketball when I started noticing a person that became a regular at our workouts. Finally, one day I stepped away from workout and went over to introduce myself. It was Greg Sherwood and I was shocked. My wife was an English Teacher at Plainview High School and I heard about how great of a coach/person/ administrator/ and teacher he happens to be every day. From that day forward Greg Sherwood became a hero in my mind. I really think he and some of his coaches were just trying to get away from it all so they could concentrate on football and I must admit that he picked a spot that was safe, but regardless I did get to know him and it was my pleasure.

Greg Sherwood is a legend among legends in the Texas Panhandle/ Plains region. Greg was born in Woodward, Oklahoma, graduated from Panhandle High School in 1955, and received his BA from University of Texas. Later he attended West Texas State University to get his master's in education. It was at West Texas State University that I ran into him in a class I was taking but it didn't ring a bell in my mind at that time. Greg married Jacquelyn Harstsell and they had two sons, Scott and his wife Brenda, Panhandle, Texas, and Stan and his wife Kelly, Celina, Texas. He has a brother, Marshall Sherwood from Panhandle, Texas.

Coach Sherwood started is coaching career at Baker Junior High School in Austin, Texas. Then he jumped to high school coaching in Comanche but finally got his first Head Coaching job in Dalhart. The person that hired him was Doug Ethridge who as Sherwood said, "The greatest break I ever got in the coaching world was working for Doug Ethridge." He continued, Doug was a man that was ahead of his time and he really laid the foundation for success at Dalhart." Greg backed up that statement with a 41- 9-1 record in five years at Dalhart. After that, Coach Sherwood started taking on jobs that very few would be interested in like Liberal, Kansas. He said more than once that he loved taking on jobs that presented huge challenges. At Liberal he stayed two years and compiled 13 wins, but he started a saying that stayed with him for the rest of his career. It was called the "The Angry Red." From Liberal High School, Greg went to Kermit High School for one season then took the Principals position at Vega High School. In 1973 Coach Sherwood took another job that people really questioned when he accepted the Head Football position at Spearman High School. Spearman was on hard times and very few people thought this was a good move for Greg Sherwood. Forty-eight wins later and a trip to the State 2A State Championship in 5 years put Spearman on top of the map concerning high school football. Of course, after that type of success, football positions started looking for him but instead of taking several opportunities to advance his career with already successful football programs he decided on Plainview High School in Plainview, Texas. Sherwood himself said this about taking the Plainview football position, "That seemed like a challenge I couldn't pass up." Plainview had 58 years without a play-off berth and this time almost everyone thought Greg had bit off more than he could chew. In his first year at Plainview his Bulldogs made history because they advanced all the way to the Class 5A state quarterfinals. It was at Plainview that his "Angry Red theme" took hold and spread across the State of Texas, not just the Panhandle/Plains region. To back up that year, the "Angry Red" either won or tied for the district championship 5 times in 10 seasons. He is still the winningest coach in Plainview history with 66 wins. Sherwood said this about his stay in Plainview. We had a lot of success in Plainview, but I stayed because it became home to my family and me. My sons Scott and Stan both played football for Plainview and I cried when we left, but

I usually cried when I left a coaching position. After it was all said and done, his football coaching career ended with a record 174-64-2.

Then after 23 years of coaching, Greg Sherwood decided to take on another challenge, because he was selected as the Athletic Director of the Lubbock ISD school district in 1988. He stayed on that position until his retirement in 2001. One of the challenges Greg had to face was the football situation in Lubbock. He had first-hand knowledge of how down football was in the city three 5A schools. He was 27-3 versus Lubbock Coronado, Lubbock High and Monterey during his tenure at Plainview.

It was during this time that I started paying attention to the athletic situation in Lubbock. Since I graduated from Amarillo High School in 1958, I knew first-hand how the Amarillo felt about playing the Lubbock Schools in football. I promise you, there was no fear from the Sandie's point of view. Then I worked at Hereford, Odessa Permian and Midland High and the same attitude existed in those schools

about playing the Lubbock schools in football. As a former Athletic Director and basketball coach I always pay close attention to how athletic directors handle tough situations. Greg Sherwood was awesome in his approach to the total school situation and won everyone over to his side as quick as you can say [Skit-Scat-how about that]. First and foremost, he hired coaches that had the same mindset as he had, and then he let them coach. It is not as easy to win at football as one might think. You must compete against the Amarillo schools and the West Texas Schools, Odessa High, Permian High, Midland High, Midland Lee, San Angelo, Abilene Cooper and the legendary Abilene High. You don't have to be a rocket scientist to understand that winning is tough when competing with those schools. It was slow moving but eventually the Lubbock Schools started competing and winning more games than they lost, and you could tell a different kind of attitude was developing in the football programs. This past year in 2017, Coronado and Monterey had great football seasons. In my opinion the Sherwood influence is still part of those programs even though the Lubbock ISD has had different Athletic Directors since his death.

Coach Sherwood was the President of the Texas High School Coaches Association, inducted into the THSCA "Hall of Honor", and later into the Texas High School Football "Hall of Fame". What he was very proud of was the ASCO All-Star football classic where the "Greg Sherwood Service Award" was given to the person that epitomizes what service, leadership, and character are about in the educational field. But wins, play-offs trips, and honors were not what Greg Sherwood was about. It was a small part of it but not even close to the Sherwood people knew and loved. As one write said, it's what was underneath; it's what inside that makes him so special, so unique.

Clark Mires, a former assistant coach said this, "He's the greatest person of any guy I've even known in my life." He continued, "There's not another Greg Sherwood in the world, and I meant that. Greg was a great [X and O] coach but what made him so successful is that he cares so much about people and could get so much out of them." Coronado football coach Butch Henderson [who is a legend himself] marveled at the way he could sell community or school personnel in the direction he thought a program needed to go. Steve Parr played for Sherwood at Dalhart and later was an assistant coach under him at Plainview said this about Greg, "I learned more about life than anything else", "he taught you about people and to believe in God." Ines Perez who worked for Coach Sherwood in the LISD athletic department said, "He had so much influence on me and my career and all Lubbock athletics." "It was always about the way he treated people, he loved people-coaches were his hero's." Another coach that Sherwood hired, James Morton [a legend himself] who coached at Monterey said, "A better boss hasn't existed." He continued, "As a coach he set the bar high for all of us because he was such a humble man, a great person."

But the lucky ones were his former players. Most all his former players see him as a second father. He turned about programs but in doing so he turned around lives. Not only would they run through a wall for him but do it again if needed. Greg himself said this about his former players, "My goal was to set players up for success in life and make football a great experience but what happened was they made football a great experience for me." Ex-Superintendent of Schools, E.C.

Leslie at Lubbock ISD said this about Sherwood, "His genuine love and interest in others influenced so many that it will be a heritage passed on for generations." "He dreamed big about influencing total school and community environment." John Hill who worked for Sherwood for 8 years in Plainview and 14 in Lubbock said, "If you worked for him, you knew how special he made you feel, you also knew and felt you were a great coach just walking the sidelines with him."

But the story that best describes Greg Sherwood is the story when his son, Scott returned from his first semester at West Point. The first thing Greg did was to take Scott along with him to deliver 30 meals, coats, hats and even a hot water heater to the needy. As John Hill said, "There are thousands of people that know he never thought of himself first." That sums it up about Greg Sherwood.

OTHER FOOTBALL COACHING LEGENDS

The next category is **called Others**-meaning just that. Football high school football legends in the Texas Panhandle/Plains region are plentiful to say the least. We can't write about each one, so we sent out e- mails to every high school athletic director and coach in the Panhandle/Plains region that has been part of the UIL in Texas. We ask for nominations with a questionnaire included. We don't want to miss anyone because that is what this book is about, and we apologize if we miss anyone, but they needed to be nominated for us to write about them. The following are the high school coaches that were nominated as a legend: **Bill Spann**-Dumas, **Larry Wartes**-Stamford and Hereford, **Don Cumpton, Bobby Davis**- Frenship, **Pete Shotwell**-Abilene, **Jim Eddins-Seagraves, Louis Kelley**-Estacado, **Tom Ritchey**- Sweetwater, **Leo Brittain**-Vernon, **Harold [Chesty] Walker**-Philips, **Butch Henderson**-Borger and Coronado, **Johnny Taylor**-Idalou, **Eddie Metcalf**-Stratford, **Bill Anderson**-Stamford, Rising Star, Graham, Hereford, **Ron Mills**-White Deer, Groom, Canyon, Panhandle, **Gene Mayfield**-Littlefield, Borger, Permian, Levelland.

BILL SPANN-DUMAS

Coach Spann had a reputation for toughness as a football coach. He demanded a lot of his players and they responded in the proper way. His teams were mentally and physically tough. They had to be because he expected a lot from them. His son, Carl Spann said this of his father, "It was a great experience, but he was tough." Then Carl continued, "I probably had to play a little harder to keep my position", because I was his son.

The last year Dumas was in the football play-offs was in 1933. Spann was a line coach on the Dumas team that won the state championship in 1961. In 1962 Spann was elevated to the head coaching position. Bill seemed to fit the job like a glove because Dumas didn't miss a beat, going 13-1 and winning a second straight Class 3AAA state championship in football. In the eight years that followed Bill Spann posted a 74-16-2 record, winning seven district titles and tying another.

In the championship years of 1961 and 1962, the Dumas Demons averaged 33.3 pts per game while giving up only 6.2. Over the next four seasons, Coach Spann proved that those championship teams were not a happen chance deal. The Demons were a combined 39-1 in the regular season from 1963-66. During that period, Spann's teams were known as "The Black Knights of the Panhandle". His teams were a legend in the Panhandle, but they didn't always have a good run in the play-offs. Twice Dumas lost play-offs games by a point, one time by two points and once on first downs tiebreaker.

Bill Spann resigned from Dumas after the 1975 football season, then went to Burleson but eventually moved to Texarkana where he was a coach/teacher until his retirement in 1988. Spann was inducted into the Texas Panhandle "Sports Hall of Fame", and the Dumas ISD, "Hall of Fame".

LARRY WARTES-STAMFORD/HEREFORD

Coach Larry Wartes was my hero so it's easy for me to write about him. Larry hired me as the Head Basketball coach/assistant football coach at Hereford High School from 1968-72. Not only that I had the pleasure of coaching his son, Mike Wartes in football and basketball. Larry was one of a kind and I remember him so well from the first day I witnessed his coaching when I was coaching football at Albany, Texas and he was the Head Football Coach at Stamford until the last day of his coaching when I saw him stand on his head during a football game at Clovis, New Mexico. He was my hero because he talked the talk as good as anyone, but he also walked the walked better than anyone. He set the background for my career in coaching and I was the lucky one just being a small part of his coaching staff.

Larry Wartes was more than a football coach but was more about being right with life and God. He was an assistant football coach under Gordon Wood where they won two state football championships then when he took over as the head coach, they won two more state championships in 1958 and 1959. Later he left Stamford for Hereford in 1967. At Hereford he coached for another four years before taking an administration position as assistant superintendent of schools. When it was all said and done, his overall football coaching record as an assistant football coach and head football coach was 165-60 with four state championships.

In college Larry was an "All Border Conference basketball player" at Hardin Simmons University then was inducted in the Hardin Simmons "Hall of Fame", the Texas High School Coaches "Hall of Honor", and the "Big County Hall of Fame". Larry was Hereford's "Citizen of the Year" in 1991 and 1994, then eventually was selected "Hereford Whitefaces Fan of the Year" in 2008-09. Larry was a giant in the coaching world in the Panhandle/Plains region.

DON CUMPTON-MULESHOE/HEREFORD/ABILENE/HEREFORD

You can't write about Larry Wartes or Larry Dippel without mentioning Don Cumpton. Don was an assistant football coach on the same staff as Wartes and Dippel. Those three on the same staff was awesome. I was part of that staff and without a doubt that coaching staff might be the best ever-I'm sure I will get some argument on that issue but it is hard to argue with three football coaching legends on the same staff at the same time.

Coach Cumpton was also an assistant football coach at Tulia and Stanford Fritch. In 1975, Sanford Fritch advanced to the regional finals and in 1976 Don was named the Athletic Director and Head Football coach at Muleshoe High School. From that point on coach Cumpton stated making a name for himself in the world of coaching high school football. From Muleshoe, he moved back to Hereford as the Athletic Director and Head Football coach then he jumped to the "Little Southwest Conference" when he was named the Head Football coach Abilene High School in 1983. Don couldn't stay away from Hereford and decided to return to Hereford as the Athletic Director and Head Football coach in 1986. His first year back Hereford advanced to the State Semi Final championship game.

Coach Cumpton overall football coaching record is 115-61 with two state semi-finals, one regional finalist, and several district championships. Don was selected as the Amarillo Globe News "Coach of the Decade 1980's", and the Panhandle Sports "Hall of Fame Coach" of the Year in 1981. In 1986 he was selected as the SWOA "Sportsmanship Award" and in 1981, the WTSU Alumni "Coach of the Year". In 2010 he was selected for the "Greg Sherwood Award". He was the Texas High School Coaches Association Director from 1980-1982.

BUTCH HENDERSON-BORGER/CORONADO

The first time I heard about Butch Henderson was when he was hired by Jim Breckenridge as an assistant football coach at Borger. I knew about that hiring firsthand since Butch took my place as an assistant football coach at Borger so I could accept the position of Head Golf/ Assistant basketball coach at Midland College. The next time I heard his name was when Borger was in the State Quarterfinals vs. Brownwood. I thought it was a misprint. Come to find out Butch had the Borger team in the play-offs four of the last six years he was the head coach.

Next time I heard about Butch he was coaching at Coronado High School in Lubbock, Texas. I thought to myself "another coach bites the dust". Several good coaches had been at Coronado before Butch, but those same good coaches had a difficult time winning football games. In the first 22 years at Coronado, the football program had only one play-off appearance and one winning season. The next thing I know Butch is taking the Head Football position at Wayland Baptist University but not before he compiled a won-loss record of 141-105 at Coronado High School. What was impressive to me was the fact that during his stay at Coronado the football program had 11 play-off appearances and 4 regional/area championships. His overall coaching record in 32 years is 196-153.

Butch was the "South Plains/Top of Texas Coach" eight times. He was the recipient of the "Coaches Care Award" presented by Gatorade in 1992 and was selected for the "Greg Sherwood Award" in 2016. Beside his coaching awards, he was selected three different years as the "Teacher of the Year Award".

BOBBY DAVIS-WILSON/POST/CORPUS CHRISTI CALALLEN/ FRENSHIP

Bobby Davis could write a book about two subjects that we could all learn from. One, he came up the hard way proving his ability as a football coach starting at Lockney Junior High School. Then he was an assistant football coach at Lockney then finally got his first head football position at Wilson. What is impressive to me is that he was successful along the way but hit pay-dirt at Wilson with a 22-8 record. From Wilson, he was selected as the Head Football coach at Post and from Post he became the Head Football coach at Corpus Christie Calallen with a record of 28-19. Then he came back to the Panhandle when he accepted the Head Football position at Frenship. In summary, he starts his football coaching career in Lockney as a junior high school coach then finishes his high school career at Frenship High School where he builds a powerhouse football program. Dave Campbell "Texas Football Magazine" lists his record as 247-163 in thirty-eight years. His record at Frenship was 131-98.

Along the way on his journey to becoming a football legend in the Panhandle/Plains region he had three sons by his wife Delmarie of which they were married over 50 years. His and her leadership didn't stop on the football field because all three sons are successful educators in the arena of education. Bryan, Brad and Brent have already made a huge positive mark in the world of athletics and in my opinion that is a powerful statement coming from the Bobby Davis household.

Coach Davis served on the Texas High School Coaches Association Board of Directors along with being on the THSCA Football Advisory Committee. One of his biggest achievements came when he was inducted into the THSCA "Hall of Honor" in 1999. In 2002 he won the "Tom Landry Award" and his staff coached the THSCA North All Star football team in San Antonio in 2005, then he coached for the South All-Stars in the ASCO West Texas Football Classic in 2006. Other awards given to Bobby Davis was in 2001, he was named "Legendary Coach of the Year" presented by Texas Tech University. In 2005, he was named the "Football Coach of the Year" presented by the Sports Express Radio Network, then in 2006

he was named "Man of the Year" presented by Wolforth Chamber of Commerce and Agriculture. Finally, in 2008 he received the "Legacy of Excellence Award" presented by Team Rehab and Sports Medicine.

EDDIE METCALF/STRATFORD

Eddie Metcalf loves living in Stratford and his talk is above the normal talk when a football coach talks about living in a city like he plans on living there the rest of his life. But he also walks the walk as his ex- superintendent says, "Eddie is not just active in school but active all over the town". Coach Metcalf came to Stratford as an assistant coach in 1994 and was elevated to the Head Football Coach in 2004. The Panhandle native didn't come by this position by accident as he had been an assistant football coach at Lubbock Roosevelt, Brownwood, Morton and Stratford.

Eddie didn't disappoint anyone because he led the Elks to the state championship game his first year as a head coach. There was no drop-off for the fans of the Elks. Stratford had already established a football dynasty by going 74-12 over the last six years of football competition.

Then in 2005, Metcalf and his young group of players won the State Championship. What was special, they had to win a three-way flip of the coin just to get in the play-offs. When he raised the Championship State Championship Trophy "He said that he wasn't even sure they could win this thing himself even when I was holding that trophy, I thought the alarm would go off and I would wake up."

In 2008, the Stratford Elks won their second state championship under Coach Metcalf and became one of the Panhandle/Plains multiple state champions in the Panhandle/Plains region with three state championship wins. Eddie Metcalf record at Stratford was 115-31. He resigned his position as the Head Football coach in 2014. Coach Metcalf said that all he tried to do was teach intensity to play the game right for the right reasons. He wanted his players to act right on the field and off the field but most importantly he wanted them to win graciously. Eddie was selected as the "Amarillo National Bank "Coach of the Year" in 2006.

LUIS KELLEY/ESTACADO

I personally have been a fan of Luis Kelley for many years. I eat at the Red Zone cafe, located in Lubbock, Texas and every time I eat there, I am reminder of Coach Kelley. He has a picture of himself and a picture of his state championship team picture on the wall of the Red Zone café. Then my wife took an English teaching position at Estacado and I continued to hear about Luis Kelley. Everything I heard from him was above the norm especially what coaches like to hear from teachers. That really got my attention.

Coach Kelley played at Cisco Junior College then went to New Mexico State University where he was voted the "Most Valuable Football Player". According to his teammates he received that award because of his determination, passion, hard work, high fives, and humor. To this day his teammates hail his selfless and humble attitude. He graduated from NMSU in 1961 and started his coaching career. He started as an assistant coach for eight years at Lubbock Dunbar then became the Head coach for six years, 1969-1974. Then he went next door to Lubbock Estacado and had a great career for twenty-six years. Totally he coached for forty years and compiled 235-111 coaching record. Coach Kelley's teams won 17 district championships and were in the playoffs 17 times. He had four state finalist and one state championship team.

Luis Kelly was the Avalanche Journal "Coach of the Year" eight times, was selected by the Texas High School Coaches Association "Hall of Honor", in 1997. In 1988 he was selected to the Abilene ISD "Hall of Fame" in 1988, and he NMSU "Hall of Fame" in 2004. In 2001 he was named the Texas Tech Chapter Legendary "Coach of the Year", and later was named for his "Outstanding Contribution to the Amateur Football Award".

TOM RITCHEY-SWEETWATER

Everybody that is a football fan knows about "Friday night Lights" but how many know that a full-length film about the football powerhouse "Sweetwater Mustangs almost became a real deal. There was some opposition because some old timers were very uneasy about that situation, but the school board voted 5-1 to cooperate. Then before two-a-days started in August, the directors called and said they hadn't been able to raise enough money for the project. One thing for sure Tom Ritchey doesn't need a film about his coaching career to get the attention of the Panhandle/Plains football fans. He has already done that with a big bang.

Coach Ritchey was an Abernathy graduate and played his high school football for Curtis Davenport and basketball for Wayne Preston. He ended up at Southern Methodist then transferred to North Texas where he graduated from college. In 1972, he was named the Head Football Coach at Ft. Stockton High School. After two years at Ft. Stockton he took an assistant football position at Midland Lee and from there in 1975 he landed the Head Football position at Idalou High school. After eleven seasons with Idalou he finally hit pay-dirt when he was hired as the Sweetwater Head Football Coach.

At Sweetwater he led the Mustangs to eleven playoff berths, four unbeaten regular seasons and a 38- game regular season winning streak. At Sweetwater alone, his football record was 120-24. His over-all record was 208-64. Totally his teams won 13 district championships and went to the playoffs 16 times. Buster Leaf who was an assistant coach under Ritchey at Idalou said this about Coach Ritchey. "Coach Ritchey strongest attribute is his compassion for the players." "He always put them in front of everything else-he wanted to win as bad as anyone, but he always did what was best for the kids." Tom was selected into the Texas High School Coaches "Hall of Honor" in 2000. He said himself, "That being selected into the "Hall of Honor" was huge in his mind because I have always idolized the people in the "Hall of Honor". In 2003 Coach Tom Ritchey was selected to the Big County Athletic "Hall of Fame".

LEO BRITAIN-VERNON/WICHITA FALLS/GRAHAM/RICHLAND

I remember it like it was yesterday. Amarillo had two high schools, a new one called Palo Duro and Leo Brittain was headed to Palo Duro. I graduated from Amarillo High School in the same year as Leo graduated except, he graduated from Palo Duro. I still remember the coaches crying about losing Brittain in football. He didn't let anyone down and became a football legend at Palo Duro. Leo coached 19 years and won one state championship at Vernon so we can consider him a coaching legend from the Panhandle/Plains region although he had great success at Wichita Falls which some feel that city is located in the North Texas Region of Texas.

Not many coaches get a football stadium named after them but Coach Brittain did at Vernon called the "Leo Brittain Field at Lions Stadium". In his career as a football coach Leo had 34 playoff wins putting him close to the top in that category of Texas High School Football. Not only that, his 34-13-1 record in playoffs is high on the list of the legends of Texas Football. Leo overall football record was 208-106. He led Vernon to two back to back state final appearances in 1989 and 1990 winning the title in 1990.

Coach Brittain won at Vernon leaving a strong winning tradition he created, then won at Wichita Falls more than he lost, and finally retire after two years at Richland. He was selected into the Texas High School Coaches Association "Hall of Honor" in 1997.

JOHNNY TAYLOR-IDALOU

If you live in the Panhandle close to Lubbock, from 2000 – 2011 the city of Idalou was dominated by winning football. Although Idalou was located just outside the city of Lubbock, Idalou had its own identity and its own personality. Johnny Taylor the head football coach at Idalou for twenty-two years brought out the best of the bunch and finished his career at Idalou has a big-time winner, the State Football Championship in 2010.

With his retirement in 2010 Coach Taylor has the distinction of being able to go out on top. Most of the time, when a coach is winning usually, they want to stay another year [which seems normal] but not coach Taylor. He made up his mind before the season started, didn't tell anyone until they had won the State Championship. He knew it was time to hang up the whistle and he stayed the course to the end with outstanding success. He finished his coaching career with 189-65 record. His teams qualified for the play-offs sixteen times, including eleven straight seasons from 2000 to 2010. His team finished with four trips to the regional finals then to the state finals and the finals. His final ten years at Idalou, his teams won 101 games.

Johnny Taylor coached the game of football for thirty-eight years before he decided to retire but did get to coach another football game in the Annual ASCO West Texas Football Classic, an all-star game for the regional high school graduates. Coach Taylor was a co-founder of the ASCO classic which benefits some medical needs by high school football players that was seriously injured on the field. Coach Taylor was inducted into the Texas High School "Hall of Honor" in 2016. He gives credit to all the coaches helping him in those years, the community of Idalou, players that stuck with him and worked hard to get better each year, family and his wife.

L.G. WILSON-FLOYDADA

I personally never knew L.G. Wilson, but I feel like I knew him very well. His daughter was our Head Women's Basketball Coach when I was the Athletic Director at Wayland Baptist University. She is responsible for my first education about women's basketball [Five on Five]. She put on a clinic every day and I benefited by watching her coach. The rumor was that she was a splitting image of her dad when he coached football. L.G. graduated from Abilene Christian University in 1950. He played football, basketball, and baseball.

Coach Wilson overall football record was 207-102. He was the head football coach, athletic director at Winters High School from 1960-1967, Floydada High School from 1968-1982, and Tulia High School from 1983-1990. He is the 12th winningest coach in the Panhandle/Plains region as of 2016. L.G. also coached at Brownfield High School, Weatherford High School and Temple High School. Coach Wilson retired in 1990.

He was a World War II veteran serving in the U.S. Navy from 1944 to 1945. He married Elaine Halbert in Sweetwater on June 16, 1949. The Texas High School Coaches Association inducted L.G. Wilson into the "Hall of Honor" in 1979. In 1999 the Lubbock Avalanche-Journal newspaper named Coach Wilson as one of the sixty most memorable contributors to South Plains athletics. He was also an outstanding track and field coach.

BILL ANDERSON-STAMFORD, RISING STAR, GRAHAM, HEREFORD

Of the many years that I coached, 53 totally, I don't remember hearing a negative comment concerning Bill Anderson. Matter of fact, all I ever heard was nothing but great things, particularly from fellow coaches.

Coach Anderson coaching career extended 50 years at stops in Stamford, Rising Star, Graham, South Taylor, Palestine, Rivera, Abilene Christian University, West Texas State, Cisco Junior College, Howard Payne, and Tarleton State. He was an outstanding coach that gave of himself to all the schools that he coached. Everyone loved Bill Anderson. We mention him even though he coached in college because he was nominated three times by different coaches at different schools.

Bill was selected in the Big Country Athletic "Hall of Fame", also named to the Texas High School Coaches "Hall of Honor". The football stadium in Stamford was dedicated and renamed "Bill Anderson Stadium."

RON MILLS-WHITE DEER, GROOM, PANHANDLE, CANYON, BAY CITY, SAN MARCOS, BRENHAM

Ron Mills was a great running back for White Deer and West Texas State University. After his college days he started his career in coaching as an assistant coach at White-Deer. Then he went to Groom as a Head Football Coach and his career as a coach was never questioned after that. Groom advanced as far as the UIL allowed Class "B" football by winning the regional championship.

Coach Mills team at Bay City was semifinalist 1978, finalist in 1979, semifinalist in 1980 and state champs in the 4AAAA division in 1983. What was Ironic to the fans in the panhandle was the fact that his team at Bay City defeated Estacado in the finals.

Mills overall coaching record was 203-115-14. He was inducted into the Panhandle Sports "Hall of Fame" in 1996.

Bill did what most of our legends do and that is to surround himself around good people, both coaches and players.

GENE MAYFIELD-LITTLEFIELD, BORGER, PERMIAN, LEVELLAND

Gene Mayfield had a great career as a football Quarterback at West Texas State University, only to be overshadowed by his performance as a football coach. Success was second nature for coach Mayfield starting with Littlefield where he had an overall record of 32-13-2. All he did was step it up when he went to Borger.

It was when he was at Borger that I first heard of his coaching accomplishments. At Borger he had a 62-13-2 record making the play-offs four times and a state finalist in 1962. Then Coach Mayfield elevated his coaching taking Odessa Permian to another level of play in football. His Permian football team won the State Championship in 1965. In 1968 and 1970 played for the State Championship losing both games and finished as runner up State Champs.

Gene Mayfield was President of the Texas High School Coaches Association in 1964 and his over-all won lost record in high school was 178-71-8. He was named by the Texas Sportswriters Association "High School Coach of the Year in 1970." He was inducted by the Panhandle Sports Hall of Fame in 1981.

JIM EDDINS-SEAGRAVES

Coach Eddins spent three decades coaching high school football and basketball around the South Plains. He compiled a career record coaching football of 141-30 at Seagraves High School, and then in basketball he coached Seagraves to 16 district championship or a playoff wins.

Jim coached at Seagraves from 1972-1986 as the Head Football Coach. What is impressive is that he never had a losing season at Seagraves taking the Seagraves Eagles to the Playoffs many years. His teams reached the UIL State Football semifinals in Class 2A in 1975, 1976, and 1979. Then in 1979, Seagraves played for the UIL State Class 2A championship.

Unique was the word for Coach Jim Eddins as he was named "All South Plains "Coach of the Year" twice in football and twice in basketball. This is what a real coach happens to be especially a coach that is recognized in two sports such as basketball and football.

Coach Eddins grew up in Sudan and gave credit to Francis Smith, a former coach at Sudan. Also, in the same statement, he gave legendary basketball coach Polk Robinson credit for helping him become the coach he was. As usually, Coach Eddins gave lots of credit to his assistant coaches Jim Draper and Jim Hamilton.

He said that his players at Seagraves had a deep sincere desire to perform in the heat of a competitive game, and the fans always supported the teams giving those teams a winning environment to compete in both football and basketball.

BILL PEARCE-BRECKENRIDGE

Can you be a legend at the school you coached but very few people know who you are? That is a question that is easy to answer, and Bill Pearce is one of many that are legends in the sport that they coach. There are more legendary coaches that fit this kind of characteristic than the ones that get media attention giving them exposure to the public and exposure in other cities.

In Breckenridge, Texas at Breckenridge High School Bill Pearce is a legendary coach, particularly the Big Country region. He has been everything to Breckenridge, starting in 1977 as an assistant football coach. Then Head Football Coach, then trainer and now a contract trainer.

Coach Pearce is known in the area as an outstanding football coach and an outstanding citizen, where the community of Breckenridge appreciates him for his work with kids, parents, community and assistant coaches.

What program had a winning football program that was a dynasty but now, who knows about them?

Who remembers Phillips High School? Who remembers Harold "Chesty" Walker? I really doubt if many readers will remember but they should. But if you lived from the span of 1939-1956, and you were a football fan in Texas, you would remember. During those seasons Phillips High School produced 18 district championships and one state championship. Walker's teams were a combined 172-23. During those 18 seasons three times, Phillips was undefeated. What is impressive is the fact that Coach Walker's teams played in 28 playoff games and posted a 23-5 record but what is even more impressive is after the worst season in his career in 1939 when they went 5-4-1; Phillips never lost more than two games in the next 17 years. His teams were 67-7 from 1950-56, which included a 15-0 record in 1954 winning the schools only state football championship. In Coach Walker's final five years at Phillips his teams were 10-1, 10-1, 15-0, 10-1-1 and 8-1-1. That impressive record in that time frame was 53-4-2.

His overall coaching record was 207-34 but what makes this record outstanding is the fact that his teams could not advance further than the regional championship. His teams did win 6 regional championships.

One of Walkers strong characteristics was the fact that he produced some outstanding coaches. There were 24 former Phillips players who were coached by Walker that went on with a career in the coaching world. Coach Walker's legacy in the Panhandle of Texas should never be forgotten.

One of the playoff games that seemed to grab the attention throughout the State of Texas was held in Vernon, Texas. The official football program in Big Black letters said this:

PLANO WILCATS VS PHILLIPS BLACKHAWKS CLASS AA SEMI-FINALS
SATURDAY, DECEMBER 9, 1967 8:00PM
LION STADIUM, VERNON, TEXAS

One sportswriter called this game "The story of the Texas transformation"

Plano is now one of the top football programs in the State of Texas and Phillips no longer exist. What this is saying that high school football as we knew it then would never be the same and that story line is so true today.

Phillips was a company town, created in the 1920's by the Phillips Petroleum Co located a few miles north of Borger and an hour out of Amarillo. The idea was to give the refinery workers a cheap place to live and a school for their children to attend. The company did everything for the workers, providing housing at cheap rate, and no police to monitor the community. They didn't need it because if someone got out of line, they were removed and sent to another facility. Soon the school was everything in Phillips, Texas. Phillips, the school became a legend from the standpoint that they got whatever they wanted. The little school was classified 2AA, but it had three choirs, a 120-piece marching band, which would be decked out in the Phillips 66 colors, black and orange.

Phillips was good at everything and took pride in that issue. In 1939, they had six trophies at the school but in 1975 they had over 600.

Phillips was so good, and the company's reputation was so widespread, that the opponents got suspicious. It seemed that the families with the best athletes ended up at Phillips and not at some of the other Phillips petroleum companies. The truth is the families decided where they wanted to be and all they had to do was asked for a transfer. But the truth is most of the athletes were born in town at the medical center, but people always heard rumors of company move-ins.

Plano won that game and then continued to move up the notch of the UIL classification system winning a state title in 1971, 77, 86, 87 and 94. On the other hand Phillips had shrunk to a small Class A school. In 1987, the school closed for good. Then in 1980, there was an explosion at the plant that just about destroyed the school and many homes. No one was seriously hurt but that was it for the company. All that's left now besides the refinery is steel tentacles reaching out in the school building. What's left of Chesty Walker stadium are trees growing up in place of the grandstands of the stadium. Lest we forget and always remember the days of the Phillips Blackhawks domination in the Texas Panhandle.

"YOU GOT MY BACK" COACHING STORY—THE DENVER CITY STORY

One of the enjoyments of coaching is the brotherhood shared in the fraternity of coaching. It happens everywhere and it is a strong bond that exists between coaches regardless of any situation. Coaching young people is a challenge and that challenge brings out the best of the best. During that challenge many obstacles get in the way of success and that is where the bonding takes place because it requires a commitment from a group called a coaching staff. Denver City had such a staff and the story is finally getting out to the public. Just like the Littlefield connection, Denver City had a 36-year period where several coaches made their mark in their football program. The ironic twist to this story is that it started when Mike Wartes hired Mike Mayberry as the Head basketball coach at Muleshoe. Wartes already had Alan Cornelius on the staff at Muleshoe, which meant that Muleshoe had three coaches that graduated from Hereford, Texas. Now guess who influenced those three guys in their coaching philosophy? Mike's father Larry Wartes was the head coach at Hereford and his assistants Larry Dippel, Don Cumpton, David Bornstein, and Fred Upshaw gave those young guys a tremendous education in football philosophy and knowledge.

Then Mike Mayberry was hired at Denver City as the Head Boys Basketball Coach and assistant football coach. Mr. Kelly, the Denver City Superintendent liked what he saw in Coach Mayberry, not just the way he was coaching basketball but also football. Finally, one day Mr. Kelly asked Coach Mayberry where he learned his philosophy about football. Coach Mayberry said, "It all started at Hereford and then transferred to Muleshoe though Mike Wartes." He continued, "I really don't know too much else except what I learned from those coaches at Muleshoe and particularly those coaches that played their high school football at Hereford." "It's all about family and treating everyone like family." That spring Mike Wartes was hired as the Head Football coach at Denver City and he brought two assistant coaches, Steve Taylor and Alan Cornelius. Later Terry Summers joined the other three moving from Hereford. That was the start of one of the most successful football programs in the history of that area.

Hundreds of young lives were guided by those guys and the school board and administration took notice. Liking what they witnessed and wanted to keep the continuity of the program together, each time the head coach left the program the next assistant in line would be elevated to the Head Coaching position. The first to leave was Mike Wartes when he accepted a Head Football position with Saginaw Boswell. Wartes ended up with a 25-17 record at Denver City.

Next in line was Alan Cornelius who was the Head Football Coach for the next seven years compiling a 58-18 record. Cornelius left DC for the Canyon Randall head football position and Steve Taylor was named the Head Football Coach. Coach Taylor took over the position in 1992 and stayed until he left for Ozona in 1997. I was the lucky one when Steve Taylor hired me as the Head Boys basketball coach and assistant football coach at Ozona. I wanted to be part of his program and I was not disappointed. It didn't take Coach Taylor long to turn the corner at Ozona which soon started producing play-off team's year in and year out. Then in 2011 Coach Taylor returned to Denver City as the Head Football coach for another five years. Twice Coach Taylor had undefeated teams in regular season at DC and his overall record for eleven years as the head coach was 82-33.

When Taylor left Denver City, the school board hired Mike Royce, but he left after one year which opened the door for Terry Summers. The Superintendent and the board at Denver City hired Coach Summers in 1999. Twelve years later after finishing 66-60 at DC, Coach Summers resigned his position and that is when Coach Taylor came back to Denver City.

Altogether, Wartes, Cornelius, Taylor, and Summers compiled a 231-128 record over 36 years for a 64% winning percentage. That included 8 district championships and 22 play-off games. In our current system, the top four teams in the district gained play-off spots but not in the days of those coaches. One team advanced and that was the winner. There was another hero in the group, and he was vital to the success of their program. Bill "Doc" Scott was the athletic trainer and tended to injuries. It was his decision from his diagnosis if a player continued to play or not. His word was final, and he was respected by the entire staff. His job was to get them back on the field as soon as possible, but only when he felt they were healed.

Denver City might have had one of the youngest football staffs in the state in 1981. Wartes was 28, Taylor 27, Cornelius 26 and the youngest was Summers at 23. Not to mention that the guy that started all this Mayberry was 26.

Cornelius and Taylor ended up with the best winning percentage of the four with a 75% winning percentage while Taylor had a 73% winning percentage. The legacy was not about winning percentage but more about the family attitude they had for everyone involved with the school. It was like a domino effect where one affected the other and it was contagious. All four felt it was an honor to be at Denver City and they were all outstanding teachers as well as coaches. Coach Summers retired from coaching and is now in the oil field related work for Oxy. Coach Wartes just retired from the Superintendent of Schools at Canyon which is a position he held for many years. Cornelius is retired but went back to work at Canyon ISD as their Discipline Coordinator. Coach Taylor just retired from his Athletic Director's position at Denver City. One thing is for sure and that is everyone associated with the Denver City schools were blessed by those four outstanding coaches-everyone benefited included themselves.

LESS WE FORGET LEGENDARY ASSISTANT COACH

DON BLACK-FRENSHIP

Don Black did the impossible. He was an assistant football coach and was elected into the Texas High School Coaches Association "Hall of Fame." It's an honor to just be elected as a head coach but to be elected as an assistant coach, is awesome.

Coach Black coached at Lubbock High, Roosevelt High, and Post High then went with Coach Bobby Davis to Corpus Christie Calallen in 1976. Then in 1981 he followed Coach Davis to Frenship. At Frenship he was the man behind the defense at Frenship as he ended his career being the defensive coordinator for 37 years. What makes his story so unreal is that he joined Bobby Davis at Post and the next 40 years he was his assistant coach and then when Bobby Davis retired coach Black was the right-hand man for Bobby's son, Brad.

From 1981 – 2009 coaching years, Frenship made the play-offs 17 years. What made everyone notice was that they made the play-offs 13 straight years from 1996 – 2008. Frenship had nothing but success in those years, being ranked #1 in the state in 1999, which included 4 trips to the state quarterfinals and 3 trips to the state semifinals.

In addition to Coach Black's football duties, he was the Head Track and Field coach at Frenship. Coach Don Black was liked and appreciated by everyone he encountered as witnessed by Bobby Davis. Coach Davis said this about Coach Black, "Everybody that ever played for him loved him, just thought the world of him." Coach Davis continued, "He was very friendly with the kids, and the kids really liked him. If there ever was a coach that kids like more, I don't know who it was, because they loved Don Black."

After retirement, Coach Black died on a Friday morning unexpectedly, something that caught everyone by surprise. His death was thought to be because of heart problems.

NOTE: FROM THE AUTHOR

If for some reason a Legendary Coach is left out- the following could be the reasons

1. The main reason is information is limited and resources are limited
2. The person you wanted to be listed is still coaching
3. The person you wanted to be listed was more successful in another region than the Panhandle Plains Region
4. The person you wanted to be listed wasn't nominated by their peers
5. The person you wanted to be listed didn't coach in the Panhandle/Plains region
6. You will see the word None many times and it means that no school from the Panhandle/Plains region qualified for the State Championship or played for the State Championship
7. If a person was considered a college legend, they were given limited coverage unless they were a legend in the high school arena first.

Boys Basketball

PANHANDLE/PLAINS HIGH SCHOOL BASKETBALL HAS a strong tradition and just like football, the coaching legends are numerous. Coaching legends are more isolated in boys' basketball in terms of winning big because of the high demand for success in football. In the early stages in the history of basketball in the state of Texas, some coaches felt basketball was just a way for the athletes to stay in condition before track season started. The thought process was you couldn't pick up a basketball until basketball season started and that kind of thinking doesn't lead to a skilled basketball player. You could almost hand pick the schools that had a different mind- set because they had basketball programs that usually won in basketball on a consistent basis. "It is what it is", would be a statement that explains the thinking during that period.

Then in 1974-75, an organization called the Texas Association of Basketball Coaches was organized and through that organization, basketball in Texas started playing catch-up to many surrounding states in Texas. Now, in 2019, Texas has caught up and passed many states in terms of developing high school boys' basketball.

Just like we did in football, first we are going to look at all the Panhandle/Plains cities that played for the State Championship from 1920-to 2017. In basketball, it is simple because in most all states including Texas, they have what they call a State Basketball Tournament where teams qualify by winning district, bi-district and regional. Then they have a four- or eight-man tournament to determine the winner.

The following teams qualified for the Texas State tournament from 1921-2017 that are from the

PANHANDLE/PLAINS REGION.

All schools competed vs. each other regardless of size.

Highlighted number gives the times a school made the state tournament

[None] means that no school/Panhandle/Plains region qualified for the state basketball tournament Listed below are the [Year-School-results] of participation in the State Boys Basketball tournament

From 1921-1925, no Panhandle/Plains team qualified for the Texas state tournament

1926	Canyon-Semifinals
1927	Cisco -Quarterfinals, Ralls-Semifinals
1928	Cisco [2]-Quarterfinals
1929	Cisco [3]-Semifinals
1930	Estelline-Semifinals [close to Plainview, Texas]
1931	Plainview-Quarterfinals
1932	Ropesville-Quarterfinals
1933	Lamesa -Semifinals, Crowell-Quarterfinals
1934	Lamesa [2]-Runner-up
1935	Lamesa [3]-Runner-up
1936	No Panhandle/Plains team qualified for the Texas State tournament
1937	No Panhandle/Plains team qualified for the Texas State tournament
1938	Abilene-Semifinals
1939	Abilene [2]-Semifinals, Vernon-Quarterfinals, Dalhart-Quarterfinals
1940	Crowell [2]-Semifinals

Summary of the first twenty years of UIL state tournament basketball in Texas. Lamesa had 3 trips with 2 Runner- up appearances and 1 semi-finalist exit.

Cisco had 3 trips with 1 semi-final appearance, and 2 quarterfinalist exits. Abilene had 2 trips with 2 semi-final exits.

Crowell had 2 trips with 1 semi-final appearance and 1 quarter-final exit.

**In the first twenty years, only 11 different teams qualified for the State tournament

Canyon, Estelline, Vernon, Dalhart, Plainview, and Ralls all had one trip to the State Tournament

1941   Pampa [1]-Quarterfinals, Abilene [1] [2]-Runner-up

1942 **UIL divided schools into 1A, 2A and B**

1942   B-Stratford [1]-Quarterfinals
            1A-none
            2A-Childress [1]-Quarterfinals,
1943   B-Idalou [1]-Semifinals
            1A-Anson [1]-Quarterfinals
            2A-Amarillo [1]-Quarterfinals
1944   **B-Stratford [2]-Quarter finals,** Roscoe [1]-Semifinals
            1A-Dimmitt [1]-Semifinals,
            2A-Childress [2]-Runner-up
1945   **B-Roscoe [2]-Quarterfinals**
            1A-Canadian [1]-Quarterfinals
            2A-Pampa [2]-Quarterfinals
1946   **Stratford [3]-WINNER**
            1A-Levelland [1]-Runner-up
            2A-Abilene [2]-Quarterfinals, Amarillo [2]-Semifinals
1947   B-Gruver [1]-Semifinals
            1A-Levelland [2]-Quarterfinals
            2A- Amarillo [3]-Semifinals
1948   B-none
            1A-Dimmitt [2]-Semifinals
            2A-Amarillo [4]-Quarterfinals
1949   B-Shallowater [1]-Quarterfinals
            1A-Memphis-**WINNER**
            2A-Lubbock [1]-**WINNER**

[1950-UIL added another category called "City"]

1950   **B-Gruver [2]-WINNER**
      1A-Canyon [1]-WINNER
      2A-Vernon [1]-Runner-up, Sweetwater [1]-Semifinals, City-none

1951   B-Stanton [1]-Semifinals, Adrian [1]-Quarterfinals
      1A-Canyon [2]-Quarterfinals
      2A-Lubbock [2]-Semifinals
      WINNER, Borger [1]-Semifinals, San Angelo [1]-Quarterfinals City-none
      [1952UIL divided teams into 1A-2A Division 2 and 3A-4A Division 1 and B]**
      B-Hawley [1]-Quarterfinals
      1A-2A-D2-Dimmitt [3]-WINNER, Levelland [3]-Semifinals
      3A-4A-D1-Borger [2]-Semifinals
      1953** **[UIL added PVIL]**

1953   B-Stinnett [1]-Quarterfinals
      1A-Denver City [1]-Runner-up
      2A-Dumas [1] – Runner up
      3A-Vernon [2]-Semifinals
      PVIL-3A-Lubbock Dunbar [1]-**WINNER**
      4A-Pampa [3]-WINNER

1954   B-Plainview [1]-Runner up,
      1A-Sundown [1]-Runner up, PVIL-1A-Stanton [1]-Runner up
      2A-Childress [3]-Semifinals
      3A-Plainview [2]-Semifinals
      4A-Pampa [4]-WINNER

1955   B-Bovina [1]-Semifinals
      1A-Sudan [1]-Semifinals
      2A-Seminole [1]-**WINNER**
      3A-Plainview [2]-Semifinals
      4A-Pampa [5]-Semifinals

1956   **B-Gruver [2]-Quarterfinals**
      1A-none
      2A-Phillips [1]-Runner up
      3A-Amarillo Palo Duro [1]-**WINNER**
      4A-none

1957   B-Meadow-Runner up, B-PVIL-Panhandle Douglasville [1] - **WINNER**

1A-Ropesville [Ropes] [1]-Semifinals

2A-Seminole [2]-Runner up,

3A-PVIL-Lubbock Dunbar [2]-WINNER

4A-Pampa [6]-Runner up

1958   B-Claude [1]-Quarterfinals

1A-Plains [1]-Semifinals

2A-Seminole [3]-Semifinals

3A-Hereford [1]-Semifinals

4A-Pampa [7]-WINNER

1959   B-Hedley [1]-Quarterfinals, B-PVIL-Colorado City Wallace [1]-**WINNER**

1A-Plains [2]-Runner up

2A-Seminole [4]-Semifinals

3A-Hereford [2]-Runner up, 3A-PVIL-Amarillo Carver-Runner up

4A-Pampa [8]-WINNER

1960   B-McAdoo-**WINNER**, B-Wink [1]-Quarterfinals, B-Jim Ned [1]-Quarterfinals,

B-PVIL-Colorado City Wallace [2]-WINNER

1A-Sunray [1]-Runner up

2A-Dimmitt [4]-Runner up

3A-Lamesa-**WINNER**, 3A-PVIL-Lubbock Dunbar [3]-**WINNER**

4A-Borger [3]-Runner up

Listed above are the schools that played for the UIL State Championship located in the Panhandle/Plains region from 1941-1960.

The dominate team in this era was Pampa with 8 State Tournament appearances. Pampa had 4 State Championship rings, 1 Runner up, 1 Semifinalist, and 2 Quarterfinal appearances. Close behind were Seminole and Dimmitt each with 1 State Championship ring, 1 Runner up, and 2 Quarterfinal appearances. Amarillo was next with 2 Semifinal and 2 Quarterfinal appearances. Next were Stratford, Levelland, Borger, Childress and Gruver with 3 state appearances. Stratford and Gruver each won a State Championship with Borger and Levelland being the runner up 1 time. Lubbock Dunbar in the PVIL sector won 3 state championships in this era.

Lubbock, Colorado City Wallace, Hereford, Plains, Childress, Plainview, Roscoe and Vernon had 2 State Tournament appearances. Lubbock and Colorado City Wallace won 1 State Championship ring.

1961   B-Aspermont-Semifinals, B-PVIL-Munday Dunbar-Runner up

1A-White Deer-Semifinals

2A-Dimmitt-Runner up

3A-Dumas-Semifinals

4A-Amarillo Palo Duro-Runner up

1962   B-Hawley-Quarterfinals, Aspermont [2]-Semifinals, Quitaque-Quarterfinals

1A-White Deer [2]-WINNER, 1A-PVIL-Colorado City Wallace- **WINNER,**

2A-PVIL- Lubbock Dunbar- **WINNER, 2A-None**

3A-Dumas [2]-WINNER

4A-Lubbock Monterey-Semifinals

1963   B-McAdoo-**WINNER,** Talpa-Centennial-Quarterfinals

1A-Stratford-Semifinals

2A-Canyon-Runner up

3A-Seminole-Semifinals

4A-San Angelo Central-**WINNER**

1964   **B-McAdoo [2]-WINNER, Hawley-Semifinals,** B-PVIL-Paducah-**WINNER**

1A-Sanford Fritch-Semifinals

2A-Canyon [2]-WINNER

3A-none, 4A-none

1965   B-Meadow-Semifinals

1A-Gruver

2A-Phillips-Semifinals

3A-PVIL-Lubbock Dunbar [2]-WINNER

1966   B-Channing-Runner up, **B-PVIL-Colorado City Wallace [2]-WINNER**

1A-Gruver [2] WINNER

2A-none, 3A-Andrews-Semifinals

4A-Lubbock Monterey [2] Semifinals

1967   B-PVIL-Plainview Washington-Runner up

1A-Lorenzo-Semifinals

2A-Dimmitt [2]-Runner up

3A-Lamesa-**WINNER**

4A-Abilene-Semifinals

1968   B-Darrouzett-Semifinals

1A-Aspermont [3]-WINNER

2A-Colorado City-Semifinals

3A-PVIL-Lubbock Dunbar [3]-Runner up

4A-none

1969   **B-Meadow [2]-Semifinals**
1A-Clarendon-Semifinals
2A-none, 3A-Perryton-Semifinals, 4A-none

1970   B-Ackerly Sands-Semifinals, Pvil
1A [2] Clarendon-Runner up
2A-Morton-Semifinals
3A-Lamesa [2]-Semifinals

1971   **B-Ackerly Sands [2]-Semifinals**
1A-none, **2A-Dimmitt [3]-Semifinals**
3A-Dumas [3]-WINNER
4A-Plainview-Semifinals

1972   B-Anton-Semifinals
1A-Sanford Fritch [2]-Semifinals
2A-Morton [2]-WINNER
3A-none, 4A-none

1973   B-Spade-Semifinals
1A-Sanford-Fritch [3]-Semifinals
2A-Morton [3]-Semifinals
3A-Lamesa [3]-Runner up, 4A-none

1974   B-Hedley-Semifinals
1A-Paducah-Semifinals
2A-Friona-Runner up
3A-Andrews-Semifinals
4A-none

1975   **B-Spade [2]-Runner up**
1A-Shallowater-Semifinals
2A-Dimmitt- [4] WINNER
3A-Lamesa- [4] WINNER, 4A-none

1976   B-Brownfield-Semifinals
1A-Crowell-Runner up
2A-Morton [4]-Runner up, 3A-none, 4A-none

1977   **B-Hedley [2]-Runner up**
1A-Seagraves
2A-Morton [5] WINNER
3A-Borger-Runner up

1978   B-Silverton-Semifinals
1A-none, **2A-Dimmitt [5]-Runner up**
3A-none, **4A-Abilene [2]-Semifinals**

1979	B-Whitharral-Semifinals
	1A-Vega-**WINNER**
	2A-Seminole [2]-WINNER
1980	B-Nazareth-Semifinals
	1A-Memphis-Semifinals
	2A-Abernathy – **WINNER**
	3A-Snyder-Runner up, 4A-none

Summary: In the third twenty years of competition from the Panhandle/Plains region of the UIL Texas State Boys tournament the following teams dominated this era.

The big winners in this time period were Morton and Dimmitt with 5 state tournament appearances. Morton had two State Championship rings, 1 runner up, and 2 semifinals. Dimmitt had 1 Championship ring, 2 runner ups, and 2 semifinals. Next and right behind those two was Lamesa with 2 Championship rings, and 2 semifinals. Next was Dumas with 2 Championship rings and 1 semifinal appearance.

Aspermont was next with 1 State Championship ring and 2 Semifinal exits. Sanford-Fritch was next with 3 semifinal appearances. In the PVIL, class 3A-Lubbock Dunbar was the star again with 2 State Championship rings and 1 runner up appearance.

Schools with 2 state tournament appearances were Spade, Hedley, Ackerly Sands, Clarendon, Meadow, Lubbock Monterey, Abilene, McAdoo, Canyon, White Deer, PVIL Colorado City Wallace. McAdoo and Colorado City Wallace won 2 State Championships.

1981	1A-none, 2A-Shallowater-Runner up
	3A-Perryton-Semifinals
	4A-Canyon-Runner up
1982	1A-none, 2A-Morton-Semifinals [UIL changed to 5A and no class B]
	3A-Dimmitt-**WINNER**
	4A-Andrews-Semifinals
	5A-Pampa-Semifinals
1983	1A-Turkey-Quitaque Valley-Semifinals
	2A-Morton-**WINNER**
	3A-Dimmitt [2]-WINNER
	4A-Borger-Runner up

1984   1A-Nazareth-Runner up
          2A-Morton [2]-Semifinals
          3A-Dimmitt- [3] - Semifinals,
          4A-none,
          5A-none

1985   **1A-Nazareth [2] Runner up,** Munday-Semifinals
          2A-Morton [3]-Runner up
          3A-Seminole-Semifinals
          4A-Lamesa-Runner up
          5A-None

1986   **1A-Nazareth [3]-WINNER**
          2A-Morton [4] WINNER
          3A-Dimmitt [4] Runner up,
          4A-none
          5A-Amarillo-**WINNER**

1987   1A-Paducah-**WINNER**
          2A-Morton [5]-WINNER
          3A-Dimmitt [5] Semifinals,
          4A-none
          5A-None

1988   **1A-Paducah [2] WINNER**
          2A-Haskell-Semifinals,
          3A-none, 4A-none, 5A-none

1989   1A-New Home-Semifinals
          2A-Farwell-Semifinals
          3A-Brownfield-Semifinals
          4A-Andrews [2]-Semifinals,
          5A-none

1990   1A-Vega-Semifinals
          2A-Abernathy-Semifinals
          3A-Lamesa [2] Runner up
          4A-Pampa- [2] Semifinals,
          5A-none

1991   **1A-Paducah [3]-Semifinals**
          2A-Abernathy [2] WINNER,
          3A-none
          4A-Pampa [3]-Semifinals,
          5A-none

1992 1A-Petersburg-Runner up
2A-Abernathy [3]-Semifinals,
3A-none
4A-Pampa [4]-Semifinals,
5A-none

1993 **1A-Petersburg [2]-Semifinals**
2A-Amarillo Highland Park-Runner up,
3A-none
4A-Plainview-Semifinals,
5A-none

1994 **1A-Nazareth [4]-Runner up**
2A-Shallowater-semifinals
3A-Littlefield-Runner up
4A-Plainview [2]-WINNER,
5A-none

1995 1A-Sudan-**WINNER**, Robert Lee-Semifinals
2A-Earth-Springlake- Semifinals
3A-Seminole [2]-Semifinals,
4A-none,
5A-none

1996 **1A-Nazareth [5] Runner up**
2A-Haskell [2]-Semifinals, 3A-none
4A-Pampa [5]-WINNER,
5A-none

1997 **1A-Nazareth [6]-Runner up**
2A-Tahoka-Semifinals
3A-Tulia-Runner up
4A-Sweetwater-Semifinals,
5A-none

1998 1A-Gruver-Semifinals
2A-Lockney-Semifinals
3A-Tulia [2]-Semifinals
4A-Lamesa [3]-Semifinals,
5A-none

1999 1A-**Paducah [4]-Semifinals**
2A-Wellington-Runner up
3A-**Seminole [3] Runner up,**
4A-none,
5A-none

2000 1A-Happy-Semifinals
     2A-Hale Center-Semifinals
     3A-None
     4A-None
     5A-None

The third 20-year era the Panhandle/Plains teams that played in the UIL Texas State tournament are as follows:

Nazareth proved that you can win in both girls' and boys' basketball during this period with the boy's team taking the top spot with 6 trips to the boy's state tournament. Nazareth won 1 State Championship ring and was the runner up 5 times for the State Championship. Guess what, Dimmitt, Morton, and Pampa finished with 5 trips to the state tournament. Morton had 3 State Championship rings, 1 runner up, and 1 semifinal appearance. Dimmitt had 2 State Championship rings, 1 runner up, and 2 semifinal appearances. Pampa had 1 Championship ring and 4 semifinalist appearance. Next in line is Paducah with 4 state tournament appearances, finishing with 2 State Championship rings and 2 semifinal exits. Seminole, Lamesa, and Abernathy, each had 3 state tournament appearances, with Abernathy winning 1 State Championship and 2 semifinal exists. Lamesa had 2 runner ups and 1 semifinals appearance while Seminole had 1 runner up and 2 semifinal appearances.

Plainview, Tulia, Petersburg, Shallowater, Andrews and Haskell each had 2 state tournament appearances with Plainview winning the State Championship ring 1 time.

2001 1A-D1-Stratford-Runner up [UIL divided 1A into two divisions]
     1A-D2-Nazareth-Runner up
     2A—Hale Center-Semifinals
     3A-Dimmitt-Semifinals
     4A-Hereford-Semifinals,
     5A-none

2002   **1A-DI-Stratford [2]-Semifinals**
1A-D2-Nazareth [2]-WINNER, 2A-none
3A-Dimmitt [2]-Semifinals,
4A-none,
5A- none

2003   1A-D1-Morton-Semifinals
1A-**D2-Nazareth [3] WINNER**
2A-Abernathy-Semifinals,
3A-none,
4A-none,
5A-none

2004   1A-D1-**Morton [2]-Runner up**
1A-D2-Grady-**WINNER**
2A-Shallowater-**WINNER**, 3A-none
4A-Lubbock Estacado-Semifinals,
5A-none

2005   1A-D1-**Morton [3]-WINNER**
1A-D2-Paducah-Runner up, 2A-none, 3A-none
4A-Amarillo Palo Duro-Semifinals,
5A-none

2006   1A-D1-Gruver-Runner up

1A-D2-**Nazareth [4]-WINNER**

2A-Tahoka-Semifinals,

3A-none,

4A-none,

5A-none

2007   1A-D1-New Deal-Semifinals

1A-D2-**Nazareth [5]-Winner**

2A-**Shallowater [2]-Runner up**

3A-Abilene Wylie-Runner up,

4A-none,

5A-none

2008   1A-D1-White Deer-Semifinals

1A-D2-Paducah [2]-Semifinals,

2A-none,

3A-none,

4A-none,

5A-none

2009   1A-D1-Plains-Runner up

1A-D2-Nazareth [6]-Runner up

2A-Shallowatr [3]-Semifinals

3A-Lubbock Estacado [2]-Semifinals,

4A-none,

5A-none

2010   **1A-D1-Gruver [2]-Semifinals**

1A-D2-Nazareth [7]-WINNER, Grady-Runner up

2A-Idalou-Runner up

3A-Lubbock Estacado [3]-WINNER

4A-none,

5A-none

2011   1A-D1-Clarendon-Semifinals

1A-D2-Paducah [3]-WINNER

2A-Idahou [2]-WINNER

3A-none,

4A-none,

5A-none

2012   1A-D1-Olton-Semifinals

1A-D2-Grady [2] Semifinals

2A-Idalou [3]-Semifinals

3A-Estacado [4] Semifinals

4A-none,

5A-none

2013   1A-D1-none

1A-D2-Texline-Semifinals, Water Valley-Semifinals

2A-Idalou [4]-Semifinals

3A-Abilene Wylie [2]-Semifinals,

4A-none,

5A-none

2014   1A-D1-Smyer-Semifinals

1A-D2-Water Valley [2]-WINNER, Nazareth [8]-Semifinals

2A-Bushland-Semifinals, 3A-none

4A-Amarillo-Runner up,

5A-none

2015   **1A-Texline [2] WINNER**

2A-Canadian-**WINNER**

3A-Childress-Semifinals,

4A-none,

5A-none,

6A-none

2016	1A-Happy-Semifinals, **Grady [3]-Runner up**
	2A-Canadian [2]-Winner
	3A-Brownfield-**WINNER**
	4A-none,
	5A-none,
	6A-none
2017	1A-Borden County-Semifinals, **Happy [2]-Runner up**
	2A-Clarendon-Semifinals
	3A-none,
	4A-none,
	5A-none,
	6A-none
2018	**1A-Borden County- [2[-Semifinals**
	1A-Nazareth- [9]-Runner up
	2A-Stinnett West Texas-**WINNER**
	3A-Seminole-Semi Finals
	4A-None
	5A-None
	6A-None
2019	1A-Jayton-Runner up
	1A-Nazareth- [10]-Runner up
	2A-Gruver- [3]-Runner up
	3A-None
	4A-None
	5A-None
	6A-None

During the time period of 2001-2017, the Panhandle/Plains region was dominated by Nazareth at the UIL State of Texas basketball tournament. Nazareth had ten state tournament appearances winning the State Championship 5 times with 4 Runner up exits and 1 Semifinal appearance. Next was Idalou with 1 State Championship ring, 1 Runner up exit, and 2 Semifinal appearances. Estacado also had 4 state tournament appearances with 1 State Championship ring, and 3 Semifinal exits. Close were Grady, Paducah, Shallowater and Morton with 3 state tournament appearances. All four schools had 1 State Championship ring, 1 Runner up exit, and 1 Semifinal appearance. Gruver had 3 state tournament appearances also, with 2 runner up metals, and 1 semi-finals medal.

Canadian made two trips to the State tournament and won 2 State Championship rings. Texline won 1 State Championship ring and had a Semifinalist exit. Happy, Abilene Wylie, Dimmitt, and Stratford had 2 state tournament appearances.

TEAMS FROM THE PANHANDLE/PLAINS REGION THAT HAVE MADE THREE OR MORE STATE TOURNAMENT APPEARANCES FROM 1920-2017

UIL STATE BOYS TOURNAMENT APPREARANCES [3 OR MORE]		UIL STATE CHAMPIONS 1920-2017 [2 OR MORE]	
DIMMIT	17	NAZARETH	6
NAZARETH	16	MORTON	6
MORTON	13	PAMPA	5
PAMPA	12	DIMMITT	4
LAMESA	11	MCADOO	3
SEMINOLE	10	LAMESA	3
PADUCAH	8	PADUCAH	3
GRUVER	8	SEMINOLE	2
SHALLOWATER	7	GRUVER	2
STRATFORD	6	CANYON	2
ABILENE	6	DUMAS	2
CANYON	6	ABERNATHY	2
AMARILLO	6	CANADIAN	2
BORGER	5	AMARILLO	2 * PALO DURO & AMARILLO HIGH
PLAINVIEW	5	LUBBOCK	2* ESTACADO & LUBBOCK HIGH
ABERNATHY	5		

AMARILLO PALO DURO	4
CHILDRESS	4
CANADIAN	4
IDALOU	4
LUBBOCK ESTACADO	4
ANDREWS	4
CHILDRESS	4
CLARENDON	4
LEVELLAND	4
HEREFORD	3
DUMAS	3
BROWNFIELD	3
DUMAS	3
HAPPY	3
WHITEDEER	3
ASPERMONT	3
SANFORD FRITCH	3
MEADOW	3
CISCO	3
PLAINS	3
HEDLEY	3

BASKETBALL Coaching records of coaches that were successful in the Panhandle/Plains region. Note: Some coaches made their mark in other regions but for listing purposes all names that we can associate with the Panhandle/Plains region will be mentioned, particularly where they finished their high school coaching. Also, the records listed are from Texas Basketball Magazine [Bob Springer is the editor & publisher] He is also the organizer of "Texas Basketball Museum". If mistakes are made, it is not the fault of the Texas Basketball Magazine but rather the fault of the editor of this book.

High School coaching records of Boys from the Panhandle/Plains region. - [Combined-HS boys and girls*] [Active coaching UP TIL 2019 **] [****Combined HS boys and girls-College Men/Women]

TOP HIGH SCHOOL COACHING WITH 400 WINS OR MORE

Name	School	Wins
Carl Irlbeck *	Hart/others	1014
Ron Mayberry****	Permian/Hereford/others	906
Ken Cleveland	Dimmitt	886
OW Follis	Lamesa	857
Danny Nix **	Burkburnett	800+
Tony Mauldin	Morton /others	746
Rocky Rawls	Bronte	700+
Allen Simpson	Amarillo/Canyon	697
Robert Hale	Pampa	664
Rocky Rawls	Bronte	651
Micky Baker	Water Valley	636
Gano Tubb	Levelland	630
Randy Dean	Coronado	562
Dan Hamrick	Canyon	549
Duane Hunt	Borger	548
Leslie Broadhurst **	Canyon Randal	559
Doug Gordon**	Stanton/Wall/Midland Lee	526
Terry Collins	O'Donnell	519
Ricky Guy	Claude/Memphis/River Road	517
Doug Gordon **	Stanton/Midland Lee	526
Kim Nichols	Coahoma	509
Wayne Tipton	Gruver	500
Randy Dean	Coronado	500
Jeff Evans **	Amarillo Palo Duro	475
Bubba Edwards**	Borden County	423
Jim Reid	Dumas	420

High School boys' basketball coaching legends in the Panhandle/Plains region deserve a big pat on the back saying, "good job". Basketball is a skilled athletic sport and often the skill part requires many extra hours in the gym which means long hours of work for the player and the coach. In the smaller divisions of the state of Texas most athletes play all the sports which mean schools have a better chance to win in their division. In that situation the Panhandle/Plains athletes compete very well often excelling in many cases. If the playing field is level, the Panhandle/Plains athletes hold their own but the larger divisions struggle on the state level. Simply put. in cities like Ft. Worth, Dallas, Houston, and San Antonio have better numbers in term of athletes. The higher classifications usually must yield to the other regions in the state of Texas because the larger metro schools have a huge advantage over the Panhandle/Plains regions. The big cities in the Panhandle/Plains region are Abilene, Lubbock, Wichita Falls, Amarillo and San Angelo. Those cities provide excellent competition but when you compare them to Ft. Worth, Dallas, San Antonio, and Houston the Panhandle/Plains athletes don't get the same level of completion. It doesn't take a rocket scientist to figure out that the better competition you play the better chances you have in order to improve your talents you have. With that said we have many basketball coaching legends in the Panhandle/Plains region. Too many to just name a few so we will put them in categories just like we did football legends. Those categories are:

- LARGE SCHOOL COACHING LEGENDS SMALL SCHOOL COACHING LEGENDS
- SCHOOLS THAT BECAME A LEGEND IN BASKETBALL
- TRADITION AND LEGEND ALL IN ONE-62 YEARS OF WINNING BASKETBALL
- FATHER/SON WINNERS IN THE STATE TOURNAMENT
- A LEGEND TO REMEMBER AND NEVER FORGET
- OTHER COACHING LEGENDS THAT WE SHOULD NEVER FORGET

LARGE SCHOOL COACHING LEGEND: CLIFTON MCNEELY-PAMPA

A trivia question that can stump almost everyone in today's world of Texas high school basketball is asked the following question. What School dominated the Texas State Championship in the large school division of the UIL in the 50's? Of course, the answer is Pampa and the coach was Clifton McNeely. It was a time like no other time in the history of Texas high school basketball located in the Texas Panhandle. I know first-hand because I was playing my high school basketball at Amarillo High School and guess who we couldn't beat? My junior year, Pampa was runner-up for the Large School [4AAAA] State Championship and my senior year Pampa was the large school division State Championship.

Clifton McNeely was born in Greenwood, Texas, graduated from Slidell High School, Decatur Baptist Junior College, and Texas Wesleyan University in Fort Worth, Texas. He left the University after the 1941-42 basketball season and joined the United States Army Air Corps becoming a World War II veteran. He returned to Texas Wesleyan for the 1946-47 basketball season where he led the nation in scoring and led his team to a school best 30-4 record.

Clifton was the 1st pick of the inaugural 1947 BAA draft by the Pittsburg Ironman-becoming the first player ever drafted in the NBA. However, he was not interested in the signing and never played in the NBA. After working for Phillip 66 in Bartlesville, Oklahoma for four months in 1947, McNeely returned to Texas and became the Head Coach at Pampa High School. His 13-year record at Pampa was 320-43.

McNeely teams advanced to the State Championship 6 times winning 4 state championships. Following his coaching career, he was assistant principal at Castleberry High School in Fort Worth, principal at Bridgeport High School, principal at Denton High School, and retired as an administrator in the Irving Independent School District.

Pampa celebrated the 50's state titles recently with one of the main attractions being the signing party of Teddy McIlvain book called **"22: E. Jay McIlvain Story of Faith and Inspiration"**. The book emphasizes the influence of former Pampa coach Clifton McNeely on McIlvain and his Pampa teammates. McIlvain thinks the success of those Harvester teams can be directly traced to McNeely. McIlvain said, "We started out in junior high and the football coach was coaching the basketball team and he told me I was too little to play". McIlvain ended up making the Pampa varsity for three seasons and he was a state championship game MVP. During this celebration a video was shown featuring the highlights of those championship teams who won 72 straight games from 1952-55. Those Pampa teams had success which most likely never be matched by other Texas Panhandle teams. Jim Bond, who became a minister and is also a Panhandle Sports Hall of Fame member officiated McNeely's funeral in 2013 said, "It's very rare to have the kind of relationship we all had together, we were a family all put together by McNeely".

I can testify to his coaching ability and his loyalty of the players he coached. I played at TCU on the same team as Jerry Pope who played for McNeely during those days. Jerry and I were very good friends and all he talked about was Coach McNeely. I was so full of his stories about coach McNeely that I had to find out firsthand, so I arranged to meet with him when he was the assistant principal at Castleberry High School. It was an awesome experience for me to sit next to him and hear his words about basketball. I knew I was going to coach and I wanted to hear from the best. It was the smartest things I ever did in my coaching career. I found out two things that have carried me over into my entire career in coaching regardless of what sport, what gender or where I coached. First, I found out why Pampa was better than we were when I played against the Pampa teams in the 50's. They were more dedicated, better conditioned, and were committed to getting better by hard work and time in the gym. They had a gym that was available 24-7. They outworked us, out played us, and were far more dedicated to winning than we were. It wasn't even close. Second, I learned the secret to winning from him and have used his formula for my entire life. All the above is what makes the difference in winning but it will not work if you don't have a commitment from the entire group including the coach and community. When you get both the coach and the players committed to the goal they want, it can happen, but the coach must lead and be an example for all to follow. So, you really thought there was a secret to winning. No, it is the same thing you hear from all great coaches. The only problem with doing what was suggested is getting it done. That is not easy, and it takes lots of folks to really get that accomplished but the bottom line is the leadership of the head coach and the relationship that coach has with the players, administration, and community.

During his coaching career at Pampa Coach McNeely was offered coaching positions at University of Texas at Austin, University of Texas at El Paso, and Rice University. Instead he would decide to stay at Pampa. McNeely was inducted into the Texas High School Hall of Fame, Slidell ISD Hall of Fame, The Panhandle Sports Hall of Fame and the Texas Wesleyan University Hall of Fame. In 1960 Pampa renamed the

Basketball field house giving it the name of McNeely Field house in his honor.

THE PAMPA CONNECTION:
ROBERT HALE-PAMPA-EVERMAN-SEYMOUR-LEWISVILLE-
BURLESON-DALHART

Robert Hale came on board at Pampa in July 1986 already owning a basketball record of 182-110 coaching record. In 13 seasons at Pampa Coach Hale compiled a basketball record of 289-123. His Pampa teams won 8 district titles in a row, seven of which reached the regional finals in the play-offs. Pampa was a powerhouse basketball team between 1991 and 1996 under Coach Hale. The Harvesters played as good as they could advancing to the State Semifinals in 1991 and 1992 losing over- time games in both games. The 1991 game was a triple over-time game that will be remembered in history as one of the greatest Pampa high school games ever played. Then in 1996 under the direction and coaching of Robert Hale, Pampa won the Gold [4AAAA State Championship] once again in the 1996 Texas State Basketball Tournament with a record of 33-3.

In doing so, Robert Hale became a legend in the basketball world of the Texas Panhandle/Plains region. Since I know Robert Hale very well this is easy for me to write because he deserves the best of everything. That is the kind of person he happens to be. My connection with him was through Larry Wartes wife Joyce, who is Roberts's sister. Not only that, my brother Mike Mayberry and Robert are the best of friends, so it was easy for me to stay in contact with him.

What he did at Pampa is awesome. It's one thing to win at a school but to follow a legend and win, then keep on winning it is almost impossible to believe. He was named the Texas Sports Writers Association "Coach of the Year" and honored as the TABC "Coach of the Year for all Classifications". Robert was a three-time selection as Globe-News Super Team Boys Coach of the Year. In 1997 he was honored as the Panhandle Sports Hall of Fame basketball coach of the year.

In 1992 he coached the North basketball team in the McDonalds Texas All-Star game held in conjunction with the Texas High School Coaching Association clinic. In 1963 he coached the Texas Association Basketball all-star game.

When Robert left Pampa for Weatherford high school in 1999, he told everyone that he thanked the players for playing with so much heart and then thanked his assistant coaches finally saying that the fans at Pampa were the greatest in the world.

One tradition that I enjoyed that Robert Hale started at Pampa was the concept of using the # 5 on every jersey on each player or a number that added up to a 5. It was a simple way to back up the thought of playing like a team with is composed of 5 players. I witness this at Denver City when my brother, Mike Mayberry started doing the same thing attempting to get the message over to everyone that it takes a team to win, not individuals.

SMALL SCHOOL COACHING LEGENDS
DIMMITT COACHING LEGENDS:

JOHN BLAINE

Everyone associates Dimmitt with Ken Cleveland and rightly so. But before there was a Cleveland there was another legend that few know except those living in the Dimmitt area. His name is John Blaine and most folks give him credit for starting the rich tradition at Dimmit. Of course, Cleveland took to another level.

In June 2006, a group of friends, family, and former players gathered around the former Dimmitt high school building, now part of the Dimmitt Middle School complex to rename the old building in the memory of John Blaine. John Blaine served as principal, superintendent, and eventually as a full-time coach in the old building.

During the ceremony to rename the building, Blaine's daughter was talking to the crowd and said, to quote one of my dad's favorite players, Pat Tate Truelove, on the occasion where she was inducted into the 34th Panhandle Sports Hall of Fame, "He was the very best coach I have ever played for anywhere I played." "Every coach I played for I called "coach", but his name was Mr. Blaine."

Blaine received his B.S. from West Texas State Teacher's College in 1935, and his master's degree in education from Colorado State in 1941. He began teaching and coaching at Friona at the junior high in 1936. The next year he moved to Dimmitt where he was a coaching assistant. In 1940 he took on the role of high school principal for three years then was selected as the superintendent for five years. In 1948 he returned to coaching. Blaine was an old school coach which means he coached everything, both genders and all levels.

Many people agree that Coach Blaine was the first to introduce the "T" formation in football around the Panhandle of Texas. Coaches would crowd into the stands just to watch the formation and see for themselves concerning this new type of football formation. One thing for sure, his return to the athletic scene in Dimmitt totally went up several notches all for the good. He was the head coach in football, girls' and boys' basketball, and track. Later, Aubrey Lester joined him as an assistant coach. Then, between the years of 1948-1952, Dimmitt became a house- hold name in athletics across the State of Texas.

During that period, the Dimmitt Bobcats won 48 games while losing 6 in football. The boys' basketball team had 163 wins and only 13 losses. His girls' basketball team had 105 victories and only 7 defeats. His track teams won honors ranging from second in district to second in state. His girls' basketball teams won the Texas State Basketball Championship in 1950, 1951 and 1952. During that five-year period, the boys' basketball teams won the district every year, the bi-district title three times and in 1948 they were defeated at the Texas State Tournament. But in 1952, Dimmitt won the gold and was declared the boys State champs. There have been very few teams win the state championship in both the girls and the boys' championships but how many win the championship with the same coach? To make everything sweeter from the boys' basketball perspective, that year in 1952 the UIL decided that the Class A Champ needed to play the Class AA Champ who would be called the Divisional Champ. Dimmitt was undefeated with a 36-0 record and Bowie was undefeated with 35-0 record. Dimmitt had not been beaten in the last 65 boy's games and Bowie had a 70-game winning record. Dimmitt won the game 59- 54 to stay undefeated.

In 1952, Dimmitt under the direction of John Blaine set a record that has never been broke and I don't think will ever be broke. Coach Blaine coached the football team to an 11-1 championship year and then he was the head coach of both the girls and boys state championship teams who had a combined 72-0 record. Coaching all three sports his coaching record was 83 wins and one loss. That says it all.

What people didn't know except the players that played under his direction was his main assistant coach was his wife, Juanita. He would send her out on scouting trips to scout the opponents for the coming game. When they came home, it was like one coach talking to another coach and she took much joy in his successful career. Any kind of award he received should also have her name on it and very few would disagree with that statement.

If he was living in our day and time, his awards and recognition would be awesome for sure, but in those days, athletics was not put on such a high level of appreciation. However, he was named the Texas "State Coach of the Year" including all sports and all districts. He was named the "Winningest Coach in America" and in 1977, he was selected into the "Panhandle Sports Hall of Fame." In 1979, he was selected in the Texas High School Coaching "Hall of Honor" by the coaching association of Texas. He coached 16 "All-State players and three of those became All-Americans' in college.

DIMMITT COACHING LEGEND: KEN CLEVELAND

If there has ever been a legend in the world of coaching boys' basketball it has to be Ken Cleveland. He did more for basketball in the Panhandle of Texas than anyone in our present time and day. Before he was selected as the head boy's coach, Dimmitt was already known for its basketball, but Cleveland took the program to another level. I know first-hand because I was the head boys' basketball coach at Hereford which was only 25 miles from Dimmitt. We played them once a year and we never beat them. I respected him a great deal and admired what he did at Dimmitt. What I liked was the way he did it with just sound fundamentals and sound defensive philosophy. Nothing was complicated and it was a piece of work to set back and study his program. I had something happen in a game that I have never seen in my coaching career when playing Dimmitt at Hereford one year. We had the ball out of bounds and Dimmitt was pressing our offensive players trying to create a turnover on the sideline out of bounds play. Time was running out; we were out of time-outs and our player [Hereford] was starting to panic trying to throw the pass to a Hereford player and in his panic just dribbled the ball inbounds instead of passing the ball. Everyone was in shock as I was. Officials hesitated for a second and finally called a violation. Most everyone laughed, even Ken smiled at me. That was Dimmitt basketball for sure.

Ken Cleveland was born and raised in Coleman, Texas where he played football, basketball and tennis. Not to mention he was an outstanding student and a school leader. He married Libby Pegram in his second-year college. After being named All-State in basketball his senior year Ken received a basketball scholarship to Texas University and was co-captain and All Conference for the Texas Longhorns. Ken started his coaching career at Sonora high school and after three years he became the Head basketball coach at Dimmitt. Soon after moving to Dimmitt Vicki was born and then two years later Kevin came into the Cleveland Household. Then in 1967, Ken Cleveland coached his Dimmitt Bobcats to the Championship game in boys' basketball and from that point on, Coach Ken Cleveland legacy started.

Over the next 26 years, they made ten trips to Austin winning the State Championship in boys' basketball three times, 1975, 1982 and 1983. Ken coached at Dimmitt 32 years and his team won the District Championship 27 times. His overall coaching record of 887-277 is one of the best in the USA.

The thing that was most important to Cleveland was his family and his players. There is a book called "Letters for Coach" that remembers the legacy of Coach Cleveland through the eyes of the people he touched in his lifetime. I know I was touched when I read some of the thoughts and words from some of his players. One of those players I recruited when I was the Head men's basketball coach at South Plains College was Pat McDonald. Pat wrote his letter he was in the Army located in Saudi 23 miles from Kuwait. He was writing to Libby and thanking her for all she had done for him but never got away from the "Pride and Poise" that he inherited from the Dimmitt Bobcats basketball program coached by Ken Cleveland. He said that this was the biggest challenge he had ever faced, and he felt confident because of his background in Dimmitt. He talked about moving from one position to another every hour on the hour. He said, "My Company is set ready to attack the best Iraqi men." "My platoon is leading the company and I feel like I am a lucky guy." He continues, "I am not worried too much, but I do think a lot about my father when he was killed in Vietnam when I was 18 months old." Pat said in his letter that he was 99.99999% sure he would return healthy. That was the Dimmit way of thinking. One of the things that impressed me about Ken was his legacy concerning his former players that became outstanding coaches. Not wanting to leave anyone out, please understand that these are the ones that were mentioned in the book, "Letters for Coach." John Smith, Amarillo; Jerry Schaeffer, West Texas A&M; Rocky Rawls, Bronte; David Land, Denison; Jeff Bell, Brock; Larry Birdwell, Lorenzo; Steve Myatt, Clarendon; Johnny Hampton, Canyon; Blake Brown, Wayland Baptist University; David Bellingshausen, Fort Worth; Kevin Cleveland, Wayland Baptist University; Dwight McDonald, Palo Duro; Alan Steinke, Dimmitt; Richard Wood, Dimmitt.

Ken Cleveland has been called the John Wooden of Texas high school basketball but most basketball fans from the Panhandle of Texas think it is just the opposite. They think that John Wooden is the Ken Cleveland of college basketball. To be honest there are some outstanding characteristics each had that were similar. Both were humble, polite gentlemen on the court and off the court and both were outstanding players in high school and college. Both coaches used calm approaches to their coaching technique without raising their voices or using profanity. Both proved over and over that they could win with talent and without talent. There were many others but the one that stood out to me was they both had a long-lasting impact on everyone they surround themselves around in a positive way.

Coach Cleveland was the second president of the TABC, Texas Association of Basketball Coaches serving in 1977-78. He was inducted into the Texas High School Basketball Hall of Fame one month before his death. Two TABC scholarships are awarded in his name annually. In 1988, he was inducted into the Texas High School Coaches Association Hall of Honor as a basketball coach. He had the Dimmitt gym named after him, he had a book come from his lifetime as a coach, and he has a legacy that can't be denied. Just before his death, Ken told a pastor friend in Dimmitt that his life was complete and if the Lord took him, he would be ready. Ken's son Kevin said, "He may have been ready, but we weren't." But the statement of the century was made by his granddaughter Lacy Buckley saying, "the chance of being struck by lightning is one in a million. That's what Granddaddy was, one is a million."

LARGE SCHOOL LEGEND: O.W. FOLLIS-LAMESA

Lamesa was another city in the Panhandle/Plains region that was known for its basketball. When Coach Follis was playing high school basketball at Hughes Springs, his team advanced to the State Basketball Championship tournament in 1935. Never did he dream that one day he would be the head coach at Lamesa which is the team that defeated his team that particular year.

Follis was a star athlete at College of Marshall, now called East Texas Baptist University. He played football and basketball and earned his master's degree in physical education and industrial arts at East Texas State University. He served in the United States Navy from 1942-1946 where he was stationed at the Naval Training Station in Chicago. Turns out that was a good thing as he married Mildred Winton from Waukegan, ILL on July 17, 1945.

Coach Follis was hired at Lamesa in 1946 and he stayed on board until 1982. During that period, Follis put together a high school boys basketball record of 857-216. He now has the 24th best boys' high school coaching record in the United States of America. From 1952 to

1959 he was the head football coach at Lamesa High School where he had a record of 39-39. Then in 1960 he gave up his football duties and concentrated on basketball.

During his 36 years as head coach he never had a losing record. He teams at Lamesa won 20 district championships and advanced to the Texas State tournament five times. Coach Follis and his Golden Tornadoes brought home the gold in 1960, 1967 and 1975.

In 1960 Lamesa won its first State Championship defeating South San Antonio, 56-54 in the final game and defeated Aldine in the semifinals 51-48. To get to the State Tournament the Golden Tornado's had to defeat Dumas and Brownwood. The first championship is always the hardest and that story held true when Lamesa won its third State Basketball Championship in 1975. In 1975 they defeated South Grand Prairie and Cleveland to win the Gold. In regional they beat Brownwood by 17 and Levelland by 9 in order to qualify for the State Championship.

Follis was involved in community work in Lamesa. He was an active member of the noon Lion's club for 45 years and he was a former director of the Lamesa Boy's Club. His wife Mildred taught English at Lamesa High School from 1946-1982. Many of those years his wife was also the high school Cheerleading Sponsor.

O.W. Follis was inducted into the Texas High School Coaches Association Hall of Honor in 1975 and the Texas Basketball Hall of Fame in 1986. In 1997 the Lamesa Middle School gym [where they play the high school games] was named O.W. and Mildred Follis Gymnasium.

LARGE SCHOOL LEGEND: GANO TUBB-LEVELLAND

If you mention O.W. Follis when talking about great basketball coaches, in the same sentence Gano Tubb would be talked about. They were like two peas in a pod. Matter of fact, the team that usually went to the UIL Texas State Boys' Basketball tournament was usually decided in the Levelland vs. Lamesa game. I was a lucky guy because I knew Gano and his family very well. My first year in Hereford we were already scheduled to play Levelland and when we played them, we beat them in

Levelland. I had heard so much good about Gano that I started getting the big head. Little did I understand at that time that we were just lucky and soon that became clear to me because we didn't beat them the next three years.

Gano Tubb graduated from Levelland High school. He attended Southeastern Oklahoma where he lettered in football, basketball and track. He was named "The Little All-American" in football his senior year. He started his career in coaching as an assistant at Levelland High school from 1938-1940. Then he was named the Head football and basketball coach in Levelland from 1941-1947. His basketball teams won the district six straight years and advanced to the State UIL Basketball tournament in 1946 and 1947. They were runner-up champs in 1947. His football teams compiled a won-lost record of 33-22 which included a regional runner up and a district championship. Then for a short period of time Gano moved to O'Donnell where success followed him again. Levelland hired him back two years later and Gano started his real career at Levelland. His basketball teams won the district championship 1949,1950,1952,1954, 1965, 1967, 1972, and 1973. His 1952 team advanced to the UIL Texas State Basketball tournament. In 1972 Gano was named "The South Plains Coach of the Year" and was nominated to coach the Texas High School basketball All-Star game. Finally, after his 1973 team that had a 29-1 record, and was a regional finalist, Gano Tubb retired. He ended his basketball career with 630- 248 record and a 43-27 record in football.

If ever there was a legend in the high school basketball coaching legends that was loved any more than Gano, it would be hard to find. Many coaches often make people mad or disappointed in something they do most often by accident. It is what it is and mostly it's just human nature. Gano Tubb was one of the most liked citizens of Levelland each year he coached. He was loved by his players, his family, the Levelland students, the Levelland administration, the Levelland community and even his opponents. At the time of his death Gano was the Hockley County Judge but he could have been the mayor if he so desired.

He was described as a calm and determined coach that never yelled, cussed or mistreated any of the players he coached. If he had something to say, he said it one on one and face to face. He used inspiration to gather their attention and to get them to play to their potential. The only thing negative was he carried a small knife with him and in the early days of his coaching he would throw the knife into the floor in a nervous habit while coaching. Later, that stopped and then he just used it to clean the bottom of his shoes. The greatest asset he had was that he kept everything simple. He often just told them to just put the ball in the hoop boys. That is all you must do.

During his 35 years of coaching his teams won 16 district championships, three regional championships and guided his teams to the State UIL Basketball Championship three times. In 1979 Gano was selected to be in the Texas High School Coaches Association Hall of Honor and in the same year, the new gymnasium at Levelland High school was named "The Gano Tubb Gymnasium." Gano Tubb was an active member of the community of Levelland in more ways than one. He was a member of the Levelland Country Club and after his death the Levelland members created a golf tournament called the "Gano Tubb Invitational." One of my biggest thrills came when I was invited to play in the Gano Tubb golf tournament in Levelland, Texas.

SMALL SCHOOL LEGENDS: THE MORTON CONNECTION: TONY MAULDIN AND COMPANY: TED WHITLOCK

Tony Mauldin began his coaching career at Boerne Junior High in 1971. After two years he traveled to Merkel, Texas then he hit the jackpot going to Morton, Texas. At Morton history was made and he was a huge part of it while winning the gold in boys' basketball three times at the Texas UIL State Boys Basketball tournament. At Morton during his last six years [82-87] his teams advanced to the state tournament and included state championships in 1983, 1986 and 1987.

In 1987 Coach Mauldin moved to Western Texas Junior College in Snyder, Texas. That is where I first met him since I was coaching at South Plains College and I still remember the wars we had in recruiting and playing vs. each other. I learned to respect that guy for who he was as a person and who he was as a coach. From WTC, he moved to Abilene Christian for five seasons. Then he went to Kenya doing missionary work, but he ended up leading a technical school in Nairobi, Kenya to three boy's national titles and two girls' national titles. The next thing I know he is back in the States and signed on with Lakeview Centennial, Garland, Texas where had several playoff teams, one going all the way to the state championship game.

Tony has 746 wins in his career coaching high school boys' basketball. He was named the "National Coach of the Year" by the National Federation of State High School Associations while coaching at Lakeview Centennial. Winning basketball games just came natural for Tony Mauldin. During his playing days at Howard Payne University, members of the National Association of Intercollegiate Athletics, Howard Payne either won or shared the Lone Star Conference Championship all four years he was at Howard Payne. From the start of Mauldin's basketball coaching career after Howard Payne he became the at Head basketball coach at Boerne leading his team to the District Championship. Then he did the same thing at Merkel, and then to Morton. At Lakeview Centennial his team was in the playoffs five of seven years, two of which ended playing for the state championship at the Texas UIL State Championship tournament.

Mauldin abilities as a coach became well known throughout the state of Texas and many coaches used his style of coaching thinking that was the answer. Soon they would learn that it wasn't just his style but the way he put everything together. Tony is the first to tell you that the relationships he built with his players was the highlight of his career. Many of those players whom he formed a strong bond with during his years of coaching reached out to him before and after his retirement from the coaching world.

TED WHITLOCK-MORTON

Ted graduated from Clinton High School in 1954 then played on Kilgore's College 1956 National Championship team where he was named to the All-American team in 1956. He graduated from East Texas State University, starting his coaching career at Morton, Texas.

Whitlock is the one given credit for starting the Morton basketball dynasty. He started his coaching career at Morton as a Junior High School Boy's coach and the Head Girls Basketball in 1960. Under his direction Morton dominated for nearly 20 years. Coach Whitlock guided his Morton Indians to the Texas UIL State Tournament four times from 1970-1976. They lost in the state semi-finals in 1970, won the State Championship in 1972, lost in the semifinals in 1973, lost in the finals in 1976. In 1972, Ted Whitlock was named the Texas State Coach of the Year.

Coach Whitlock was a member of the Hall of Fame at Kilgore College. He died on June 11, 2014.

In 1977 Morton had another State Championship under the leadership of Dan Smith, then in 2005, Ignatius Caraway, who graduated from Panhandle State won the boys State Championship at Morton.

SMALL SCHOOL-LARGE SCHOOL LEGEND:

CARL IRLBECK-NAZARETH/CLARENDON/ABERNATHY/ PLAINVIEW/PLAINVIEW CHRISTIAN/MONTEREY/HART

If there is such a thing as a coaching legend, then Carl Irlbeck gets my vote. He was someone special in the basketball coaching world located in the Panhandle/Plains region. I first met him when he was coaching at Abernathy and I was coaching at Wayland Baptist University. I asked him if he would work our basketball camps at Wayland. It was not an easy chore since we went back to back three straight weeks with overnight campers. Matter of fact it was hard work and tough. If anyone has worked an over- night camp they will understand. Carl's youngest son Bruce was enrolled in our camp, so Carl decided to coach that same week. After the first day of working 18 hours-from getting the campers up in the morning for breakfast to putting the campers in bed at night, I knew why Championships followed Carl Irlbeck. Even at his age, not counting me, he was the oldest one working the camp, and no one was disappointed in his work ethic, his enthusiasm, his dedication, his command of basketball knowledge, and his ability to communicate. He was excellent in all regards. I became a Carl Irlbeck fan. Then several years later I recruited two of his players when I was the head coach at South Plains College, and he was the head coach at Plainview. Those two players led South Plains College to a region 5 championship and a record of 4-1 at the National tournament finishing 5th in the Nation. It was the first trip ever to the National JC tournament for SPC, a huge breakthrough. Then later after both of us retired we went into business together and nothing, but a strong professional attitude was seen by me in Carl Irlbeck after 35 years.

Irlbeck a Happy native who has coached at Nazareth, Clarendon, Abernathy, Plainview, Plainview Christian, Monterey, and Hart has a won lost record of 1014-449 in 37 years. At this point in time that stands 11th in the nation coaching high school girls' and boys' basketball. Long before that his coaching nearly came to an end. He retired after the 1994 season at Plainview where they won the Texas State UIL basketball tournament in the 3AAAA classification. He had diabetes and it was taken a toll on his health. He said, "I thought I was done with coaching after his teams had made 28 playoff appearances, won 25 district titles and 3 state championships.

However, Hart needed a math teacher and he was available, so he started another career as a math teacher. It didn't last because soon he became the Hard Boys' basketball coach and finished his career at Hart, Texas. He said, "They needed a boy's coach that could help them learn and get better, so I felt needed and just did it." "I never say what I am going to do, but I have never said no to something that affects kids in a positive way."

Irlbeck proved over and over to everyone that he had a winning touch and a winning philosophy in coaching. He made six state tournament appearances and took four different teams to the state basketball tournament. He took Clarendon, Abernathy, and Plainview to the UIL State Basketball tournament winning two. Then he took Plainview

Christian Academy girls to the TAPPS State Championship and won the championship in 1996-97 basketball and volleyball. He coached a cross-country team to a state title in 1984 at Abernathy. Then he won state titles in tennis at Abernathy 1979, 1980, and 1981.

If we could give an Old School Coaching award it would go to Carl Irlbeck for sure. Carl said, "I always enjoyed the game of basketball more than the average person." He continued "Since I was a little boy, I always dreamed of playing on a state championship basketball team." "But I wasn't good enough to play, so I just concentrated on being a coach that could lead a group of players to the state championship."

SMALL SCHOOL LEGENDS
NAZARAETH IS A LEGEND IN BOY'S BASKETBALL

If a school could be called a basketball legend, then Nazareth would win hands down in the State of Texas much less the Panhandle/Plains region. The total is 23 state championships total for the Boys and Girls basketball program in Nazareth which is the best in the USA according to many opinions but for sure the best in Texas. In the boys alone, Nazareth has made 15 state tournament appearances winning six State Championships being in the final two nine times.

Let's start with Johnny Hampton who graduated from West Texas State University. He won the first boy's state championship while coaching the Nazareth boys in 1986. Nothing but class and championships follow Johnny Hampton as his name is well known though out the State of Texas and the Panhandle/Plains region. He is still coaching and still winning state championships as an assistant girls' basketball coach at Canyon high school working with the Legend of all legends Joe Lombard. Next a guy by the name of Mike Scarborough who graduated from Texas Tech University won state championships coaching the boys at Nazareth in 2002, 2003 and 2006. He was inducted into the Panhandle Sports "Hall of Fame. Zack Boxell was the boy's coach winning the state championship in 2007 and 2010. The interested thing about Zack is that between Zack's and Doug [his father], they have a combined 8 state championships. The last state tournament appearance for Nazareth was in 2014 under Coach

Nathan Branum. None of the above coaches fall into the category of "less we forget" because they are alive and making a difference with everyone within their reach but the history of Nazareth boys' basketball in the Panhandle/Plains region is something that we always want to remember.

MCADOO

McAdoo defeated Midway [Henrietta] 58-42 for the State Championship in 1960. It was their first of three in five years [1960, 1963 and 1964]. Fabian Lemley from Texas Tech University was the head coach in all three championship years. He was a legend in his own rights by winning 243 games at McAdoo in his first seven years. McAdoo had only 38 students in the high school with only 15 boys which 13 played basketball. George Scott was only 5'10" but he scored 88 pts [43, 31, and 14] in three games at the state tournament and broke the 1947 state tournament record for a 3-game series and his 43 pts in the semi-finals win was a class B record. George later graduated from West Texas State and became a high school coach.

CAREY [LOCATED IN CHILDRESS COUNTY]
[A HOOSIER'S REAL STORY IN TEXAS]

In 1937 when all schools in Texas regardless of the number of students in the school played for the UIL State Championship Basketball Tournament Carey was the State Champion. With an enrollment fewer than 100 students Carey won the championship by defeated Fort Worth Poly in the semi - finals and Gober in the finals. The 1937 State Championship remains the only state championship ever won in any sport in the history of Childress County. Carey was coached by the legendary Albert "Catfish" Smith who became the head coach at Carey in 1934 at the age of 22. In 1936 he guided the Carey Cardinals to a 40-8 record and to the state semifinals. Coached Smith later coached at Mt. Vernon. In 1947-1948 his football team was 11-0 and his basketball team was 30-0. That feat has never been duplicated in the history of Texas sports.

GRUVER – THE TIPTON CONNECTION +
LAWRENCE BROTHERTON

Wayne Tipton is a legendary coach who had a wonderful career coaching boys' basketball in the Texas Panhandle. He coached at Samnorwood, Briscoe, Sunray, White Deer Gruver, Cisco Junior College, Dalhart and Meridian. He coached both girls and boys with over 500 wins to his credit. He has coached teams in the Texas UIL State Basketball tournament at three different schools. In 1960 his Sunray boys' team was the runner-up champion. Then in White Deer he won his first state championship in 1962. That was when I became a huge fan of Wayne Tipton. In my opinion, it is one thing to win a championship at one school but to do it at another school is awesome. Then to top that, he goes to Gruver and takes the greyhounds to the state tournament in 1965 and puts the icing on the cake by winning the state championship at Gruver in 1966. In 2006 Coach Tipton was selected to be in the Texas High School Basketball Hall of Fame.

Wayne Tipton will always be remembered by all those that he touched, and he touched so many students everywhere he coached. Wayne Tipton is a coach that we never want to forget. But we are reminded of his legacy because he has a son named Sam Tipton who has taken his legacy in the world of coaching to another level. We will cover that issue when we write about the girls coaching legacy of the Panhandle/Plains region.

THE COACH THAT BROKE THE ICE WINNING THE FIRST STATE
CHAMPIONSHIP AT GRUVER WAS LAWRENCE BROTHERTON.

Gruver won the UIL State Boys' basketball tournament in 1950 by defeating Waelder 43-34 in the finals. What made the victory so sweet was that Gruver won two games earlier both by one pt. when they were not expected to win. The Austin Newspaper said this about that Gruver team in 1950. The Greyhounds were a "diminutive but scrappy" squad which relied upon their "ball-hawking play."

GRUVER TRADITION IS MARKED BY THE NEW BASKETBALL ARENA IN GRUVER.

In 2010, the Amarillo Globe News wrote a sports article about the new gym that Gruver build. The new gym cost $4.9 million and has 36,000 square feet with a walking trail built above the gym floor. It has four scoreboards, multiple docking stations for iPads which are linked to speakers that come on when hooked up. There are 13 flat screen TV's and the facility touts upholstered seats. Sheryl Honeycutt, editor of Texas Coach, a publication of the Texas High School Coaching Association said this about the new Gruver Gym. "There is nothing to compare it to it is a cut above the rest."

LARGE SCHOOL LEGEND:
JIM REID-DUMAS/KERRVILLE TIVY/INGRAM MOORE

My association with Jim Reid goes back to 1956 when he was a senior at Palo Duro High School playing under the legendary Tom Gilley. That was when Amarillo High School split into two schools. I remained at Amarillo and he went Palo Duro. Then Palo Duro won the UIL State Basketball Championship in 1956. Then in 1963, we ran into each other again at Perryton Middle School. He was the Head basketball coach at the Middle school and assistant high

school coach under Roy Pennyton. Some coaches you meet never have a bearing on your career, but Jim did on mine. He was instrumental in my getting the Head Basketball position at Adrian, my first head job and then he influenced me into making some changes [that needed to be made] when I was the head basketball coach at Permian High School.

Jim was a loss to everyone that knew him. I had the opportunity to coach against him while I was the head coach at Hereford High School in 1971. We were defeated by Dumas to an over- time game at Dumas and I predicted they would win the State Championship which they did. While coaching at Dumas, he had a tradition where he would put a fireman's hat when he knew the game was won during the game. The fans loved it and often would start yelling for him to put the hard on his head.

In our game, he never put the hat on, and I guess that was one good thing in our defeat. Jim won four championship titles putting himself in a small group of coaches. He and Doug Boxwell are the only two coaches to win state titles in three different schools. Coach Reid won a state title at Dumas in 71, two state titles at Kerrville Tivy, and one state title at Ingram Moore. By the way, he is the only coach to win three back-to-back state championships with two different school districts [Dumas and Kerrville].

Superintendent Bruce Faust said this about Jim. "He made athletics relevant to real life because there was always a lesson to be learned, whether it was during practice, riding on the bus, in class or just talking. He had a gift for that, because he was a great listener as well as a great communicator."

Teams under his guidance won over 400 games in his 27 years of coaching. He also led McMullen County volleyball team to a runner-up state championship in 1992. He was the TABC All Star Coach in 1993, inducted into the Texas High School Basketball Hall of Fame in 1996, Amarillo Globe-News 100 Best Sports Legends of the 20th Century, Panhandle Sports Hall of Fame in 2002, Palo Duro High School Hall of Legends in 2008 and Tivy High School Athletic Hall of Fame in 2007.

He was a deacon and Sunday school teacher, a Lions Club member in Dumas, the Director of the Dumas Chamber of Commerce, on the YMCA board and the First National Bank board of directors in Dumas. He served on the Dumas ISD school board and was awarded the Lamar Award of Excellence for Personal Achievement in 1990.

Jim Reid died on April 25, 2008. What says everything about Jim was during his funeral, four of the Pallbearers were Gene Arrington, Robert Echols, Robert Hover and Paul Hyatt. The reason I mention this is that those four men and Jim Reid were the starting five when Palo Duro won the State Basketball Championship in 1956, exactly 52 years later.

JERRY HALE-DUMAS TRADITION AT ITS BEST AND THE START OF IT ALL-

Jerry Hale broke the ice in two ways in 1962. He coached Dumas to their first UIL State Boys' basketball tournament and at that time Dumas was the first to win both the UIL State in both football and basketball in the same year. Since then three other teams have accomplished that feat but Dumas was the first. In 1962 under Jerry Hale's coaching, Dumas defeated Waxahachie 58-38. The 20-pt. win in the final featured a defense which held Waxahachie to 31% shooting and stopped the outstanding offense of the Indians from Waxahachie. Several of the basketball players played on the State Championship football team also

LARGE SCHOOL LEGEND

ALLEN [BONES] SIMPSON- BORGER/CANYON/BIG SPRING, SPEARMAN, PERRYTON AND AMARILLO

Allen Simpson won everywhere he coached and won big. He had a system and he stuck with his system and it paid off for him winning two state championships and qualifying for the UIL State Basketball tournament four times. He believed in making the most of each possession you have in basketball on the offensive end of the court then he coached that importance to his players then they gave him a career coaching record of 697-372. I started following him when he coached at Spearman and then to Borger. I went to Borger and visited with him about his philosophy of basketball trying to steal all I could from him. That is when he showed me his possession chart and I starting using one myself. When he won the State Championship in the large school division while at Amarillo High School I was in awe because I didn't think that feat was possible.

Coach Simpson was born in Spearman, Texas and graduated from Borger High School. He was a two-time all-district basketball player at Borger. In 1958 he graduated from West Texas State University and took on the nickname of "Bones." He was a two-time all-border conference player and continued at WTSU getting his Master of Education degree in 1963. In 1958 he began his teaching and coaching career for the next 36 years. Coach Simpson had coaching stints in Borger, Canyon, Big Spring, Spearman, Perryton and Amarillo. His basketball teams won two state basketball championships, Canyon in 1964 and Amarillo in 1986. All together he took four teams to the UIL Texas State Basketball tournament, Canyon in 1963/1964, Perryton in 1981 and Amarillo High in 1986.

In 1994 Allen retired from coaching. He was named the 1964 2AA Texas Coach of the Year by the Texas High School Coaching Association and in 1986 the Texas Sports Writers Association Coach of the Year. In 1988 he was inducted into the West Texas State University Athletic Hall of Champions in 2006, and he was the 142nd member inducted into the Panhandle Sports Hall of Fame. One of my biggest pleasures was coaching Sammy Simpson, Coach Allen Simpson's son at South Plains College. Sammy was a delight to be around and he was everything that is good in life, humble and a good example for athletes to follow.

SMALL SCHOOL LEGEND:
RICHARD POTTER-SUDAN/NAZARETH/IDALOU/LEVEL LAND/ SONORA/VEGA

Richard Potter was nominated not once but twice by coaches in the Panhandle/Plains region. Coach Potter was a true down to earth Panhandle, Texas product. Graduated from high school in Tulia where he was an All-District football and basketball player. Continued his upper level education at West Texas State University, started his coaching career while making several stops along the way at Sudan, Nazareth, Idalou, Levelland, Sonora and Vega.

In that period, his 1979 team at Vega won the UIL State Basketball Championship. They defeated LaPoynor in the finals 52-33. No one thought Vega would win the game since LaPoynor had been to the tournament seven times with five state championships to their credit. Since it was Vega's first appearance everyone figured that Vega would be nervous and scared.

Don't get me wrong, Coach Potters teams had won district many times in his lifetime but winning at the state tournament was another thing altogether. Vega didn't disappoint anyone winning the championship by 19 pts. Vega created 23 LaPoynor turnovers and what one Austin Newspaper called "deadeye gunnery throughout the game."

Richard Potter was district "Coach of the Year" five times and he was a Captain in the Army but more than anything else, his fans remember him as a darn good basketball coach

LARGE SCHOOL LEGEND: DUANE HUNT-BORGER

Duane Hunt made an impact in the world of basketball at Borger and then made an impact in the world of evangelism. He had a career basketball coaching record of 548-236 with three trips to the UIL State Basketball tournament being the runner up state champ twice. He was at Borger for twenty-three years with a record of 507-206.

Coach Hunt is a past president of the Texas Association of Basketball Coaches. He served from 1982-1983. He graduated from Oklahoma City where he played for the late legendary Abe Lemons. Duane was one of the original organizers of the Texas Association of Basketball Coaches where he was instrumental in starting the top 20 rankings and the academic all-state teams.

In 1989, Coach Hunt retired but starting working for the good of all mankind. He became the director of missions for the Larry Jones International Ministries. He and his wife have traveled over 68 countries on six continents. He recently has served as the Immediate Past President of the Fellowship of Baptist World Ministries. Duane is known as a gifted master at bringing evangelical leaders, from diverse backgrounds, together, and managing the multiple details of a major crusade.

In 2012 Duane Hunt was honored in San Antonio, Texas by selected to the Texas High School basketball "Hall of Fame."

LARGE SCHOOL LEGEND:
DAN HAMRICK-CANYON/PLAINVIEW/CHILDRESS/
ELECTRA/ATHENS

Dan Hamrick graduated from Olney High School and Midwestern State University making a huge impact coaching boys' basketball at Canyon High School. His Canyon teams made the play-offs nine of 14 years. He coached 30 years and has had a strong influence over many ex- players and coaches in the area. Randy Dean who had a tremendous coaching stop at Coronado High School, Lubbock, Texas said this about Dan Hamrick. "Dan made a huge impact on my coaching career in a positive way so much that I will always owe him for his knowledge and style in coaching."

Coach Hamrick moved to Athens located in East Texas and retired after 30 years in the coaching business. Before he retired, he served as the boys' basketball coach, co-athletic director, assistant athletic director, head athletic director and then consultant to the athletic department.

His career record coaching boys' basketball was 549-301 with 18 play-off appearances. Dan served as the Regional Director for the Texas Association of Basketball Coaches Association and two years on the all-star player selection committee for the Texas High School Coaches Association. In 1994 he was selected to coach the North All Star Basketball Team.

SEMINOLE LEGENDARY CONNECTION-SIXTY-TWO YEARS OF TEXAS BASKETBALL DYNASTY-ELEVEN DIFFERENT COACHES

37 DISTRICT CHAMPIONSHIPS-21 REGIONAL TOURNAMENT APPEARANCES-NINE STATE TOURNAMENT APPEARANCES-2 STATE CHAMPIONSHIPS

HERE ARE THE NAMES OF THOSE COACHES:

Coach FaFollette-Six district championships, 2 regional finalists, 2 regional championships, 1 state finalist, and 1 state championship.

Coach Reneau-Two district championships, 2 regional finalists.

Coach Lominack-Three district championships, 2 regional finalists, 1 state finalists.

Coach Ingle-One district championship, 1 regional finalist.

Coach Caffey-Four district championships, 1 bi-district championship, 1 regional finalist, 1 state championship.

Coach Byerly-One district championship, one regional championship, one state tournament appearance.

Coach Isbell-One district championship, one co-district championship, one area finalist, one regional finalist.

Coach Waldrip-One district runner up, 5 district championships, 1 bi-district championship, 2 regional quarterfinalists, 1 regional finalist, 1 regional championship, 1 state tournament appearance.

Coach Clark-Five district championships, 1 regional quarterfinalist, 1 regional finalist, 1 state runner up championship.

Coach Page-One district runner up, 7 district championships, 2 bi-district championships, 5 regional quarterfinalists, 1 regional finalist.

Coach McWilliams-Three district championships, 2 bi-district championships, 1 regional finalist.

In 1955 Seminole defeated San Marcos 50-49 for the State Championship. Metz LaFollete of West Texas State University was the head coach and the district championship were the first for Seminole. The Austin paper said that Seminole "outhustled" and "outshot" Atlanta in the semi- final win. The Indians lost in the finals in 1957 [to Buna], 1963 [to Clear Creek} and in 1999 [to Mexia]. On that team in 1955 Leland Caffey was a member of that Championship team then he coached Seminole to a State Championship in 1979.

In 1979 Coach Caffey led his Seminole State Championship team defeating Altair Rice Consolidated 47-42. The Austin Newspaper reported that the "physically superior" Rice was stifled by the Seminole defense. Two members of that State Championship team, Danny Wrenn and Mike Grass played for Wayland Baptist University and later, Danny Wrenn became the head girls' basketball coach at Plainview High School. He is now a legend in his own right and still coaching girls' basketball in Plainview, Texas.

PANHANDLE/PLAINS LEGENDARY MOMENTS OF THE UIL STATE BOYS BASKETBALL TOURNAMEN. LEAST WE FORGET

WHAT DO ALL THE HEAD BOY'S BASKETBALL COACHES BELOW HAVE IN COMMON THAT HAPPENED AT THE STATE UIL CHAMPIONSHIP GAME WHICH THEY WON?

SHALLOWATER -2004-Ray Morris was the coach of this championship team and his son Eric Morris led the way for the championship. 1st Eric made a 3pt shot to put the game in overtime then Eric made a twisting jump shot in the lane with 6 seconds on the clock to win the game. Eric was awarded All-State in 2004

DIMMITT-1982/1983-Ken Cleveland was the coach of these championship teams and his son Kevin led the way for both championships. Kevin was an All-State basketball player in 1982 and 1983.

PADUCAH-2011-Jay Cantrell was the coach of this championship team and his adopted sons,

Cantrell and Willie Cantrell led the way for the championship. Willie was an All-State basketball player in 2011.

AMARILLO-1986-Allen Simpson was the coach of this championship team and his son Sammy led the way for the championship. Sammy was an All-State basketball player in 1986.

LUBBOCK ESTACADO-2010-Tony Wagner was the coach of this championship team and his son Kevin led the way for the championship. Kevin was an All-State basketball player in 2010.

GRUVER-1966- Wayne Tipton was the coach of this championship team and his son Sam led the way for the championship. Same was an All-State basketball player in 1965 and 1966.

ABERNATHY-1980-Carl Irlbeck was the coach of this championship team and his son Cletus helped Abernathy win the championship in 1980.

WATER VALLEY-2014-Andy Copley was the coach of this championship team and his son Cameron helped Water Valley win the championship in 2014

CANADIAN-2015/2016-Andy Copley was the coach of these championship teams and his son Cameron led the way for the championship. Cameron was an All-State basketball player in 2015 and 2016.

A LEGEND THAT NEEDS TO BE REMEMBERED -DUNBAR HIGH SCHOOL-LUBBOCK

A legend that reminds us of where we have been and where we are now is Dunbar High School that was in Lubbock, Texas. In 1920, the first school in Lubbock for black students opened in the Flats Neighborhood in Lubbock and later was given the name "Dunbar" named for Laurence Dunbar, an American Poet, novelist and playwright. Then in 1930 Dunbar became a four-year high school and later had its first high school graduation.

Soon Lubbock Dunbar still segregated began a remarkable run in athletic competition all in the Praririe View Interscholastic League. In 1920 it was called the Texas Interscholastic League of Colored Schools but later came under the authority of PVIL.

Dunbar was one of the largest schools in the PVIL classified as 3AAA and won its first state championship in basketball in 1957 then won the state track meet in the same year. In 1960 the Panthers won another state basketball championship by defeating Houston Elmore 74-71. In 1962

Dunbar won another state basketball championship by defeating Galena Park Fidelity Manor 63-52 and in the spring won the state track title.

In 1940 Dunbar using used uniforms handed down from Lubbock High School lost to Wharton Trainer in the state football championship game. But in the spring Dunbar won its second straight state track championship in 1963. Then in the fall of 1963 they won the football state championship defeating Conroe Washington 19-14.

In 1965 Dunbar won its fifth state championship in basketball by defeating Cartage Turner 82-66. According to resources in 1968 Dunbar won its fourth state track meet. Then in 1970 Dunbar became part of the University Interscholastic League called the UIL.

Dunbar High School compiled an outstanding athletic record in 15 years ranging from 1953-1968 winning 11 state championships. During that time period for most of the seasons Prof Struggs was the principal at Dunbar. George Scott was the head football coach from 1953-1964. Damon "Professor" Hill Sr. coached football, basketball and track. Ernest P. Mallory was the basketball coach for most of the championship seasons

A COACHING LEGEND THAT WON THE STATE CHAMPIONSHIP IN THE FIRST YEAR THAT THE SCHOOL OPENED

TOM GILLEY-BULA, SUDAN, PALO DURO [AMARILLO]

Coach Gilley was a coach that was promoted from Junior High School basketball to High School basketball and won a state championship his first year. No one has ever questioned Coach Gilley about paying his dues as a coach before he hit the big-time lights. He spent 13 years at Horace Mann Junior High School coaching all sports in a tough part of the city of Amarillo. He was a fearless leader at a school that needed leadership and he didn't mind demanding their attention with tough love.

Coach Gilley was a strong personality and was very volatile, but his strong suit was he was an outstanding motivator. He was the perfect fit for a group of high school players transferring to Palo Duro from

Amarillo High School because they now lived in the Palo Duro school district. Gilley was like a second father to many young players that didn't have a dad. Like one of his ex-players said about Tom Gilley, "Coach Gilley was our mentor, our coach, and our dad."

What made his first state championship so great was Palo Duro made another appearance five years later when Palo Duro lost in the state championship game to Houston Austin, 68-60. Gilley an extremely intense coach was also very vocal on the sideline sometimes giving him a negative reputation. But it was never negative to his players who understood him and accepted his ways. Tom died in 1995 ending 53 years in Amarillo, all colorful and all respectful to the game of basketball and life.

A COACHING LEGEND THAT ESTABLISHED FIRST CLASS RELATIONS TO EVERYONE HE MET

RANDY DEAN-CHILDRESS-HEREFORD-LUBBOCK CORONADO

If you have ever met Randy Dean, you would know that the statement above is so true. He demonstrates a first-class attitude as well as anyone in the coaching world. He is also a huge winner coaching boys' basketball.

His claim to fame other than his first-class attitude and his winning ways around the basketball- court, is the fact that he coached Jarrett Culver who helped Texas Tech play for the National NCAA basketball championship. He spent 32 years in the coaching business, 16 at Coronado having success at each school ending up with over 500 wins.

Coach Dean put Coronado basketball on another level of success by taking Coronado to the regional tournament in 2011, 2014, 2016, and 2017 where his Coronado team had a 30-4 record. Taking your team to the Regional tournament is an accomplishment in the large school division not to mention coaching Hereford to the UIL State Tournament in 2000-2001. Dean is quick to point out that he had two great coaching mentors in Charlie Johnson and Dan Hamrick.

Coach Dean said, "I never wanted to do anything other than coach." He then said, "What made coaching so special for me is the fact that I had the best assistant coach that exists, my wife Kayle who was always there for me win or lose."

Coach Dean just retired from coaching and soon will receive recognition for his accomplishment as a basketball coach that made a huge difference especially to the young men he coached. He was named All-City Boys Basketball "Coach of the Year" in 2011.

Girls Basketball

LEGENDS IN GIRLS BASKETBALL IN the Panhandle/Plains region are plentiful. So many that I know we will miss someone and that isn't what I want to happen. If it does, please accept my apology now. Simply put, there are so many, it is impossible to name them all so please forgive me.

Ask any old timer sports fan this question. Thinking just about the Panhandle/Plains region which sport has been the consistent dominate sport that has competed on the Texas state level in the last fifty years? No doubt about it, girls' basketball wins the prize. Not that the other sports haven't had their moment of glory, but girls' basketball has been consistent on all levels of play throughout the existents of UIL athletics.

The first recorded UIL high school Texas State championship in girls' basketball was the 1950-51 school year.

None-Means that no school from the Panhandle/Plains region qualified for the State Tournament

**FORMAT: [YEAR – CLASS – SCHOOL – PLACE – HOW MANY [TOURNEY TRIPS]
WIN-FINALIST-SEMIFINALIST**

1951	B	Claude –Winner	1
	1A	McLean -Finalist	1

UIL moved to three divisions

1952	B	Claude Winner	2
	1A	McLean-Semi Finals	2
	2A	Morton –Finalist	1
1953	B	Claude- Winner	3
	1A	New Deal-Winner	1

	2A	Muleshoe-Semi Finals	1
1954	B	Claude-Finalist	4
	1A	None	
	2A	Dimmitt- Winner	1
1955	B	Cotton Center-Finalist	1
	1A	Dimmitt-Winner	2
	2A	Abernathy-Semi-Finals	1
1956	B	Ropesville- Semi-Finals	1
	1A	New Deal-Finals	2
	2A	Tulia-Semi-Finals	1
1957	B	Roosevelt-Winner	1
	1A	Ropesville-Winner	2
	2A	Dimmitt-Semi-Finals	3
1958	B	Bovina-Semi-Finals	1
	1A	White Deer-Semi-Finals	1
	2A	Abernathy-Winner	2
1959	B	Bovina-Finals	2
	1A	Sudan-Finals	1
	2A	Abernathy-Winner	3
1960	B	Claude-Finalist	5
	1A	Hale Center-Semi-Finalist	1
	2A	Friona-Finalist	1
1961	B	Claude-Finalist	6
	1A	Sundown-Winner	1
	2A	Spearman-Finalist	1
1962	B	Claude-Winner	7
	1A	Sundown-Winner	2
	2A	Friona-Semi-Finalist	2
1963	B	Claude-Semi-Finalist	8
	1A	Sundown-Winner	3
	2A	Friona-Semi-Finalist	3
1964	B	Trent-Winner	1
	1A	Abilene Wylie-Semi-Finalist	1
	2A	Friona-Winner	4

UIL WENT TO FOUR CLASSIFICATIONS

1965	B	Trent-Winner
	1A	Roosevelt-Winner
	2A	Friona-Finalist
	3A	Tulia-Semi-Finalist
1966	B	Sundown-Semi-Finalist
	1A	Earth-Springlake-Finalist
	2A	Spearman-Winner
	3A	Tulia-Winner
1967	B	Quitaque-Finalist
	1A	Springlake-Earth-Winner
	2A	Spearman-Finalist
	3A	Tulia-Winner
1968	B	Lamesa-Klondike-Finalist
	1A	Springlake-Earth-Winner
	2A	Spearman-Semi-Finals
	3A	None
1969	B	Lamesa-Klondike-Winner
	1A	Straford-Winner
	2A	Spearman-Semi-Finalist
	3A	Canyon-Winner
1970	B	Follet-Winner
	B	Trent-Finalist
	1A	Abilene-Wylie-Winner
	2A	Spearman-Finalist
	3A	Canyon-Finalist

The first twenty years [1951-1970] in the UIL representing girls' basketball, the Panhandle/Plains region dominated the state tournament.

1951 there were only two divisions in girls' basketball but by 1965, it had expanded to four divisions. Here is a summary of those first twenty years.

Claude was the dominate girls' basketball city from 1951-1970. They had 8 appearances in the State UIL tournament playing for the gold seven times winning the Girls UIL State Championship trophy four times finishing second three times. Also, Claude did have one semi-final appearance.

Spearman was second with six state tournament appearances. Spearman won one Texas State UIL championship ring, finished as runner-up three times, and had two semi-final appearances.

Friona had five appearances winning the Texas State UIL championship one time, then had two silver finishes and two semifinalist appearances.

Sundown won the Texas State UIL Championship three times with one semi-finalist appearance. Tulia tied with Sundown with four appearances. They won the Texas State UIL tourney two times, with two semi-finalist appearances.

Dimmitt, Abernathy, Trent, and Abilene Wylie had three appearances at the Texas UIL State Basketball tournaments during the first twenty years. Abilene Wylie, Dimmitt and Abernathy had two gold trophies and one semi-final trophy at the state tournament. Trent won two gold trophies and one silver championship to add to their trophy case.

Schools with two appearances were Canyon [1W, 1F], New Deal [1W, 1F], McLean [1F, 1S], Ropesville [1W, 1S], Roosevelt [2W], Springlake-Earth [2W], Bovina [1F, 1S], Lamesa-Klondike [1W, 1F].

What stands out is the fact that the Panhandle/Plains region had 27 total State Championships and 17 runner-up championships in that period. That means that the region of the Panhandle/Plains region won the state championship 27 times out of 66 opportunities. That means that region won the state championship 41% during that era. In that same period, the Panhandle/Plains teams had a state champion crowned in one of the divisions every year except in 1956, and 1960. Also, in both of those years, teams from the Panhandle/Plains region were in the finals in two of the three divisions.

The second twenty years in the UIL Texas State Girls basketball tournament

1971	B	Follett-Semi-Finalist	1
	1A	Claude-Winner	1
	2A	Spearman-Winner	1
	3A	Canyon-Finalist	1

1972	B	Follett-Semi-Finalist	2
	1A	Claude-Winner	2
	2A	Spearman-Winner	2
	3A	Canyon-Winner	2
1973	B	Follett-Semi-Finalist	3
	1A	Turkey-Valley-Finalist	1
	2A	Spearman-Semi-Finalist	3
	3A	Canyon-Finalist	3
1974	B	Lamesa-Klondike-Finalist	1
	1A	Turkey Valley-Semi-Finalist	2
	2A	Slaton-Winner	1
	3A	Canyon-Winner	4
1975	B	Lamesa-Klondike-Semi-Finalist	2
	1A	Vega-Finalist	1
	2A	Borger-Phillips-Semi-Finalist	1
	3A	Canyon-Finalist	5

1976	UIL moved to five divisions		
	B	Nazareth-Semi-Finalist	1
	1A	Straford-Winner	1
	2A	Borger-Phillips-Winner	2
	3A	Canyon-Finalist	6
	4A	None	

1981	UIl dropped the Class "B" classification moving it up to "1A" & adding a "5A"		
	4A	None	
	2A	New Deal-Finalist	1
	3A	Abernathy-Winner	1
	4A	Canyon-Winner	8
	5A	Lubbock-Monterey-Winner	3
1982	1A	Nazareth-Winner	7
	2A	Borger-Phillips-Finalist	
	3A	None	
	4A	Levelland-Semi-Finalist	1
	5A	Amarillo-Semi-Finalist	1
1983	1A	Sudan-Winner	1
	2A	Hale Center-Finalist	2
	3A	Slaton-Semi-Finalist	5
	4A	Levelland-Winner	2
	5A	None	
1984	1A	Nazareth-Winner	8
	2A	Hale Center-Finalist	3
	3A	Abernathy-Winner	1
	3A	Abernathy-Winner 1	
	4A	Levelland-Finalist 3	
	5A	None	
1985	1A	Nazareth-Winner	9
	2A	Abernathy-Finalist,	2
		Seymour-Semi-Finalist	1
	3A	Vernon-Winner	1
	4A	Sweetwater-Finalist	1

	5A	Lubbock-Monterey-Semi-Finalist	4
1986	1A	Nazareth-Finalist	10
	2A	Abernathy-Winner	3
	3A	Vernon-Semi-Finalist	2
	4A	Levelland-Winner	
	5A	None	
1987	***All five State Championships were won from the Panhandle/Plains region		
	1A	Sudan-Winner	2
	2A	Morton-Winner	1
	3A	Slaton-Winner	6
	4A	Levelland-Winner	5
	5A	Plainview-Winner	2
1988	1A	Nazareth-Winner	11
	2A	Shallowater-Winner	1
	3A	Brownfield-Winner	1
	5A	None	
1989	1A	Nazareth-Winner	12
	2A	Abernathy-Finalist	4
	3A	Canyon-Finalist	9
	4A	Levelland-Winner	7
	5A	None	
1990	1A	Nazareth-Winner	13
	2A	Wall-Semi-Finalist	1
	3A	Abilene Wylie-Winner	1
	4A	None	
	5A	Lubbock-Monterey-Semi-Finalist	5

The second twenty years [1971-1990] was almost the same as the first twenty years with the Panhandle/Plains dominating the Texas UIL State Girls basketball tournament. During this period, the UIL dropped the "B" classification and added another classification.

Nazareth put on a clinic in how to win state championships during this period. They were in the Texas UIL State Girls championship thirteen times winning it eleven times and finishing second twice. The city of Nazareth is a proud city and they have every right to be proud of their girls' basketball tradition.

During the second twenty years Canyon comes in second with nine appearances in the Texas UIL State Girls championships winning five and coming in second four times. Also, since Canyon made two appearances in the first twenty years, that would give Canyon eleven appearances, six wins, and five runner-up spots.

Levelland started late then came on strong with seven appearances in the Texas UIL State Girls championships. What was awesome is they won the gold six of seven appearances at the state tournament. However, they did have a semi-final year on one trip.

Slaton had six trips to the Texas UIL State Girls basketball championship winning the gold five of six times and one semi-final performance.

Always playing in the awesome large school division, Lubbock Monterey had five Texas UIL State Girls basketball championship appearances. In this period Monterey high school had one win, one finalist appearance, and three semi-finalist appearances.

Spearman had four appearances in this time period with three wins, and one semi-final. But what is most impressive abut Spearman is when you combine the two twenty-year sessions Spearman has ten Texas UIL State Championship appearances with four championships, three finalists, and three semifinalists.

Abernathy had four appearances in the second twenty years of the Texas UIL State girls' basketball championships. They had two championships, one runner-up trophy, and one semi-finalist performance. Also, Abernathy had three appearances in the first twenty years giving them a total of seven appearances in the Texas UIL State Girls Championships. Over this period, they had four state championships, one runner up, and two semi-finalist appearances.

Also, Borger-Phillips had four appearances in this period. They won one Texas UIL State Championship girls' basketball, finish second once and had two semi-finalist results.

Follett had three appearances in this period at the Texas UIL Girls State basketball tournament. Three times in a row they were semi-finalist in the second twenty years, but Follett did the win the state championship the last year of the first twenty years which gives them four state appearances total.

Hale Center made three appearances in this period at the girls' state basketball tournament. They played for the state championship three times winning the championship once, being runner-up twice.

Follett played in the state tournament three times in this period finishing with three semi- finalist appearances.

What stands out is the fact that the Panhandle/Plains region had 46 state championships and 32 runner-up trophies in this period. That means that 48% of the time, a state champ is crowned from the Panhandle/Plains region during that period.

The last twenty-eight years [1991-2019] of the Texas Girls UIL State Basketball tournament

	*	All five winners are from the Panhandle/Plains region	
1991	1A	Nazareth-Winner	1W
	2A	Abernathy-Winner	1W
	3A	Tulia-Winner	1W
	4A	Levelland-Winner	1W
	5A	Amarillo Tascosa-Winner	1W
1992	1A	Claude-Semi-Finals	1S
	2A	Panhandle-Winner	1W
	3A	Canyon-Winner	1W
	4A	Canyon Randall-Winner	1W
	5A	Plainview-Semifinalist	1S
1993	1A	Nazareth-Semifinalist	2
	2A	Panhandle-Semifinalist	2
	3A	Dimmitt-Winner	1W
	4A	Levelland-Finalist	2
	5A	Amarillo-Winner	1W
1994	1A	Sudan-Winner	1W
	2A	Tuscola-Jim Ned	1F
	3A	Canyon-Finalist	2
	4A	Borger-Semifinalist	1S
	5A	Amarillo-Winner	2
1995	1A	Sudan-Winner	2
	2A	None	
	3A	None	
	4A	None	
	5A	None	
1996	1A	Nazareth-Winner	3
	2A	None	
	3A	Slaton-Finalist	1S
	4A	Canyon-Winner	3
	5A	Amarillo-Semifinals	3

1997	1A	Whiteface-Winner	1W
	2A	Shallowater-Finalist	1F
	3A	None	
	4A	Levelland-Winner	3
	5A	None	
1998	1A	Nazareth-Winner	4
	2A	None	
	3A	None	
	4A	Canyon Randall-Winner	2
	5A	Amarillo Palo Duro-Finalist	1F
1999	1A	Vega-Winner	1W
	2A	None	
	3A	Shallowater-Semifinals	2
	4A	Canyon-Finalist	4
	5A	None	
2000	1A	Nazareth-Winner	5
	2A	None	
	3A	Perryton-Semifinals	1S
	4A	Canyon-Winner	5
	5A	None	

2001 UIL divided 1A into two divisions, division one and division two.

	1ADI	Sudan-Semifinalist	3
	1AD2	Nazareth-Winner	6
	2A	Wall-Semifinals	1S
	3A	Abilene Wylie-Finalist	1F
	4A	Plainview-Winner	2
	5A	None	
2002	1AD1	Sudan-Semifinalist	4
	1AD2	Nazareth-Winner	7
	2A	Abernathy-Finalist	2
	3A	Perryton-Semi-Finalist	2
	4A	Plainview-Winner	3
	5A	None	
2003	1ADI	Hedley-Semi-Finals	1S
	1AD2	Gruver-Semi-Finals	1S
	2A	Shallowater-Finalist	3
	3A	Canyon-Winner	6
	4A	Plainview-Winner	4
	5A	None	
2004	1ADI	Sudan-Semi-Finalist	5
	1AD2	Water Valley-Semi-Finalist	1
	1AD2	Earth-Springlake-Finalist	1F
	2A	Shallowater-Winner	4
	3A	Canyon-Winner	7
	4A	Plainview-Finalist	5
	5A	None	
2005	1AD1	Seagraves-Winner	1W
	1AD2	Nazareth-Winner	8
	2A	Canadian-Finalist	1F

	3A	Canyon-Winner	8
	4A	None	
	5A	None	
2006	1AD1	Claude-Semi-Finalist	2
	1AD2	Water Valley-Semi-Finalist	2
		Earth-Springlake-Finalist	2
	2A	Wall-Finalist	2
	3A	Abilene Wylie-Finalist	2
	4A	None	
	5A	None	
2007	1AD1	Sundown-Finalist	1F
	1AD2	Nazareth-Winner	9
	2A	Panhandle-Semi-Finalist	3
	3A	Canyon-Winner	9
	4A	None	
	5A	None	
2008	1AD1	Sudan-Finalist	6
	1AD2	Follett-Winner	1
	2A	Tuscola-Jim Ned-Winner	2
	3A	Canyon-Winner	10
	4A	Plainview-Semi-Finalist	6
	5A	None	
2009	1AD1	Sudan-Winner	7
	1AD2	Vega-Semi-Finalist	2
	2A	None	
	3A	Lubbock Estacado-S	1S
	4A	None	
	5A	None	
2010	1AD1	Smyer-Winner	1W
	1AD2	Turkey Valley-Semi-Finals	1S
		McLean-Finalist	1F
	2A	Wall-Finalist	3
	3A	Abilene Wylie-Finalist	3
	4A	None	
	5A	None	
2011	1AD1	Smyer-Winner	2
	1AD2	Whitharral-Finalist	1F
	2A	None	
	3A	Abilene Wylie-Winner	4
	4A	Canyon-Winner	11
	5A	None	
2012	1AD1	Sudan-Winner	8
	1AD2	Whitharral-Semi-Finalist	2
	2A	Tuscola-Jim Ned-S	3
	3A	Abilene Wylie	5
	4A	None	
	5A	None	
2013	1AD1	Smyer-Finalist	3
	1AD2	Whitharral-Winner	3
	2A	Merkel-Finalist	1F

	3A	None	
	4A	None	
	5A	None	
2014	1AD1	Plains-Winner	1W
	1AD2	Nazareth-Winner	10
	2A	Wall-Winner	4
	3A	Abilene Wylie	6
	4A	Canyon-Winner	12
	5A	None	

2015	UIL added another division called "6A" and dropped the 1A division one and two		
	1A	Nazareth-Winner	11
	2A	Gruver-Finalist	2
	3A	Shallowater-Finalist	5
	4A	Abilene Wylie	7
	5A	Canyon-Winner	13
2016	1A	Nazareth-Finalist	12
	2A	Panhandle-Finalist	4
	3A	Wall-Winner	5
	4A	Abilene Wylie-Semi-Finalist	8
	5A	Canyon-Winner	14
	6A	None	
2017	1A	Nazareth-Winner	13
	2A	Panhandle-Winner	5
	3A	Canadian-Winner	2
	4A	None	
	5A	Canyon-Winner	15
	6A	None	
2018	1A	Nazareth-Winner	14
	2A	Claude-Semifinals	2
	3A	None	
	4A	Denver City-Semi-Finals	1S
	5A	Amarillo-Winner	4
	6A	None	
2019	1A	Nazareth-Winner	15
	2A	Panhandle-Semifinals	6
	3A	Wall-Semi-Finals	6
	4A	None	
	5A	Amarillo-Winner	5
	6A	None	

UIL Texas State Girls basketball summary of the last twenty-eight years.

Canyon first appearance in the Texas UIL State Girls championship was in 1969. Since then, 49 years later, Canyon has been in that championship 26 times winning the championship 18 times. That means that Canyon has a 53% chance of playing in the State Tournament and a 37% chance of winning the big prize before the season starts. Add to that fact is when Canyon wins the regional championship qualifying for the state championship, Canyon has a 69% chance of winning the gold. What is even more impressive is the fact that Canyon usually plays in a large school division which means that the competition is usually stronger simply because of size and number of students. In this period, [1991-2018] Canyon was dominate without a doubt, so dominate that the opponents often wondered if they would ever have a chance to play for the championship. During this time period, Canyon made fifteen appearances winning the gold thirteen times and two runners up trophies. That means that when Canyon won the regional tournament qualifying for the state tournament, their chances of playing for the state championship was 100% with an 86% chance they would win the gold.

Nazareth totally dominated the small school division. They were so dominate that almost everyone started getting bored with Nazareth winning except Nazareth. They made their first appearance in 1976 and for the next forty-two years they won twenty-four championships but played for the title twenty-five times. That means that before the season started in girls' basketball in the city of Nazareth knew that they had a 55% chance of winning the state championship. In this period, [1991-2018] Nazareth played for the State Championship fourteen times winning it thirteen times with one semi-finalist performance. Another thought about Nazareth during that period when they WON the regional championship, from that point on there was an 80% chance that they would win the gold. Now that is an impressive tradition.

When a conversation comes up concerning Texas basketball, anyone with any kind of understanding about high school basketball will always point out the tremendous influence Nazareth and Canyon had on high school girls' basketball in the state of Texas. Everything from work ethic, attitude about winning, offense, defense, team play, style of play, and coach was influenced by those two schools and their coaches.

Sudan was a small community that didn't back down from the Nazareth dynasty making eight appearances in the last period. Sudan won the Texas UIL Girls State basketball tournament four- times, finished a runner-up once and had three semi-finalist appearances. In the long run, Sudan became a force to battle in the small school basketball finally building their basketball tradition. When figuring Sudan's record from the start till now they had a total of 11 appearances at the state girls' basketball tournament. That means that Sudan played for the State Championship eight times, winning six gold, and two silvers along with three runner-up appearances.

Abilene Wylie is one school, city that has made a state tournament appearance in each twenty-year period reported in this book. But they finished up strong making eight appearances in this last period. During this time period Wylie won three gold championship rings, three silver trophies, and two semi-final appearances. Too add to that, Wylie has two more state championships, and one semi-final trophy. That gave them eleven appearances at the Texas UIL State Girls basketball tournament playing for the championship seven times and winning it five times.

Claude made two state appearances in this last period with two semi-finals appearances but over-all, Claude has ten state tournament appearances with five wins, two runners up spots and three semi-finals positions.

Plainview made six appearances in the Texas UIL State Girls basketball tournament in this period winning the gold three times, with one runner up trophy and two semi-final appearances. When you add another gold and a semifinalist appearance, Plainview has a total of 8 appearances in the State Tournament winning it four times. What one must remember is that Plainview usually had to play in the large school division, where the competition is outstanding because of the big schools involved in that division.

Shallowater has always been tough to beat and this period, was no exception. Shallowater won the gold once, finished runner-up three times and had on semi-final appearance during this last period. Also, Shallowater also won the gold earlier giving them five trips to the state tournament over-all.

Wall was a late comer but when they did get to the state tournament, they started making a habit of it. During this period Wall played for the State Championship five times winning it four times. When you add their other performance of a semi-final appearance you have Wall with a total of 5 state tournament appearances.

Amarillo had many uphill battles trying to get their noses in the State tournament and when they did get to the state tournament, they won the gold three of four times, being a runner up only once.

Panhandle made four appearances in this period winning one gold, one silver and two semi- final appearances.

Follett had three appearances all semi-finals in this last period, but they won the gold in the second twenty-year session giving them a total of four state tournament appearances.

Since 1951 Earth-Springlake has played for the state championship five times winning it two times with three runner-up silver medals to show for their efforts

Vega with four appearances since the beginning of the State tournament for girls' basketball has one gold, two silver and one semi-final trophy.

Tuscola Jim Ned, Smyer, and Whitharral had three appearances in this period at the state tournament. Tuscola Jim Ned had one gold, one silver, and one semi-final game, while Smyer played for the state championship three times winning it twice. Whitharral had three appearances in the state championship all results were semi-finalist.

Girls' basketball in the Panhandle/Plains region has a strong tradition of winning. The proof is in the pudding. Because of that many coaches deserve to be mentioned in this book and I will attempt to get it right even if some of the high school coaches advanced their career to the college level. Girls' basketball coaches in the Panhandle/Plains region have set the bar high in terms of winning at the state level. The influence coming from the coaches in the Panhandle/Plains region has been impressive to say the least.

Panhandle/Plains girls coaching records in terms of wins – Sources are [THGCA] Texas High School Girls Coaches Association and Texas Basketball

*Still coaching in 2018
If mistakes are made, it is not because of the THGCA or Texas Basketball but rather the editor of this book.

C.E. "Nig" Womach	Hawley** [National record for combined wins]	1570
Joe Lombard*	Canyon/Nazareth	1342
Dean Weese	Spearman/Levelland/Other	1207
Bob Schneider	Canyon/Other	1045
Chuck Darden*	Shallowater	878
Mike Martn	Sudan/Amarillo/Herleigh/Snyder	870
F.G. Crofford	Whiteface, Pettit, Claude, Friona, Spearman	721
Danny Wrenn*	Plainview	719
Jim Kirkland	Sudan/Spade/Frenship/Claude/Silverton/others	600
John Blaine	Dimmitt	559
Matt Garrett	Nazareth/Christoval	557
Melynn Hunt	Lubbock Cooper	527
Terry Collins	O'Donnell	519
Jim Wilcoxson	Booker/Canyon Randal	500
Dale Blaut	Amarillo High School	500
AJ Johnson*	Palo Duro	479
Jeff Williams*	Amarillo, Dumas	425
Jason Cooper*	Cotton Center, Olton, Sudan, Amarillo Tascosa, Claude	400

If you thought trying to decide whom to mention in this book as a girl's high school coaching legend in the Panhandle/Plains was easy, I salute you because I have struggled with this from the start of this section concerning high school girls' basketball. After doing the football and the boys' basketball I felt good about the coverage and information I had to present. After doing girls basketball, I feel much is left out because I don't have enough information that really separate one individual from another. Simply put, there are many good high school girls' basketball coaches from the time the UIL started covering girls' basketball which was 1951 till the present time.

When girls first started playing for a state title by the UIL, the interest by sport writers were limited in knowledge and sometimes lacked enthusiasm. Because of Title IX, they soon started picking up knowledge and their enthusiasm started to rise to the top as they started seeing a large market for their stories about girls' basketball. Then in 1978, when girls started playing five on five the girl's game changed creating more interest. During all this time, larger Universities and larger high schools started playing girls basketball, the scene at the State Tournament of Texas became awesome regarding excitement/ excellent coaching and dedicated committed athletes performing to their maximum potential.

Next a boom hit girls' basketball because athletic ability became dominate in girls' basketball particularly on the higher levels of play. Now when you attend the UIL Texas State Girls basketball tournament, it is something to witness and enjoy regardless of what level of play you are watching.

Also, now days, media and other outlets of media attention are dominate during the year providing information about different teams, coaches and schools.

We are going to divide the categories according to the following:

1. High School Coaches with the most wins in a large school environment
2. High School Coaches with the most wins in a small school environment
3. High School Coaches that made the biggest difference in girls' basketball in the Panhandle/Plains region
4. High School Coaches that have won at several schools making a difference with several school districts
5. High School Coaches that set the bar high for girls' basketball from the very start of UIL participation
6. Six on Six legacy

I want to be clear that we are talking about high school coaches first, not college coaches particularly those college coaches that have made a name for themselves in the world of college basketball. High school coaches owe so much to the following college coaches for their influence on the game and their influence on the coaches in the Panhandle/Plains region.

LEST WE FORGET WOMEN'S UNIVERSITY AND COLLEGE COACHES / PANHANDLE/PLAINS REGION

COACHES THAT HAD A HUGE INFLUENCE ON HIGH SCHOOL GIRLS' BASKETBALL FROM THE COLLEGE OR UNIVERSITY LEVEL OF COACHING

HARLEY REDIN-WAYLAND BAPTIST UNIVERSITY

What has not been said about Harley Redin that needs to be said again? His influence on girls' basketball in the Panhandle/Plains region was the shot in the arm for all girls' basketball coaches at the time he was coaching. He is a legend so big that no one can top his status in girls' basketball. He started it all in some shape or form and we should never forget his contribution to high school girls' basketball.

MARSHA SHARP-TEXAS TECH UNIVERSITY

Since the start of girls' basketball in the UIL, no one in the Panhandle/ Plains region has influenced girls' basketball more than Marsha Sharp from Texas Tech University. From the start of her coaching career till the day she retired, her influence has been the dominate factor in the Panhandle/Plains region. Because of her strong college career, her being named after a Major Highway in Lubbock, everyone knows about Marsha Sharp. She has been recognized many times over about her influence in society, not just basketball. Although she has been mostly successful on the college scene rather than the high school arena, she will not be mentioned along the other high school girl coaches in this book.

BOB SCHNEIDER-WEST TEXAS STATE UNIVERSITY

Along the same line in the same vein, Bob Schneider had the same type of influence when he coached women's basketball at West Texas State University [West Texas A&M University] The number of high school girls basketball coaches that were influenced by his coaching was awesome to say the least. His mannerism and his style of coaching was copied by many coaches both girls and boys. More will come on Bob Schneider.

DEAN WEESE-WAYLAND BAPTIST UNIVERSITY

Along in the same footsteps, no different was Dean Weese. When Dean coached at Wayland Baptist University everyone paid attention to girls' basketball even if you weren't a fan of girls' basketball, because you knew something big was going to happen. Wherever Dean stepped into the arena of girls' basketball, his teams won. More will come on Dean Weese.

KATHY WILSON-WAYLAND BAPTIST UNIVERSITY

Nothing stays the same and when Coach Wilson took the Flying Queens, women's basketball had changed like night and day. All sudden, huge large Universities started women's basketball creating a playing field that was not level for the Flying Queens. It was a transition period for Wayland Flying Queens and Coach Wilson stood firm, not giving an inch in terms of pride for the Flying Queens. They stood their ground and survived. More will come on Kathy Wilson

KELLY CHADWICK-WESTERN TEXAS COLLEGE

The only person I have seen execute the flex offense as good as Gene Gibson at Texas Tech was Kelly. He was a master coach and his influence were spread throughout the Panhandle Plains region. Kelly was one of the first coaches to really make a difference on the Junior college scene.

LYNDON HARDIN-SOUTH PLAINS COLLEGE

After winning the girls state championship at Canyon Lyndon was hired to coach the women's basketball program at South Plains College. Coach Hardin not only won at SPC but stayed true to his roots by recruiting many athletes from the Panhandle/Plains region, many who went on playing on the NCAA level of women's basketball or continued their career by coaching girls' basketball. But what stands out about

Lyndon Hardin is his sacrifice of hard work, dedicative service and loyal attitude toward women's basketball in the Panhandle/Plains region.

JOHN LOFTIN-CLAUDE/TULIA/SOUTHWESTERN OKLAHOMA STATE UNIVERSITY

How many coaches can say that they have won big at 3 different schools? After winning the girls state championship at Claude and Tulia, John was hired as the Head Women's coach at Southwestern Oklahoma State University. Although he had tremendous success at SOSU winning a national championship, John never forgot his start at in the small schools. He has been a positive influence in the Panhandle when it comes to girls' basketball.

THE LEGEND OF LEGENDS IN TEXAS HIGH SCHOOL GIRLS' BASKETBALL

DEAN WEESE

This is a no-brainer in my opinion. Weese has won on every level he has coached and won big. Not only that, his style of play, and his tough perception of control has been duplicated by every coach possible in both genders of coaching. I know because I was one of those coaches that studied him and his style of play. I had a live experience with coach Weese because he coached my daughter Kim Mayberry Arrington for two years. My wife and I were part of his team supporting the team on to two state championships. What made it more special was the fact that my daughter was not the star player but rather just part of the team. I was coaching the men's team at South Plains College, but the star coach was Dean Weese in our family for those two years. I backed that concept 100% and because of my attitude I learned so much from Dean Weese and our family including my daughter had a wonderful experience at Levelland High School. Not only that I made sure my other two daughters went to his basketball camps every year knowing that they would pick up on his disciplined methods of coaching. His demand for dedication from his players and his demand for complete commitment was second to none in any field of coaching.

But what totally sold me on Dean Weese was in influence on girls' basketball in the state of Texas, particularly the Panhandle of Texas. I am a student of basketball and since 1956; I have been studying basketball in many shapes and forms, particularly coaches. I have never witness one coach that had some much influence on one region than Dean had on the West Texas Region of Texas. What always amazed me and will continue to amaze me is when you get to the state girls play-offs and the state girls basketball championship you will witness many teams that you can see a Dean Weese basketball style in those teams. It was the same with Cotton Robinson from Buna where you could see so much Buna from many of the good high school boys' basketball teams.

The final count of his coaching record is 1207-197. That is an 85.97 winning percentage which is the proof in the pudding. Just for the record Weese had 10 state championships and 2 national AAU titles during his 42 years of coaching. He started at Higgins, then when to Spearman staying fifteen years compiling a record of 446-76. Add 3 state championships and 13 district championships to that record and you have the start of Coach Weese career as a girl's high school coach.

Dean Weese was hired and hand- picked by the legendary Wayland Baptist Flying Queen coach Harley Redin in 1973. So, you say, "Mayberry did he meet the challenge following the

Legendary coach Harley Redin?" He not only met the challenge but in his first year he led Wayland doing what he always does: Wayland had a 37-4 won lost record, which was a record for most wins, a new team offensive scoring record, their ninth AAU title, their sixth straight NWIT title, a first place finish in the Southwest Region AIAW Tournament, and a fifth place in the national tournament.

Of course, that was just the start and over the next 5 years, Dean averaged winning 32 games a season along with the following accomplishments: One AAU championship, one runner-up title, three more NWIT titles, making 4 appearances at the National AIAW Tournament finishing 3rd, 4th and 2 consolation trophies. Not only that, he was selected to coach an AAU team in a series of games in Russia, was an assistant girls' coach in the Pan-American games in Columbia and coached the Texas Oklahoma high school All-Star games for six years. For your information, under Dean Weese guidance the Queens advanced to the AIAW Final Four in 1978 at UCLA.

In 1979 Coach Weese left Wayland to take over the Dallas Diamonds in the Women's Professional Basketball League. That lasted one year, and then he returned to the Panhandle of Texas taking the Levelland high school girls basketball coaching position. At Levelland his teams won 17 district titles along with 7 State Girls Championship which included 4 straight from 1985-1989.

Dean Weese has been honored in every way possible by the fans and sport writers in every aspect known to mankind. In 2000, he was inducted into the Women's Basketball Hall of Fame in Knoxville, Tennessee. He was named the National Girl's Coach for the year by the National Federation of High School Coaches, the Texas Panhandle Hall of Fame, The Texas High School Basketball Hall of Fame and the Texas Association of Basketball Coaches Hall of Fame.

What I liked about him was his wife JoAnn Weese who kept his books for 20+ years and his three children, De Ann, Todd, and Jeremy. They led the way, especially JoAnn who was recognized by Levelland naming its [basketball court] after Coach Weese and his wife JoAnn.

Everyone in Levelland knew Dean on site and everyone that was involved with girls' basketball knew his no-nonsense approach to games and practice which brings me to a story that I must tell. Because of his non humorous approach he would get drawn into pranks by some of the staff members. Don't take this wrong because everyone loved Dean Weese so that is why it is special when someone can have a laugh at his expense. It just doesn't happen. Dean got Teed up by a basketball official for being out of his chair. It was a new rule set up by the UIL who was trying to control coaches roaming all over the place on the sideline. The rule included the Head Coach and allowed only a space to stand up to make a coaching point to the players, but they had to immediately be reseated. So, Dean gets a "T" for being out of his chair. He forgot the new rule. That was on a Friday night and then on Monday, Doc Adams who was the trainer goes to the transportation department and obtained some seat belts from an old bus that they couldn't use anymore. Then Adams, Blackshere, and Dinkins get some c-clamps and put the seat belts on the chair that goes on the floor for games that Dean always sits in because he is superstitious about keeping everything the same way. They know he will not change chairs.

Now, Dean doesn't know any of what is going during the pre-game warm-ups but almost everyone from administration, assistant coaches, players are in the know. So, after visiting with the officials he heads to the bench where he sees the chair and the seat belts. He was amused but not too much and immediately got that look of "OK" who's the wise guys.

So, Dean attempts to get the seat belts off, but he can't because they are clamped on tight. Everyone in the gym was watching and when he looked up all he could see were smiles coming from his action about the seat belts.

Coaches everywhere in the Nation and particularly Texas have studied and written about why Dean won basketball games. He himself admits, "I'm pretty much a perfectionist and very strong on fundamentals of the game of basketball." Then he continues, "It wasn't so much about talent, but more about determination and dedication. Our kids just expected to do things right, they just expected to win." Recently I heard a talk about mental toughness from the great football coach, Nick Saban from Alabama University. He was talking about mental toughness and explained what mental toughness is to him. He defined mental toughness to "What does it take to break you."

When he said that, I started thinking of the great coaches I have known and using that expression, it defines Dean Weese to the finest point of his coaching career. His teams handle all kinds of adversary, every kind of attack known to coaching with the grind that it takes to be a winner. It took a lot to break them down so much so that few could break them down. That is mental toughness at its best and to me that what his strength.

LEGEND OF LEGENDS IN TEXAS HIGH SCHOOL GIRLS BASKETBALL

BOB SCHNEIDER

The first thing I did when deciding to write this book was to send out questionnaires to all the coaches in the Panhandle/Plains region asking for nominees for high school legends of coaching. Then I explained that I wanted high school legends more than college legends, those that truly gave their career toward the development of high school athletes. I put no limit on any sport or any nominations except they had to be part of the UIL. The first time I did that, the response wasn't very good but the second time I sent the questionnaire; I received what I wanted with many nominations from all kinds of coaches in all sports.

The next thing I did was to contact many [old time coaches] so to speak legends of the Panhandle/Plains region getting their response about coaches that they consider legends of the high school coaching world in the Panhandle/Plains region. Then for the last contact for information I contacted some ex coaches that coached in the Panhandle/Plains region about nominations.

Bob Schneider was on every list and nominated several times. Then when I started during my research, it was clear to me why he was on every list for being named a legend in high school girls' basketball. Simply put, he was one of the true legends of high school girls' basketball setting the tone for other high school basketball coaches.

Bob Schneider graduated from Darrouzett high school in 1954. Then he attended Panhandle State University, Clarendon College, and West Texas State College on baseball and basketball scholarships. He ended up receiving his Bachelor of Science and Master of Education from West Texas State University. Later, he continued his education by finished an administration certification in All-Levels from WTSU. It was during this time that I first met Bob because I was doing the same thing, trying to get my administrative certificate. He made coaching stops first at Darrouzett High School, Clayton High School [New Mexico] and McLean High School.

Consider that his growing up stage as a coach.

Then in 1966, Bob moved to Canyon and accepted the head girls' basketball coach and track coach. To add more to his coaching career, he was also the junior varsity football coach which wasn't unusual at that time because most coaches in small schools coached many sports. What followed next at Canyon is what set the tone in girls' basketball at Canyon for many years to come. This is the results of his move to Canyon: His Canyon girls won the UIL Texas State girls basketball championship 5 times from 1969 to 1978. His girls track teams won the UIl State Track meet 3 time and his girls' basketball teams were the runner-up champions at the UIL State girls' basketball tournament 5 times. Adding that up, that means that the Canyon girls under the leadership of Bob Schneider played for the state girls basketball championship ten straight years winning it five times. Oh, and by the way, in 1968, they were the district champs and regional finalist.

Of course, that started Bob Schneider legacy and what a legacy it was by winning the state championship in girls' basketball and girls track in the same years, 1977 and 1978.

Bob became the head women's basketball coach at Texas Women's University in 1978. Then in 1981, he took the position at West Texas A&M University as the head women's basketball coach. It didn't take him long before he started making his mark at West Texas A&M. In his 25 years at WT, he posted a record of 1,045-293. During that period, his West Texas A&M teams won nine conference titles, which included eight Lone Star Conference banners. To me speaking from college coaching experience that feat is awesome. First off, the Lone Star Conference is outstanding from top to bottom, no soft opponents and extremely competitive. His teams reached the NCAA Division II Elite Eight twice, advanced to the NCAA Quarterfinals in 1997 and were National Runner-ups in 1988. Here is the part that gets my attention because it separates him from many coaches. Bob still ranks among the top coaches in the NCAA women's basketball history. Coach Schneider stands 26th in total victories, 38th in winning percentage, and 5th among all Division II coaches with 19 seasons winning 20 or more games.

Barbara McCurley and Bob met in McLean, Texas where he was coaching. She became Bob's wife and his statistician for 38 years, not to mention the three children they had named Brandon, Brett, and Brooke. I personally knew both Brandon and Brett and I can only say that it

was my pleasure to be around both. I never met Brooke but since I had three children, I attempted to keep up with all three the best I could. The one thing I know for sure is that Barbara deserves a lot of credit for Bob's success as a coach.

Doing my research on Bob Schneider I came across an article in Women's Basketball, by Tom Keegan that all readers would appreciate especially if you followed Bob Schneider coaching career. Brandon Schneider, Bob's son was the head women's coach at Stephen F. Austin when Bob came to observe his son's team during a practice workout. Bob sat close to the practice arena so that he could hear and see all that was going on. One of the players on the team found out who is was and came over to meet him. After introductions she began to complain about how hard it was. According to the story, Bob didn't raise his voice but instead said, "Well, young lady, it sounds to me like you're not very mentally tough." From what the article said, from that point on no one came to him looking for sympathy. The reason I wanted to put this in his story is because that was who he was. He didn't like excuses and he made sure everyone knew he didn't like excuses.

Coach Schneider was a believer in fundamental and conditioning. But his specially was mental toughness. The same thing that I said about Dean Weese applies to Bob Schneider when it comes to mental toughness. They both coached mental toughness in different ways but both got the job done so much that they became a legend in coaching girls' basketball. Bob's son Brandon said that Bob didn't have hobbies just basketball. Brandon also told reporters when he took the KU position that he prefers to answer to "Coach Brandon" because there is only one Coach Schneider and that was his father. To me that says it all.

Bob Schneider has many accomplishments as a coach and many honors, so many it will be easy to miss one but these are the ones that I remember, especially from the Panhandle region: He had been named

Basketball Coach of the Year by Panhandle Sports Hall of Fame 5 times. He was named the Lone Star Coach of the Year 4 times. The Texas High School Girls Coaching Association Coach of the Year 2 times. Bob was also named The Oil Country Athletic Conference and the Texas Sportswriter Association Coach of the Year one time. Along with all that he was named the Super Coach of the Year for all sports in the Panhandle Sports hall of Fame in 1995 and 1996.

It goes without saying the world of high school girls' basketball in the Panhandle/Plains region, Bob Schneider and Dean Weese are the basketball coaching legends of the past that have influenced the game of basketball to what it is now. It doesn't mean that other coaches didn't influence or make a huge difference in their perspective schools, cities, or regions but these two were on the ballot from anyone or everyone who was asked to name a high school girls basketball coach that you consider to be a legend in the Panhandle/Plains region. Of course, there are still many active coaches out there that are making a huge difference in girls' basketball creating a greater story to be told as I write this.

LEGENDARY COACH THAT HAS THE MOST WINS AT A LARGE HIGH SCHOOL

MIKE MARTIN

Mike Martin has 870 wins to his credit making coaching stops at Lakeview, Higgins, Dumas, Farwell, Sudan and Amarillo in the Panhandle/Plains region. Just in that region alone, he compiled 541-292 record. After a serious illness and death of his wife, Sherry, he resigned his position at Amarillo High School. The year before his resignation the Sandie's under Martin advanced to the regional semifinals.

He had success everywhere he coached but most fans will remember his 63-game winning streak and back to back Class IA state girls' championship in Sudan during the 1994 and 1995 season. That included a season where Sudan finished 39-0. That was a huge year for Martin as he was named the Texas Sports Writers Association "Coach of the Year" in 1994 and 1995.

During that time frame, he served on the board of directors of the Texas Association of Basketball Coaches.

But his success didn't stop there but instead he just added more victories and accomplishments particularly at Vista Ridge in 2008. He was used to winning and that is exactly what he did leading the Rangers to back- to- back Class 4A regional final appearances in 2011-2012 seasons. Mike Martin final coaching position was at a parochial school in Dallas called John Paul II.

Overall, he spent 42 years coaching girls' basketball in the state of Texas. His teams won 18 district championships, 19 regional tournament appearances and winning three of five state tournament appearances. He also coached a girls' golf state championship, assistant coach of a state championship football team, coaching a girl's state championship in tennis and a state championship girl's 800-meter relay team.

Coach Martin was a winner without a doubt and influenced many young athletes across the state of Texas and the proof is in the pudding. When a coach wins a one place, that is always a mark of a good coach but when a coach can win at several places at different sports, it simply means that coach is a winner on the highest level of coaching. That was Mike Martin who died in 2017 due to complications resulting from the neurodegenerative disease amyotrophic lateral sclerosis. Mike Martin was inducted into the Texas Girls Coaches Association "Hall of Fame" in 2017.

Legendary coach from a small school that had success everywhere he coached

F.G. CROFFORD-SUNRAY, WHITEFACE, PETTIT, CLAUDE, FRIONA, GRUVER AND SPEARMAN

Crofford won the Purple Heart and the Purple Cluster during World War II. He was a war hero for sure being in several battles, the Battle of the Bulge, the Battle of the Ruhr and the Battle of the Rhine. He was wounded twice, but that didn't stop him from going back to the battle front after his second injury, where he served under Gen. George Patton marching through France and Germany destroying pillboxes. His job-radio technician which meant he was up front and in the line of fire.

Crofford was a Lelia Lake graduate who attended Clarendon College before the war then went on to graduate from West Texas State College in 1951. Soon after that he started his coaching career coaching six-man football at Sunray. His real career started after that when he started girls' basketball making stops at Whiteface, Pettit, Claude, Friona, Gruver and Spearman.

Coach Crofford spend eight years in Friona where his teams reached the playoff six years. He coached at Gruver six years and led his teams to the state playoff four years. He coached four years at Spearman where his boys' team made the playoffs two times. But where he had the most success was at Claude where he guided the girls' basketball team to five state tournaments appearances in a row. His 1960 team had a 40-3 record and his 1962 team won the state championship. His over-all coaching record was 721-326 in 32 seasons. Only once in his lifetime, he had a losing record and he was quick to point out that that team gave it all they had on the court, it wasn't lack of effort. He now stands in 4th place from the standpoint of most wins of coaches in the Panhandle/Plains region.

He felt like his claim to national recognition was that he coached Denton Fox in his seventh grade at Claude. Of course, Denton Fox was an All American at Texas Tech who was drafted by the Dallas Cowboys in the 1969 draft. Personally, I beg to differ with him. I think he is a legend in girls' basketball where he helped the Panhandle/Plains get recognized as a state power in high school girls' basketball.

LEGENDARY COACH WITH THE MOST WINS FROM A SMALL HIGH SCHOOL CHARLES "NIG"

WOMACK-HAWLEY

Please make no mistake about Coach Womack – he has done something that no one to this day has done in the coaching world in Texas. He has won 1570 basketball games which at the time was a national record for wins combined for coaching girls and boys. Yet little is known about him and that is why I am listing him as one we should remember.

I found out who he was the hard way. I had to coach against him in a tournament when I was coaching the boys' basketball team at Albany. Don't get me wrong, I had already heard from some of my supporters that we would be lucky to beat Hawley. As they put it, they have a master coach. Well, I found out quickly because we couldn't score, and they were beating us soundly in the one game we did play them. For the life of me, I couldn't figure out how to handle their defense which was they call "Triangle and Two" defense. It's a defense where they put their two best defenders on the opponent two best offensive players guarding them like bees on honey. Then they play a Triangle zone defense guarding the other three in a zone type defense. I was so out coached it made me sick at my stomach. We had twice the talent they had but we couldn't score which created panic on our part. We won the game, but it was pure luck at the end not skill or coaching just luck. Sometimes that is what happens, and you sure don't talk about it to anyone. But what I did was to go back and practice that type of defense soon learning something new giving our team another way to win a game.

Coach Womack was inducted into the Texas High School Basketball Hall of Fame in 2005. He coached both boys' and girls' basketball at Hawley High School from 1947 – 1979. He ended up being superintendent of schools at Hawley High School but not before he compiled an 896-127 coaching the boys' basketball team and a record of 674-110 coaching the girls' basketball team. The Bearcats won 29 district titles and made 10 state tournament appearances. He also served as President of the Texas Girls Coaches Association in 1956-57.

LEGENDARY COACH WITH THE MOST WINS FROM A COMBINATION OF SMALL HIGH SCHOOL AND LARGE HIGH SCHOOLS

JIM KIRKLAND-FRENSHIP, CLAUDE, ROCKWALL, SILVERTON, CANADIAN, SUDAN, SPEARMAN, CAL ALLEN, TEXLINE, PERRYTON

Wow! He coached at all those places and still won 600 games. What most people wouldn't understand when comparing a coach about winning records where you coach has a lot to do with the chances of having a winning season. Not all high school girls' basketball programs are equal. What that means is not all high school girls program create an environment that leads to building a basketball program that leads to winning.

Jim won everywhere he coached particularly in Sudan where his teams won two state championships. It was at that period that Jim Kirkland name became a household name if you were a girls' basketball fan. He stated off at Spade High School where he was both the boys' and girls' basketball coach. Then he went to Frenship, Claude, Rockwall, Silverton, Canadian, and Sudan where he had the most success. After that he went to Spearman,

Calallen, and Texline. At Texline he was both Superintendent and girls' basketball coach. When he accepted the Superintendent position at Perryton, Jim hung up his coaching career.

But little did he know it during his early career he would find joy and pride in another way. His daughter Krista Gerlich provide many thrills for him but most important was she gave him two grandchildren, a granddaughter named Bryn and a grandson named Brayden.

LEGENDARY COACH THAT STATED THE WINNING LEGEND FROM THE PANHANDLE/PLAINS REGION

JOHN BLAINE-DIMMITT

Yes, I know this is his second time to be mentioned. His name came up on both sides of the Legend department, girls and boys. What he did will never be duplicated so it needs to be mentioned again. To be real, John Blaine was the first true legend in high school girls' basketball. His influence on basketball period was outstanding but particularly girls' basketball.

John attended Claude High school then went to West Texas State University where he participated in wrestling and football. Later he began his coaching career in Dimmitt in 1940. In those days' coaches coached every sport possible and Coach Blaine was no exception. He coached football, track, both girls' and boys' basketball. After the 1952 season was over at Dimmitt, his overall basketball coaching record was 316-26 with 3 straight girls basketball championships Not only that, his 1951 football team was 11-1 losing in the regional level in football, but his girls won the state championship at 36-0 and his boys also won the state championship at 36-0. That would mean his coaching record for 1951 at Dimmitt was 83-1. That is awesome for sure and as far as I know no one has accomplished that feat anywhere in the USA.

In 1952, Coach Blaine was named the Texas Coach of the Year. Then he was selected into the Panhandle Hall of Fame, the Texas Association of Basketball Hall of Fame and eventually almost every hall of fame that exist today.

Later Coach Blaine moved to Sundown where his boys' basketball team was state runners-up. His overall coaching record in basketball was 559-64 which is an 89.7 winning percentage.

Dimmitt honored him by naming one of the gyms after his name. [Read more about John Blaine in the Boys basketball part of this book]

LEGENDARY COACH WITH THE MOST WINS FROM A COMBINATION OF MANY SCHOOLS

MELYNN HUNT-LUBBOCK COOPER, PLAINVIEW, HALE CENTER, JACKSBORO, MONTEREY, HASKELL, WAYLAND BAPTIST U.

You name it; Melynn Hunt has done it particularly in the world of women's athletics. She is a true legend for sure and has worked hard at being a person of influence involved with girls' athletics especially women's basketball. Coach Hunt has 527 wins to her credit as a head coach which doesn't even come close to her total number of wins that she has been involved with since her career started.

Coach Hunt is a native of Hale Center, graduated from Texas Tech University and played basketball at Tech from 1968-70. Soon after graduation she took the Head girls coaching position at Plainview High School. She hit pay dirt coaching Plainview Girls advancing to the semi-finals of the UIL State Girls basketball team with a 30-3 record. After that she went to Hale Center high school [class 2A] as the head girl's coach where she led her team to two state finals at the state girls' basketball tournament. Getting used to the Girls State tournament, she moved to Jacksboro and took them to the state tournament. After that, she came home to Lubbock Monterey as the head coach then took a head job in Haskell, Texas.

In 2001 Melynn took the position of Assistant Athletic Director of Lubbock Independent School District in charge of high school sports in all areas of athletics. Melynn worked at that position for twelve years then accepted the assistant coaching position at Wayland Baptist University where she has been until this past year when she retired from coaching. At Wayland Melynn helped the Flying Queens continue their historic success in women's basketball as they climb higher into the world of records. On November 30, 2017, the Flying Queens posted their 1600 win which is 300 more wins than any collegiate basketball team in the USA.

Melynn husband Darrell is the head basketball coach at Star but his main job is taking care of his elderly parents. They have two sons' Doug who is the Athletic Director at Whitewright and is also the head girls' basketball coach. Kyler is in the oil business in Odessa, Texas. Melynn and Darrell have one granddaughter name Harper.

LEGENDARY COACH THAT WAS A LEGENDARY GOLF PRO JAMES MARVIN "JIM" WILCOXSON-CANYON RANDALL

I knew Jim as a golf pro long before I knew him as a basketball coach. I was playing golf on the Southwest Golf Course in Amarillo, Texas when I had a double eagle on one of the par fives. I was excited and when I came in the tell Jim about it hoping that he would get excited about my lucky golf shot. When I told him about the double eagle, I will never forget his expression or his comment. He looked at me like I wasn't even their and said "noted."

Coach Wilcoxson grew up in Childress graduating in 1963. He married Nicki Sooter on Jan 23, 1965 in Lubbock, Texas. Jim attended Texas Tech from 1963 to 1966 on a golf scholarship.

Jim began his coaching career as a volunteer coach for his daughters Kids incorporated team which later turned into a four team Little Dribblers franchise in Amarillo. Even later that turned into the Southwest Basketball Association and finally into the Amarillo Basketball Association. That is how Jim got his start coaching girls' basketball by coaching his daughter in the Little Dribblers association. The Amarillo Chamber of Commerce Sports Committee gave him a sports achievement award for the Little Dribbler national championship.

When I first notice Jim coaching was when he was a volunteer assistant coach for Kelly Chadwick at Amarillo College from 1983-1985. He took his first girls' high school coaching position at Booker High School, in Booker, Texas. Then he went to Tascosa high school, Amarillo, Texas from 1986-1989. That was the first time Jim hit the gold because the Lady Rebels advanced to the regional play-offs for the first time in the school history.

After that Jim served as the girls' basketball coach at Randall High School from 1989-2004. During that time, he led Randall to 15 consecutive play-offs, but the highlight was in 1992 and 1998 his teams won the class 4A state girls' basketball tournament. For his efforts in 1992, Jim received the Texas Girls Coaches Association "Coach of the Year" award then in 1998, he won the Sportswriters Association "Coach of the Year" award.

In 2004 Jim was awarded the Sportsmanship Award given by the Amarillo Basketball Officials Association. Then in 2005, Jim became the 135th inductee into the Panhandle Sports Hall of Fame. Then in 2012 Jim was inducted into the Texas High School Basketball Hall of Fame.

Jim Wilcoxson died on May 23, 2015, but not before he left his mark on the Panhandle/Plains region in girls' basketball. I personally salute Jim because of the many awards he received but what impresses me the most is the way he became a coach and I might add a very successful coach.

LEGENDARY COACH THAT WAS A LEGENDARY PLAYER DALE BLAUT-AMARILLO HIGH SCHOOL

I was coaching at Hereford High School and Mike Mitchell was my assistant basketball coach. Mike approached me about an "outsider" basketball tournament being held in Levelland, Texas. He wanted to know if I would play. I thought about it for a long time but decided to give it a go- besides we had the great Mike Mitchell [West Texas State University] playing for us so I knew that meant I didn't have to worry about scoring. We gathered up another guy, Joe Tubb who was doing his student teaching along with several others that Joe and Mike knew. That is how I met Dale Blaut because he was out ace in the hole for our team. Mike was very good but with Dale playing with him, we were very good. After that, Dale and I became very good friends and I started following his career.

After playing for West Texas State, getting drafted by the Chicago Bulls, Dale ended up started his coaching career and it was a no brainer for me to support him because I could see the talent in him right away. He was ready made for coaching and after coaching at Idalou and Sunray, he finally started putting it all together at Channing high school. Coach Blaut coached 14 years where he compiled a 233-99 record.

Then he accepted the Head Girls position at Amarillo High School as the head girls' basketball coach. He led the Lady Sandies to back-to-back state basketball championships in 1993 and 1994 compiling a record of 70-2. Coach Blaut remains to be the only basketball coach to win two state titles for Amarillo ISD. USA Today magazine ranked his 1994 team as #4 in the nation. Dale resigned in 1997 but he returned for a second attempt at Amarillo High School from 2002- 2005 before retiring from coaching. All total his teams won 13 district titles in his coaching career.

Then as old coaches have a habit of doing, he volunteered his assistance with Krista Gerlich, who was the head women's basketball coach at West Texas State University. That year, the Lady Buffs advanced to the regional semifinals. Finally, Dale gave up basketball for taking care of his grandchildren. When Dale Blaut was informed, he was the 159th member of the Panhandle Sports Hall of Fame, he shed many tears. He was touched by receiving this honor and that says it all about Dale Blaut. He came to the Panhandle from New York but ended up being a Texas Panhandle citizen without a doubt.

SMALL SCHOOL LEGEND THAT STARTED THE DYNASTY AT NAZARETH CATHY WILSON-NAZARETH

The game was five on five with full court presses defensively and full court fast breaks just like the boys' game. It was my first time to witness five on five girls' basketball and at all places Wayland Baptist University. I was in awe for sure because my only experience had been at Van Horn high school watching my aunts play girls basketball. However, they couldn't go pass the midcourt line making the game a true skill game for sure. You see, my aunts were twins and one played offense and the other played defense. Cathy Wilson was the head woman's coach and I was the athletic director, head men's basketball coach at Wayland Baptist. That experience was as good as it gets.

Talking about a great start in coaching, well Cathy certainly would qualify for that award. After finishing her BS in Education in 1975, she was hired as the head girls' coach at Nazareth High School. Of course, at the time, it was just another girls program trying to win some games.

Little did anyone know 43 years later; Nazareth would be a household name when it comes time to talk about girls' basketball in the state of Texas. Wilson guided the Swiftettes to the UIL state girls' basketball tournament her first year at Nazareth. Liking the taste of that success Coach Wilson led Nazareth the next year winning the gold [state championship] in her second year of coaching at Nazareth. That was the start of a dynasty in small - school girls' basketball in the Panhandle/Plains region that has brought positive success to the city of Nazareth, Texas.

After two years at Nazareth, Wilson accepted the same position at Class 2A Slaton High School. It didn't take her long to get her way with the girls' basketball program at Slaton winning back to back state championship in girls' basketball in 1978 and 79. So, Cathy Wilson starts her career in 1975 and by 1979 she has coached a team that played for the state championship four times winning three. Simply put, that feat is awesome.

Then she was hired by Wayland Baptist University to take on the challenge facing the famous Flying Queens. Oh, by the way, she was 26 years old and was replacing the legend of legends, Dean Weese. Also, she became the first female to coach the Flying Queens.

No one knew for sure what was on the horizon for the Flying Queens because everything that existed in women's basketball was going through a transition period. For sure Cathy took the challenge to heart as she led the Queens making the best making the best of the situation going 20-15 her first year. Truth be known, she deserved "Coach of the Year" beating California University getting to the AIAW final four. Of course, she lost to Texas and Villanova during that time, but the change was coming, and it was hard to stomach for the old timers that supported the Queens. The administration knew change was due, so they made the bold move to move the Queens to the NAIA organization, the same organization the men belonged. What was fitting before she retired, she guided the Queens to the NAIA national tournament her last year she coached. After that Cathy started her own firm as a financial advisor.

LEGENDARY COACH FROM A SMALL SCHOOL THAT HAD SUCCESS EVERYWHERE HE COACHED

BUD ROBERTS-WAYSIDE, DARROUZETT, GREENVILLE, HAPPY AND TULIA

Bud Roberts coached 41years starting at Wayside in 1937. Remember, the UIL start keeping records before 1951. Roberts's next stop was in Darrouzett, then Happy, then Tulia. What was interesting is that he farmed and ranched in Swisher County from 1937 to 1975. In his 41 years of coaching through 1979 Coach Roberts had compiled 7 state championships.

He led Tulia to a record of 296-36 which included back to back State girl's championships in 1966 and 1967. Not only that his 1962 girls' team from Tulia finished runner up and his team in 1965 was a participant in the state girl's tournament. He also guided Tulia to three more state titles, one each at Wayside and Greenville who were in the "Old McCamey League which he helped in the foundation before the UIL started in 1951. Bud also help in starting girl's high school track in Texas.

For his achievements he was selected in 1990 for the Hoops Hall of Fame, then in 1995 he was selected by the Texas Association of Basketball Coaches Hall of Fame. In 1970 he was received the Texas High School Girls Basketball Coaches Award, then the Panhandle Sports Hall of Fame.

Bud was named Tulia Outstanding Citizen award in 1968 and received the Purple Heart and Bronze Star while serving in the U.S. Army veteran of World War II from 1942-1945.

Carl Irlbeck and Harley Redin both gave Bud a deep appreciation salute for the many hours he gave trying to help young coaches coming up during his coaching career. Matter of fact, Irlbeck gives Bud a lot of credit for helping him along the way in his coaching career.

JIM KIRKLAND-SUDAN/OTHERS

Jim Kirkland is a legendary coach that is still remembered at Spade, Frenship, Claude, Rockwall, Silverton, Canadian, Sudan, Spearman, Calallen, Texline and Perryton. It doesn't take a rocket scientist to understand that coach Kirkland has had a huge influence on many young athletes in the Panhandle/Plains Region.

In 1987, Sudan won the UIL girls state championship with Kirkland as the head coach. Finally, in his career he became a superintendent at Texline where he shared being a coach and handling the Superintendent responsibilities. Then in 2001 Jim Kirkland became the Superintendent at Perryton, Texas.

Not many coaches can say they coached their daughter in the UIL State Championship girls' basketball tournament, but Jim can because he coached Krista Gerlich when Sudan won the gold in girls' basketball.

LEAST WE FORGET OTHER LEGENDS – GIRLS' HIGH SCHOOL IN THE PANHANDLE/PLAINS REGION

SANDY HEIMAN-

NAZARETH-THREE CONSECUTIVE STATE CHAMPIONSHIP IN 1888-1990- BASKETBALL COACH OF THE YEAR IN 1990.

LOMETA ODON-

PIONEER FOR THE QUEENS SUCCESS-COACHED AT GRUVER, SPEARMAN, WHITE DEER [COACHED THE VARSITY TO TWO DISTRICT CHAMPIONSHIPS IN 1975/1976], CORONADO JUNIOR HIGH, AND ESTACADO JUNIOR HIGH

LEGENDARY COACHES THAT MADE A HUGE DIFFERENCE IN HIGH SCHOOL GIRLS' BASKETBALL.

- **GAY BENSON-SLATON**
- **RALPH NEWTON-SPEARMAN**
- **P.D. FLETCHER-DUMAS**
- **PAT MOUSER-ABERNATHY**
- **STANLEY WHISENHUNT-WYLIE**
- **BABS LOMBARD-HALE CENTER**
- **GARY SHENBERGER-FOLLETT**
- **BILL SCHNEIDER-SANFORD-FRITCH**
- **KATHY HAIRSTON-PLAINVIEW**

LEGENDARY COACH OF THE "SIX ON SIX" GIRLS' BASKETBALL JAN IRBY NEWLAND- CLAUDE-SIX ON SIX LEGEND

If you were involved with girls' basketball when they were playing six on six, then you can understand how pure of a game six on six happened to be. It was basketball at its best - teaching the art of spacing and isolation in offensive basketball.

Newland, a great high school basketball player from Claude was a perfect example of isolation because if you could get her the ball isolated down low, it was almost automatic, said John Loftin a legendary coach himself who was her coach.

After her playing days were over, Coach Newland started her coaching career at Wheeler where she led the Wheeler girls to 9 district titles and 4 trips to the regional basketball play-offs. After that she coached at Dimmitt, Plains, and eventually Mesquite where she was the athletic coordinator and head girls' basketball coach. In 1986, she was selected to the William Penn College "Hall of Fame" and in 1995 she was inducted into the Texas High School Basketball "Hall of Fame."

A TRIBUTE TO SUCCESS AND ALL INVOLVED WITH THEIR SUCCESS-CANYON AND NAZARETH GIRLS' BASKETBALL

Both schools are sports fans hero when it comes to tradition and success. What has been accomplished at Canyon and Nazareth in girls' basketball is already history and it looks like it will never end.

Their success story is like no other in the state of Texas, much less the Panhandle/Plains region.

There are so many people that are part of these programs that are responsible for the tradition and success both schools have had, that it is impossible to name only one or two. Everyone knows who the head coaches are, and everyone knows the history that is being made by these coaches will never be forgotten. Both coaches at Canyon and Nazareth will go down in history as the greatest awesome production of success in basketball.

Joe Lombard, Canyon girls' coach is a person that I have great respect and admiration for not just his coaching but as a person. Somewhere and someday, long after I die, his records might be broken but his character and humble attitude will never be replaced. He is "One of a Kind" and that is an understatement.

Volleyball

In the early days before 1970 many schools didn't participate in volleyball on the high school level. After UIL adopted Volleyball in 1966-67 school year playing for a state championship many schools in the Panhandle/Plains region started their first volleyball program. Of course, those that already were playing volleyball had a huge advantage at the very beginning of volleyball.

Just as we have done with the other sports, we will first look at the schools and cities that played for the State UIL Texas State Volleyball championship. The first UIL recorded state championship started in 1966.

None-Means that no school from the Panhandle/Plains region qualified for the Tournament Format:

Year	Class	Name of School	Finish at the State Tournament
W-Winner,		**R**- Runner up,	**S**-Semi-Finalist
1966	B	Clyde Eula	S
	1A	Plains	W
	2A	None	
	3A	Lamesa	R
	4A	Abilene Cooper	W
1967	B	Clyde Eula	W
	1A	Plains	W
	2A	Phillips	W
	3A	Kermit	S
	4A	None	
1968	B	None	
	1A	Plains	W
	2A	Phillips	W
	3A	None	
	4A	None	
1969	B	None	
	1A	Plains	W
	2A	None	

	3A	None	
	4A	None	
1970	B	None	
	1A	Plains	W
	2A	Phillips	W
	3A	Seminole	W
	4A	None	
1971	B	Roscoe Highland	R
	1A	None	
	2A	Denver City	R
	3A	Snyder	W
	4A	None	
1972	B	None	
	1A	None	
	2A	Denver City	R
	3A	Lamesa	S
	4A	None	
1973	B	Rule	S
	1A	None	
	2A	None	
	3A	None	
	4A	None	
1974	B	Bronte	S
	1A	Plains	S
	2A	None	
	3A	None	
	4A	None	
1975	B	Bronte	R
	1A	Plains	R
	2A	Denver City	S
	3A	None	
	4A	None	
1976	B	Bronte	W
	1A	None	
	2A	None	
	3A	Seminole	W
	4A	None	
1977	B	None	
	1A	None	
	2A	None	
	3A	Seminole	W
	4A	Big Spring	S
1978	B	Bronte	S
	1A	Plains	S
	2A	Seminole	R
	3A	Snyder	W
	4A	None	
1979	B	Bronte	S
	1A	None	
	2A	Seminole	R

	3A	None	
	4A	Amarillo	S
1980	UIL dropped the word Class B and added the 5A		
1980	1A	Knox City	S
	2A	None	
	3A	Kermit	S
	4A	Snyder	W
	5A	None	
1981	1A	Bronte	W
	2A	Plains	S
	3A	Seminole	S
	4A	Snyder	W
	5A	San Angelo Central	S
1982	1A	Bronte	S
	2A	Miles	R
	3A	Seminole	R
	4A	None	
	5A	None	
1983	1A	Bronte	R
	2A	Plains	R
	3A	Seminole	R
	4A	None	
	5A	San Angelo Central	S
1984	1A	Bronte	W
	2A	Plains	S
	3A	None	
	4A	None	
	5A	San Angelo Central	S
1985	1A	None	
	2A	Plains	W
	3A	None	
	4A	Snyder	W
	5A	Amarillo Tascosa	R

The first twenty years for Volleyball to be adopted into the UIL:

During this period of times Plains had 11 appearances in the Texas UIL State Volleyball tournament playing for the state championship 8 times winning 6 state UIL championships in volleyball. Not only that they finish in the semi-finals 3 times. That means that Plains had a 55% chance of qualifying for the state volleyball tournament during the first twenty years of the UIL.

Bronte wasn't far behind in tournament appearances with 9 visits to the UIL state volleyball tournament. But what is impressive about

Bronte is that once they made it to the state tournament, they made it a habit qualifying for the tournament 9 of 11 years from 1974- 1985. They had 3 gold winners, 2 runner ups, and 4 semi-final appearances.

Seminole was like Bronte in the fact that once they made it to the state tournament, they liked it so much they decided to keep on coming year after year. Seminole qualified for the tournament 8 times from 1970-1985. Seminole played for the state championship 7 times in that period winning the gold 3 times with one semi-final appearance.

Next in line was Snyder with four appearance but all were Gold winners then Phillips who won three state championships in three appearances. Denver City qualified for the state tournament three times in this period coming away with 2 runner up trophies and one semi-final appearance. San Angelo Central made 3 appearances in this period all semi-final results.

Lamesa, Kermit, and Clyde Eula all had two appearances at the UIL State Volleyball tournament in this period. Clyde won the gold one time and Lamesa was the runner up one time.

Amarillo, Amarillo Tascosa, Abilene Cooper, Roscoe Highland, Rule, Miles, Knox City, and Big Spring all made one appearance at the UIL state girls' volleyball tournament in this period. Abilene Cooper won the state gold in their appearance.

The next twenty years 1986-2005

Year	Class	School	Result
1986	1A	Water Valley	W
	2A	None	
	3A	None	
	4A	Lamesa	W
	5A	Amarillo	R
1987	1A	Bronte	W
	2A	None	
	3A	None	
	4A	None	
	5A	None	
1988	1A	Plains	W
	1A	Windthorst	S
	2A	None	
	3A	Lamesa	S
	4A	Dumas	W

	5A	Amarillo	W
1989	1A	Plains	W
	2A	None	
	3A	Lamesa	S
	4A	Dumas	W
	5A	Amarillo Tascosa	S
1990	1A	Plains	W
	1S	Windthorst	S
	2A	None	
	3A	None	
	4A	Dumas	W
	5A	None	
1991	1A	Bronte	W
	1A	Windthorst	W
	2A	None	
	3A	Seminole	S
	4A	Dumas	S
	5A	None	
	1992	1A Windthorst	W
	2A	None	
	3A	None	
	4A	Hereford	S
	5A	Amarillo	S
1993	1A	Windthorst	W
	2A	None	
	3A	Seminole	W
	4A	None	
	5A	Amarillo	S
1994	1A	Windthorst	W
	2A	None	
	3A	None	
	4A	Dumas	S
	5A	Amarillo	W
1995	1A	Windthorst	W
	2A	None	
	3A	None	
	4A	Hereford	R
	5A	None	
1996	1A	Water Valley	S
	1A	Windthorst	S
	2A	None	
	3A	None	
	4A	Hereford	W
	5A	None	
1997	1A	Water Valley	S
	1A	Windthorst	S
	2A	None	
	3A	None	
	4A	Hereford	W
	5A	Amarillo	R

Year	Class	Location	Result
1998	1A	Windthorst	W
	2A	None	
	3A	Lamesa	R
	4A	Dumas	W
	5A	Amarillo	W
1999	1A	Water Valley	S
	1A	Windthorst	W
	2A	None	
	3A	None	
	4A	Hereford	W
	5A	Amarillo Tascosa	S
2000	1A	Bronte	S
	1A	Windthorst	W
	2A	None	
	3A	Amarillo River Rd	S
	4A	None	
	5A	Amarillo Tascosa	S
2001	1A	Water Valley	S
	1A	Windthorst	W
	2A	None	
	3A	None	
	4A	Hereford	W
	5A	Amarillo	W
2002	1A	Windthorst	W
	2A	None	
	3A	None	
	4A	Hereford	S
	5A	None	
2003	1A	Windthorst	W
	2A	None	
	3A	None	
	4A	None	
	5A	None	
2004	1A	Windthorst	R
	2A	Denver City	S
	3A	None	
	4A	Dumas	R
	5A	Lubbock Coronado	R
2005	1A	Windthorst	W
	2A	None	
	3A	None	
	4A	Dumas	S
	5A	None	

Windthorst set all kinds of records for volleyball during this twenty-year period. They had 16 state tournament appearances winning the gold 11 times. Add one runner up silver metal, and 4 semi-final appearances and you have dominance.

Amarillo playing in the large school division played for the UIL girls' volleyball state championship 6 times winning 4 gold trophies. Add 2 semi-final appearances giving them 8 state tournaments showing in this period. With one appearance from the first 20 years that give Amarillo 9 appearances in the girls' volleyball state tournament up through 2005.

Dumas had 8 appearances in this period playing for the championship 5 times winning the gold 4 times. Dumas also had 3 semi-final appearances at the state girls' volleyball tournament.

Dumas didn't reach the final four until 1988 and they made up for lost time by going to the state tournament 8 times in the next 17 years.

Hereford was like Dumas because they didn't make a state tournament appearance until 1992 but then they made 6 appearances from that point on for this period. Hereford played for the state championship 4 times winning the championship 3 times. Hereford had 2 semi-final appearances in this period.

Water Valley made 5 state tournament appearances winning the gold 1 time and finishing with a semi-final appearance 4 times. Lamesa was next with 4 state appearances winning the gold once, runner up once and had two semi-final appearances. Since Lamesa had 2 appearances in the first 20-year period that would give them a total of 6 appearances in the first 40 years of the UIL tournament. **Plains being used to playing in the state volleyball tournament made 3 appearances and won 3 gold trophies in this time frame. So, from the beginning of the state UIL girls' volleyball tournament, Plains had 14 state tournament appearances and 8 state championships.**

Not to forget Bronte because they also had 3 state appearances in this time frame, two gold trophies and one semi-final appearance. Bronte now has 12 state tournament appearances with 5 state championships in their trophy case. Seminole made 2 appearances in this period giving them 10 state tourney trips

Amarillo Tascosa had 3 state tournament appearances giving them a total of 4 in 40 years. Seminole had 2 state tournament appearances with one gold trophy to show for it. But when you add the other time frame Seminole has a total 10 tournament appearances winning the gold 4 times in the first 40 years of state tournament volleyball.

Making one state tournament appearance during this time frame was Lubbock Coronado, Denver City, and Amarillo River Rd.

UIL Girls Volleyball State Tournament participants from 2006-2018.

Year	Class	Team	Result
2006	1A	Windthorst	W
	2A	None	
	3A	Canyon	S
	4A	Dumas	W
	5A	Amarillo	W
2007	1A	Windthorst	R
	2A	Bushland	W
	3A	None	
	4A	Canyon Randall	S
	5A	Amarillo	W
2008	1A	Albany	S
	1A	Windthorst	W
	2A	Bushland	W
	3A	None	
	4A	Hereford	W
	5A	Amarillo	W
2009	1A	Bronte	R
	1A	Windthorst	W
	2A	None	
	3A	None	
	4A	Canyon Randall	W
	5A	Amarillo	W
2010	1A	None	
	2A	Bushland	S
	3A	Abilene Wylie	S
	4A	None	
	5A	None	
2011	1A	Water Valley	W
	2A	None	
	3A	Abilene Wylie	R
	4A	Canyon Randall	S
	5A	None	
2012	1A	None	

	2A	None	
	3A	Abilene Wylie	W
	4A	None	
	5A	None	
2013	1A	Windthorst	R
	2A	Bushland	W
	3A	Big Spring	S
	4A	Amarillo	W
	5A	None	

The UIL added a 6A division

2014	1A	Archer City	S
	2A	None	
	3A	Shallowater	S
	4A	None	
	5A	None	
	6A	Amarillo	S
2015	1A	Windthorst	R
	2A	None	
	3A	Denver City	S
	4A	Bushland	R
	5A	Canyon Randall	S
	6A	None	
2016	1A	Bronte	S
	2A	Archer City	R
	3A	None	
	4A	Bushland	W
	5A	None	
	6A	None	
2017	1A	Bronte	W
	2A	Archer City	S
	3A	None	
	4A	None	
	5A	None	
	6A	None	
2018	1A	Water Valley	R
	2A	Amarillo Highland Park	S
	3A	None	
	4A	None	
	5A	None	
	6A	None	

Windthorst made six appearances in the state volleyball tournament giving them 22 state tournament appearances. Oh, by the way, Windthorst played for the state championship 6 times winning the championship 3 times giving them a total of 14 gold balls.

Not to be outdone, Amarillo set the tone in this short period of time by playing for the state UIL girls volleyball championship 5 times and winning the championship 5 times. Awesome performance for sure which included another semi-finals appearance. Totally since volleyball started Amarillo has made 15 state tournament appearances playing for the state championship 11 times winning the gold 9 times. Also included to their dominate display of girls' volleyball in the state of Texas at the UIL volleyball state tournament are 3 semi-finals appearances.

Bushland located just outside the city of Amarillo made 6 state tournament appearances during this period which included 11 years. Bushland played for the state championship 5 times and won the gold 4 times. Bushland had one semi-final appearance.

Canyon Randall made 5 tournament appearances in this period. Randall won the gold once, runner up once, and had 3 semi-final appearances. **Bronte was second in state tournament appearances with 14 winning the gold 6 times since girls' volleyball started. Plains which didn't make any appearances in this last period tied with Bronte with 14 state tournament appearances, but the 8 gold championship trophies put Bronte second in that category.**

Abilene Wylie made 2 state tournament appearances. Wylie played for the championship twice winning the gold once and Bronte won the gold once and had a semi-final appearance. Archer City made two appearances in this period, one runner up and a semi-final appearance.

Making one appearance at the state girls volleyball tournament during this time frame were Dumas, Canyon, Albany, Hereford, Big Spring, Shallowater, and Denver City.

TEXAS UIL GIRLS VOLLEYBALL STATE TOURNAMENT RESULTS
[2 OR MORE]

School	Appearances	School	State Championships
Windthorst	22	Windthorst	14
Amarillo	17	Amarillo	10
Plains	15	Plains	9
Bronte	14	Bronte	6
Seminole	10	Snyder	5
Dumas	9	Dumas	5
Hereford	8	Hereford	5
Bushland	6	Seminole	4
Water Valley	6	Bushland	4
Lamesa	6	Phillips	3
Denver City	5	Water Valley	2
Snyder	4		
Amarillo Tascosa	4		
Canyon Randall	4		
Phillips	3		
San Angelo Central	3		
Kermit	2		
Big Spring	2		
Clyde Eula	2		

COACHING LEGENDS IN VOLLEYBALL

The truth of the matter is that volleyball is a young sport in the UIL. If you don't think that is true remember that football was part of the UIL in the 20's. Because of the youth involved with volleyball legends of the past are close to the present. If you started coaching volleyball in 1966 when it started being part of the UIL, by 2000, you would have been coaching 34 years. The point being that legendary coaches in the volleyball world are going to be young for the most part.

VOLLEYBALL COACHING LEGENDS FROM A LARGE SCHOOL

JAN BARKER-AMARILLO

As in most cases the scene for successful coaching is usually set up by some other coaches that took the early bumps and struggles that a program goes through before the winning takes place. They seldom get the credit for what the upcoming coach does with the program after they come on board. Jan Barker fits into that mold to some extent but what

Coach Barker accomplished was something that no one saw coming. Awesome is the word when you talk about Jan Barker.

Kim Hudson and Ann Dunavin set the tone at Amarillo High School in volleyball. No question about that issue for sure so much that a lost in the Regional quarterfinals was not good enough. That is what tradition is about. Jan Barker found that out in 1987. Matter of fact, there were several unhappy parents that thought Amarillo High School should have advanced further in the play-offs.

The next year the Sandie's won the State Volleyball Championship closing that issue never to be heard again. Soon the Class 5A Texas UIL State Championship belonged to Amarillo High School in volleyball. Who coaches 10 state championships, regardless of the sport? Jan Barker did and that puts her on the map as a legend in the world of volleyball. She won a state crown once every three years she coached. When her career was finished her record was 1,116-175 with 14 state tournament appearances. Jan Barker is the benchmark of Texas high school volleyball coaches according to Amarillo ISD athletic director. Jon Mark Beilue wrote a newspaper article from the Amarillo Globe News called "2017 Woman of the year: Volleyball coaching legend Jan Barker is more than wins." That is where I found most of my material but what impressed me the most is his statement, "Because of Barker, Amarillo wears the crown in the Texas highschool volleyball world." I think her success extends to the Panhandle/Plains/West Texas/ and North Texas.

What makes this story so special is that Coach Barker was from Yakima, Wash. She played volleyball, softball and threw the javelin. She attended Linfield College, McMinnville, Ore and started looking for a coaching position after graduation. After looking for coaching jobs in her region getting frustrated with the lack of good jobs, she accidently found out about a job in Amarillo coaching on the 9th grade level at Bowie Junior High.

At Bowie she was a success story coaching her 9th grade group to a city title which was rare. Jan wanted to be a head high school coach and she let it be known that was her desire. Of course, the AD let it be known that he couldn't hire a person for the head coaching position without quality experience. Any of us that have coached in that situation understands how frustrating it is to think that you are stuck at a Junior High position when you want to advance yourself.

Finally, she was offered a high school position at Caprock High School coaching basketball and track. She took the position but made sure that the AD knew she wanted a volleyball position. Officially Jan became the head volleyball coach at AHS in May 1987.

Jan Barker retired November 2017 after 31 years at Amarillo High. As quick as she retired, she was named in 2017, Amarillo Globe-News Women of the Year. I found it interesting that she is the first such recipient with a sports background. Not only that, personally I can't see anyone in Texas that can even come close to matching what she has accomplished.

As a former coach of 53 years I salute Jan Barker for what she accomplished. I also salute the administration for their support in her coaching career. It really takes two to be successful and the proof is in the pudding. Regardless of what you think, winning is directly related to who has the best athletes- [all things being equal in the coaching part]. To do what she did for so many years says one thing to me, and I salute her for this accomplishment because it is hard to do regardless where you coach or what sport you coach. She developed a program where her players became the kind of volleyball players, she wanted by her organization skills, her knowing exactly what she wanted in the young players making sure that each player had a chance to maximize their talents in volleyball. You can't have talent extending from her first state championship until her last state championship covering close to 31 years. It is impossible unless you have a program where you can develop athletes to the point that you can be dominate in your sport. That is what she did, and she and her staff deserve all the recognition they can get. Also, on the same note, the administration also deserves a strong salute for allowing her to have a program. Think about this for a moment. She produced 16 All Americans and she helped develop over 100 young ladies that continued their education playing volleyball. Then to add to that, she had 34 players play on the Division one level. Yes, the proof is in the pudding, she was more than just volleyball.

NITA VANNOY-SAN ANGELO CENTRAL

Make no mistake about it when you speak of volleyball particularly in the San Angelo area, Nita Vannoy is a household name. Known throughout Panhandle/Plains region from her coaching volleyball she was a gracious woman, who had a huge success story.

Nita was the first female coach hired at San Angelo Central High School. She was a very demanding coach in terms of fundamentals done right and getting the best from her players on the court. However, she was also known to relate to the players well off the court. Coach Vannoy played a big role in the building and expanding female athletics at Central High School starting with volleyball. From nothing at all, she builds the volleyball program at Central High School into a state power in the late 70's and early 80's.

Coach Vannoy had the honor of coaching volleyball in the 70's to the 80's and finally in the 90's. The humble point about Nita was that she always gave credit to her players usually staying in the background unless forced by the media. Coach Vannoy was a pioneer in the volleyball world in the Plains region even after she retired. She was known for her loyal support for all those that played or coached volleyball. One of her ex players stated, "She taught us to put our differences aside and pull together regardless of the situation. But the main reason she is considered a legend is that she touches the lives of so many people, players, coaches, students and parents alike for more than three decades.

Nita Vannoy won one state tournament but made four appearances at the state UIL girls' volleyball tournament during her coaching career of 30 years. She was at Central for thirteen years where she put San Angelo Central volleyball on the map. Her record of 395-168 included a short coaching stay at Irving High School where she won the Class 4A state volleyball championship in 1973.

But where everyone became association with coach Vannoy was when they changed the name of the San Angelo Central Memorial Volleyball tournament to the Nita Vannoy Memorial Volleyball Tournament. This tournament is known as one of the best [quality of completion] and the biggest [32 teams] in the Plains region of Texas.

Nita Vannoy died from injuries that occurred during a ranching accident on September 23, 2003.

A TRADITION TO NEVER FORGET AND ALWAYS REMEMBER WINDTHORST HIGH SCHOOL [CLASS A]

DIANE CONRADY-

If there ever was a champion volleyball coach, Diane Conrady was clearly the winner. She is a member of the Texas High School Girls Coaches Association and was selected into the Volleyball Hall of Fame in 2007.

Forgive me because I was thinking that Windthorst wasn't part of the Plains region but that was my mistake. After studying the map, it finally occurred to me that Windthorst is a big part of the Plains region and I am excited to include Diane Conrady, Volleyball coach at Windthorst for 29 years into one of our volleyball coaching legends.

When you think about Windthorst and volleyball, it is hard to even guess that they have had twenty-two UIL State Volleyball appearances winning the championship 14 times. The first seven championships came under the guidance of Coach Conrady after making thirteen state championship appearances.

When Coach Conrady retired, it was a moment in Windthorst that was scary for all volleyball followers. The thought of a new coach, a new personality, and a new style was scary for the returning volleyball players to say the least. Coach Conrady decided to stay away and allow Stacy Wolf plenty of room to be herself and add whatever she needed to add. What made the distance so much harder for retired Coach Conrady; she didn't come to workouts and stayed out of the volleyball arena, not because she didn't have the desire to go see for herself but to allow the new coach all the room she needed to be herself. Finally, Stacy Wolf called Diane Conrady on the phone and asked Diane if she wanted to come watch the girls in action. It took Diane only a few seconds to say yes, and fewer seconds to get to the gym.

From that point on, the volleyball tradition of winning continued at Windthorst with Stacy Wolf winning six championships in eight appearances.

For sure, Diane Conrady started something that will never be forgotten at Windthorst, but very important is the fact that we should remember what she did and what Windthorst has accomplished in volleyball.

PATTY JONES-LUBBOCK CORONADO

Talk about a pioneer in volleyball, Patty Jones fits that profile. Patty was the first female UIL coach hired by Lubbock Independent School District. She coached the first UIL volleyball team at Coronado High School. Before that, volleyball was an intramural sport. She was a legend in more ways than one because she was an outstanding teacher spending twenty-six years at Coronado High School as a teacher/coach.

Coach Jones had an outstanding career at Coronado high school with a record of 470 wins, which included six straight district championships, four of those undefeated in district play. She coached her teams to fourteen state playoff appearances with fifty-two players advancing to the college scene in volleyball.

Patty Jones promoted volleyball in the Panhandle/Plains region making a difference in how people perceived high school volleyball through her coaching at Coronado High School. She added so much to the game of volleyball on the high school level. She was the first to start playing music before games, making sure that the girls on the team get individual attention using video for promotion purposes giving individual attention for past achievements through volleyball.

Coach Jones obtained "Coach of the Year" awards in 1984, 1987, 1992, and 2000. She was named as an "Outstanding Teacher/Coach in Lubbock ISD by Texas Tech University in 2000. In that same line of thought, she received special recognition for her accomplishments by Senator Robert Duncan in October 1997, and Mayor David Langston in December 1992. But what I found to be awesome about her career is the fact that she never lost a game to her alma mater, Lubbock High School and lost only once to Monterey High School.

LEGENDARY VOLLEYBALL COACHING RIVALS THAT MADE HISTORY IN THE PANHANDLE OF TEXAS

JACK WILSON-DUMAS

When you start talking about competition between two schools, Dumas and Hereford volleyball comes to the front of any sport regardless. These two schools created a coaching rival unsurpassed in volleyball competition in the Panhandle of Texas.

Jack Wilson selected to the Panhandle Sports Hall of Fame came from the Dumas Junior High School program and since he was a native Dumas Demon, it was only natural for him to be named the Head Volleyball coach in 1988. If anyone had any questions about his ability to coach, he shut them up quickly by putting Dumas on the map as a volleyball powerhouse. He took the Lady Demons to three consecutive 4A UIL State Volleyball Championships Then to top that off; he added two more 4A state volleyball championships in 1998 and 2006. That included 9 UIL State Volleyball appearances and wining or sharing 16 district titles.

Matter of fact, Jack Wilson won lost record in his 24 years as a coach is 713-212 which is 68th in the nation and 2nd in the Panhandle Plains region according to the National Federation of State High School Association record books. That is a 77% winning record appearing 15 times in the Texas Regional Tournament.

When Jack found out he had been selected into the Panhandle Sports Hall of Fame he stated, "When you get something like this you feel so undeserving because there are so many other people involved in this type of success." He continued, "I don't feel a validation as much as I feel thankful."

BRENDA KITTEN-HEREFORD

Here are the facts between Hereford and Dumas. For 15 years in a row, either Hereford or Dumas was the state representative from this region meaning that one of them won the regional tournament to qualify for the state tournament. The two programs combined for 10 state championships and 17 state appearances.

Brenda Kitten 1992 team was the first Hereford High School volleyball team to reach the state tournament. Just like her rival in Dumas did, she put Hereford High School volleyball on the map. Matter of fact she was also a junior high coach and when she took the position of head volleyball coach she never looked back. After her 1992 team reached the state tournament, she took another team to the state finals in 1996 and won the first State UIL Girls volleyball championship for Hereford High School. Coach Kitten was the head volleyball coach for the Lady Whitefaces from 1985-2008. Overall, Brenda guided her volleyball teams to five state championship, and eight tournament appearances. She ended up with a record of 618-234 in 24 years along with 13 district championships.

She comes from a coaching family because her dad was a football and track coach at Texas State University, San Marcos, Texas. Coach Kitten grew up around athletics and after one semester at Texas State University she transferred to Texas Tech University. She had no plans to stay in the Panhandle/Plains region but by happen- chance she interviewed for a position at Hereford High School. She said this about her interview," When I interviewed in Hereford, my intent was to practice interviewing smiling the entire time she said this. But someway somehow, she took the job they were offering which was coaching junior high sports at one of the junior high schools. The next year, a vacancy for the head volleyball coaching position opened and she was named the head volleyball coach at Hereford High School.

Coach Kitten stayed with the volleyball program for 24 years until she was named the girls athletic director and assistant junior high principal. She was named the Texas Sportswriters

Association "Coach of the Year" in 2001 and 2008. She was also the first representative from Hereford to be inducted into the Panhandle Sports Hall of Fame.

LEGENDARY SCHOOL WHERE THE BATON WAS PASSED FROM ONE COACH TO ANOTHER KEEPING THE WINNING TRADITION GOING FROM YEAR TO YEAR

Seminole- 10 state tournament appearances
            4 state championships
            4 runner up trophies
            2 semi-final appearances

For sure Seminole Volleyball has a rich tradition in volleyball. All you must do is research their high school website [Maiden Volleyball] and the information is organized into years and accomplishments concerning the volleyball coaches in the past. They are in order:

1960-1963 **Wanda Owen**
1964-1974 **Judy Bugher** [Led her team to 1 state
            championship]
1975-1978 **Kathleen Brasfield** [Led her team to 2 state
            championships]
1979-1980 **Debbie Harris**
1980-1997 **Lynda Jackson** [Led her team 5 times to the
            state tournament winning the championship
            one time]
1998-2016 **Jacqueline Horton** [Led her team 10 times
            to the state play-offs]

At one point in time, from 1976 to 1983, Seminole dominate this region by appearing at the UIL State Girls Volleyball Tournament eight out of nine straight years. Add 25 years in the state play-offs in volleyball gives Seminole a solid mark on the Texas State Map.

JOYCE ELROD-SNYDER

When a coach wins the state championship in any sport, that championship is a huge accomplishment for any coach that coaches in the public schools but a coach that wins three should be mentioned in the same vein as other legendary coaches.

Coach Elrod put volleyball on the map at Snyder High School. She coached volleyball in Snyder for 16 years, being the Head Volleyball Coach 8 of those years.

Joyce Elrod led her teams at Snyder to seven district championships and 3 UIL State Volleyball Championships in class 4A during the years of 1976, 1980, and 1981. Her overall coaching record in volleyball was 232-64.

She was named "Honor Coach of the Year" by the Texas High School Girls Coaches Association and she was a three-time All-Star coach.

CHARLES CAIN-PLAINS HIGH SCHOOL

Charles dad was in the Navy, so they moved around a lot, but he graduated from Snyder High School and attended Texas Tech University. He graduated from Tech in 1977 and went to work at Alderson Junior High School in Lubbock, Texas. The next year he was hired in Plains, Texas at Plains High School as a junior high school coaching football, basketball and track.

In 1983 he moved to girls' athletics at Plains High School then in 1984 he became the head volleyball coach. Plains already had a strong volleyball program going and he gives Zula Blann credit for teaching him all he knows about volleyball. He stated that she was an awesome coach.

Charles must have been a good learner because the 1984 team made it to the state tournament getting beat in the first round then they made a return trip in 1985. Oh well, he coached the volleyball team to the state tournament if 1987, 1988, 1989, and 1990. Overall, coach Cain won the UIL Texas State volleyball championship four times.

When ask what his strength was in coaching those teams, he said, "He was in the right place at the right time." He continued, "There were two lady coaches that did the damage before I even came on the scene for volleyball and all I had to do is follow their lead." "Shirley Gross, Wanda Armstrong, and Zula Blann deserve all the credit because they were the ones that got volleyball going in the right direction, not me."

Charles Cain coached two All Star Volleyball games sponsored by the Texas High School Girls Coaches Association during his time at Plains, but no one really knows what his coaching record happens to be because he really didn't care what it was. He had a job to do and that is what he did giving everyone credit for any accomplishment he had. That says a lot about Charles Cain.

ZULA BLANN-PLAINS AND BRONTE HIGH SCHOOL

How does a basketball coach become a Volleyball coaching legend? Well, talk to Zula Blann and she has a story to tell about how she became a volleyball coach. In 1970 Coach Blann was considered as a girls' basketball coach at Bronte High School. But all that changed when Ballinger needed another volleyball team for their "power volleyball" tournament. The superintendent at that time was Mr. Barbee and when Ballinger called, he decided to put Bronte into that tournament even though they didn't play power volleyball. Guess who was on the list as the head coach? Right, Zula Blann and that was her start as a volleyball coach. After their first game where they were defeated by Snyder 15-0, 15-1, Zula and the team starting learning what power volleyball was about. All you can say is that the Mr. Barbee knew what he

was doing because Bronte won the Consolation Championship after that terrible start. I guess he knew more about Zula than she because from that point on, Zula Blann became a legend in high school volleyball.

After getting several nominations as a legendary volleyball coach, I became very interested in Zula Blann. Finally, after many attempts, I contacted her, and I was not disappointed. When I asked her to write down her accomplishments, she did so but also mention what the individual girls accomplished during her coaching career. To me, that tells you a lot about Zula Blann.

Zula was born in Bronte, Texas and graduated from Lake View High School [San Angelo, Texas] in 1964. She attended Angelo State University, received a BS and Med in English and Physical Education. She married Jess Blann and had two children, Delores [Delo] Dyer, [teacher and coach in the San Antonio area], and Dr. Jewel Pye, professor of Physical Education at Angelo State University.

From 1970-1980, her volleyball teams at Bronte made the play-offs 10 times, advanced to the regional tournament 10 times, advanced to the State Volleyball tournament 5 times, were runner up champions 3 times and won the State UIL Volleyball Championship in 1976. What was most impressive was the fact that Forsan was the dominate volleyball team before she became the Head Volleyball coach. Forsan had won 55 consecutive district championships before Bronte started building their own tradition in Volleyball.

She was the Head Volleyball coach at Plains from 1981-1983 and her volleyball teams were runner up two years. After Plains she landed as the Head Volleyball coach at Westwood [Round Rock] where from 1988 to 1999 Coach Zula compiled a won lost record of 346-87. Starting with a program like Bronte, a program that had never been to the play-offs, 10 times, advanced to the state volleyball tournament 2 times being the runner up champion in 1998 and winning the Texas UIL State Volleyball Championship in 1999.

In 2000, Zula Blann retired from coaching and teaching.

Baseball

IF YOU PARTICIPATE IN AN outdoor sport in the Panhandle/Plains region in the spring, your sport already has a strong handicap called the weather. If you are just competing within that region everything is fair to a point although the tip of the Panhandle of Texas is a region that is known for bad weather. What I am talking about is winter wind and cold fronts where you can't even feel your hands, they are so cold. For sure baseball has a strong handicap when competing with the other parts of Texas, particularly South Texas. It's not fair but it is what it is and anyone that lives in this region understands that before they even start.

UIL baseball started in 1948-1949 school year. At that time the UIL had two divisions, one called 2A and one called City. That lasted until the 1950-1951 school year where the UIL went to only one division, called 2A. In the 1956-1957, the UIL went to two divisions called 2A and 3A.

The first 20 years of UIL baseball at the UIL state baseball tournament. Only those teams from the Panhandle/Plains region that qualified for the state baseball tournament are listed.

Format: [Year-Division-School that represented our region in baseball-W-Won the state tournament, R-Runner up, S-Semi-final.]

[None] means that no one from the Panhandle/Plains region qualified for the state tournament

Spring

1949	2A	None	
	City	None	
1950	2A	Abilene	R
	City	None	

UIL went to one classification [2A]

1951	2A	None	
1952	2A	Amarillo	S
1953	2A	Amarillo	R
1954	2A	None	
1955	2A	Abilene	R
1956	2A	Abilene	W

UIL went to two divisions [2A] and [3A]

1957	2A	Snyder	S
	3A	Abilene	W
1958	2A	Snyder	S
	3A	None	
1959	3A	None	
	4A	None	
1960	3A	Snyder	R
	4A	None	
1961	3A	Lamesa	S
	4A	Lubbock Monterey	R
1962	3A	Seminole	R
	4A	None	
1963	3A	Lubbock Monterey	S
	4A	Dumas	S
1964	3A	Brownfield	R
	4A	None	
1965	3A	Snyder	S
	4A	None	
1966	3A	Dumas	R
	4A	None	
1967	3A	None	
	4A	Abilene Cooper	R
1968	3A	Lamesa	R
	4A	None	

The first twenty years of UIL baseball was slow to get started in the Panhandle/Plains region. During this period, Abilene played for the state baseball championship four times and won the gold twice being a runner up twice. Snyder had four appearances also with one runner up trophy and three semi-final appearances.

Lamesa, Lubbock Monterey and Amarillo had two appearances in this period, all three had one runner up trophy and one semi-final appearance.

Brownfield [R], Abilene Cooper [R], Dumas [R], Seminole [R] all had one state tournament appearance in this period.

The second twenty years of baseball state play-offs

1969	3A	Andrews	R
	4A	None	
1970	3A	Dumas	R
	4A	Lubbock Monterey	S
1971	3A	Dumas	W
	4A	Lubbock Monterey	R
1972	3A	Lamesa	S
	4A	Lubbock Monterey	W
1973	3A	None	
	4A	None	
1974	3A	None	
	4A	Lubbock Monterey	W
1975	3A	None	
	4A	None	
1976	3A	None	
	4A	None	
1977	3A	None	
	4A	None	
1978	3A	None	
	4A	Lubbock Monterey	R

UIL went to 5 classifications

1979	B	None	
	1A	None	
	2A	None	
	3A	None	
	4A	None	
1980	B	None	
	1A	None	
	2A	None	
	3A	Snyder	S

UIL dropped class "B" and added class "5A"

Year	Class	School	
1981	1A	Follett	S
	2A	None	
	3A	None	
	4A	Lubbock Estacado	R
	5A	Lubbock Monterey	W
1982	1A	None	
	2A	None	
	3A	None	
	4A	Lubbock Estacado	S
	5A	None	
1983	1A	None	
	2A	None	
	3A	None	
	4A	Snyder	W
	5A	None	
1984	1A	None	
	2A	None	
	3A	None	
	4A	None	
	5A	Lubbock Monterey	S
1985	1A	None	
	2A	None	
	3A	Graham	S
	4A	Andrews	S
	5A	Lubbock Monterey	S
1986	1A	None	
	2A	None	
	3A	Brownfield	R
	4A	Snyder	S
	5A	None	
1987	1A	Lefors	S
	2A	None	
	3A	None	
	4A	None	
	5A	Abilene Cooper	W
1988	1A	Follett	S
	2A	None	
	3A	Abilene Wylie	S
	4A	Canyon	S
	5A	Abilene Cooper	W

During this period, the second twenty-year mark of the UIL state baseball tournament Lubbock Monterey stole the show. Monterey had 8 state tournament appearances playing for the UIL State baseball championship 5 times winning the gold 3 times. Monterey also had 3 semi-final appearances.

Snyder had 3 state tournament appearances in this period winning one gold and 2 semi-final trophies.

Abilene Cooper had two appearances and won the gold both times. Dumas [W-R], Andrews [R- S], Follett [S-S], and Lubbock Estacado [R-S] also had two appearances during this period.

Those with one state tournament appearance during this time frame was Abilene Wylie [S], Canyon [S], Lefors [S], Graham [S], Brownfield [R], and Lamesa [S].

The following is the next twenty-year period concerning the baseball UIL tournament.

Year	Class	Team	
1989	1A	None	
	2A	None	
	3A	None	
	4A	None	
	5A	None	
1990	1A	None	
	2A	None	
	3A	Abilene Wylie	S
	4A	Andrews	S
	5A	None	
1991	1A	None	
	2A	None	
	3A	None	
	4A	None	
	5A	None	
1992	1A	Baird	S
	2A	None	
	3A	Graham	S
	4A	Big Spring	S
	5A	None	
1993	1A	Baird	S
	2A	New Deal	S
	3A	None	
	4A	Wolfforth Frenship	R
	5A	Abilene Cooper	R
1994	1A	None	
	2A	None	
	3A	None	
	4A	Big Spring	R
	5A	Lubbock Monterey	S
1995	1A	None	
	2A	None	
	3A	Graham	S

	4A	Lamesa	R
	5A	Lubbock Coronado	R
1996	1A	None	
	2A	None	
	3A	Graham	R
	4A	None	
	5A	Lubbock Monterey	W
1997	1A	Claude	S
	2A	None	
	3A	Abilene Wylie	S
	4A	None	
	5A	Lubbock Monterey	R
1998	1A	Rotan	S
	2A	None	
	3A	Iowa Park	S
	4A	None	
	5A	None	
1999	1A	Cross Plains	R
	2A	None	
	3A	None	
	4A	Andrews	W
	5A	None	
2000	1A	Cross Plains	R
	2A	None	
	3A	None	
	4A	None	
	5A	None	
2001	1A	Miles	S
	2A	None	
	3A	Iowa Park	S
	4A	None	
	5A	None	
2002	1A	None	
	2A	None	
	3A	Abilene Wylie	S
	4A	None	
	5A	None	
2003	1A	None	
	2A	None	
	3A	Canyon	S
	4A	None	
	5A	None	
2004	1A	Follett	R
	2A	None	
	3A	Perryton	S
	4A	None	
	5A	None	
2005	1A	New Deal	S
	2A	None	
	3A	Lubbock Cooper	R

	4A	Wichita Falls Rider	S
	5A	Lubbock Monterey	S
2006	1A	New Deal	S
	2A	None	
	3A	Abilene Wylie	S
	4A	None	
	5A	None	
2007	1A	New Deal	R
	2A	None	
	3A	Abilene Wylie	S
	4A	Canyon Randall	S
	5A	None	
2008	1A	Seymour	S
	2A	San Angelo Grape Creek	S
	3A	Snyder	W
	4A	None	
	5A	None	
2009	1A	Miles	W
	2A	None	
	3A	None	
	4A	None	
	5A	None	

Abilene Wylie had 5 state tournament appearances in this period all semi-final games. Then on the large school division, Lubbock Monterey had 4 state tournament appearances winning the gold once, runner up once, and two semi-finals contests. New Deal making its first appearance at the UIL State Baseball tournament had 4 appearances, one runner up and three semi-final contests.

Graham made 3 state appearances in this period with one runner up, and two semi-finals contests. Baird, two semi-final games, Cross Plains, two runner up trophies, Iowa Park, two semi-final games, Miles, won the UIL State baseball championship, and one semi-final appearance, Andrews, won the UIL State baseball championship and one semi-final appearance, and Big Spring, one runner up trophy and one semi-final contest. Those schools with one appearances are Claude [S], Rotan [S], Follett [R], Seymour [S], San Angelo Grape Creek [S], Canyon [S], Perryton [S], Lubbock Cooper [R], Snyder, won the UIL State baseball championship, Abilene Cooper [R], Lubbock Coronado [R], Wolfforth Frenship [R], Lamesa [R], Wichita Fall Rider [S], and Canyon Randall [S].

The last nine years in the state baseball tournament.

2010	1A	Stamford	S
	2A	Bushland	R
	3A	None	
	4A	None	
	5A	None	
2011	1A	Stamford	S
	2A	Bushland	S
	3A	None	
	4A	Wichita Falls Rider	W
	5A	Lubbock Coronado	R
2012	1A	Stamford	R
	2A	Bushland	R
	3A	None	
	4A	None	
	5A	None	
2013	1A	Stamford	R
	2A	None	
	3A	Lubbock Cooper	S
	4A	Wichita Falls Rider	S
	5A	None	
2014	1A	Dawson	S
	2A	Idalou	S
	3A	Lubbock Cooper	S
	4A	None	
	5A	None	
2015	2A	Booker	S
	3A	Littlefield	S
	4A	Abilene Wylie	S
	5A	None	
	6A	None	
2016	1A	None	
	2A	Stamford	S
	3A	Shallowater	S
	4A	Abilene Wylie	W
	5A	Amarillo	S
2017	1A	Gail Border County	S
	2A	Albany	S
	3A	Wall	R
	4A	Abilene Wylie	W
	5A	None	
	6A	None	
2018	1A	New Home	S
	2A	New Dill	S
	3A	None	
	4A	None	
	5A	None	

In this last time frame from 2010 – 2018, Stamford made 5 appearances with two runner- up trophies and three semi-final contests. Next was Abilene Wylie with 3 state tournament appearances winning the gold two times and one semi-final appearance. Also, Bushland had three appearances in this time frame with two runner -up trophies and one semi-final contest.

Wichita Falls Rider won the State baseball tournament one time during this time frame and had one semi-final appearance. Lubbock Cooper made two appearances at the state tournament in this time frame, both semi-final contests.

Those with one appearance at the UIL State baseball tournament are as follows: Lubbock Coronado with a runner up trophy, New Dill, semi-finalist, New Home, semi-finalist, Wall, semi- finalist, Albany, semi-finalist, Borden County, semi-finalist, Amarillo, semi-finalist, Shallowater, semi-finalist, Littlefield, semi-finalists, Booker, semi-finalist, Idalou, semi-finalist, and Dawson, semi-finalist.

Schools with two or more UIL State baseball appearances in the Panhandle Plains region:

Large Schools		Small Schools	
Lubbock Monterey	14	New Deal	5
Abilene Wylie	9	Stamford	5
Snyder	8	Follett	3
Abilene	4	Bushland	3
Lamesa	4	Baird	2
Andrews	4	Cross Plains	2
Graham	3	Miles	2
Amarillo	3	Iowa Park	2
Abilene Cooper	3		
Lubbock Cooper	3		
Wichita Falls Rider	3		
Lubbock Estacado	2		
Dumas	2		
Lubbock Coronado	2		
Brownfield	2		
Big Spring	2		

Schools [regardless of size] with one or more UIL State Baseball championship:

Lubbock Monterey	4
Snyder	2
Abilene	2
Abilene Wylie	2
Abilene Cooper	2
Dumas	1
Andrews	1
Wichita Falls Rider	1
Miles	1

BASEBALL HIGH SCHOOL COACHING LEGENDS IN THE PANHANDLE/PLAINS REGION

Note: Two large cities in this region, Lubbock and Abilene produced schools that had 37 of the 68 state tournament appearances starting in 1948. That means that 54% of the teams since 1948 have come from one or two cities, Abilene and Lubbock. The UIL Texas baseball state champion has been dominated by those two cities also. All together the Panhandle/Plains region has produced 16 state championships. 10 of the 16 championships have come from either Lubbock or Abilene which is 62.5%.

BOBBY MOEGLE-LUBBOCK MONTEREY

Bobby Moegle is a household name in homes that are baseball fans in the Panhandle/Plains region, but it goes further than this region concerning this legendary baseball coach. It extends into the entire state of Texas when it concerns high school baseball. Consider the fact that he is the winningest high school baseball coach in Texas but more to the point, he is ranked 5th nationally with 1115 wins. His overall record is awesome with only 266 losses with one tie in 40 years.

The fact that Coach Moegle is a legend is old hat but what always impresses me when speaking of baseball to baseball coaches, his name is always mentioned as a person that influenced everyone from baseball coaches, fans and school administration particularly in the Lubbock area more than anyone has influenced a sport regardless of the sport.

His high school record at Monterey is awesome but his result is what makes his baseball career so special. From 196-1999 his teams won the State UIL baseball championship four times and finished as a runner up for the championship four times. Not only that they made five other appearances but lost in the first round. Overall his teams won 33 district championships

Bobby was voted Texas high school coach of the year three times and selected into the Texas High School Baseball Coaches Association "Hall of Fame." Then on February 18th, 2013 he was voted into the Texas Sports "Hall of Fame" which meant he would be the first high school baseball coach ever selected for this honor.

JAMES "SPEEDY" MOFFETT-SNYDER HIGH SCHOOL

The fact remains that if you are a person of importance and we are talking about high school baseball in the Panhandle/Plains region, the name of Speedy Moffett will come up in any conversation about legendary coaches.

What coach who is named as the Athletic Director and Head football coach resigns so he can teach history and start a baseball program at the school he is teaching. WOW! When you make a comment that this coach started from the ground up, that is an understatement when it comes to the Snyder and Speedy Moffett. Not only that, coach Moffett started Snyder's Little League Baseball program at Snyder.

Speedy got his nickname at Texas Tech went a sportswriter started calling him Speedy before he knew his full name. From that point on he was nicknamed Speedy Moffett.

For the next 24 years Speedy Moffett baseball teams won 13 district championships and at one time, he was the winningest baseball coach in the great state of Texas. When he retired in 1976 his teams had won a total of 474 games which was a record at that time.

His accomplishments didn't go without notice because he was selected into the Texas High School Coaches Association "Hall of Honor in 1983." Not to mention he was also selected into the Snyder Athletic "Hall of Honor", and the Texas High School Baseball Coaching Association "Hall of Fame."

One last comment on Speedy Moffett, the baseball field at Snyder is named after him. Is there a greater accomplishment in the world of sports?

BLACKIE BLACKBURN-ABILENE HIGH SCHOOL

It seems reasonable to assume that someone from the Abilene region was instrumental in the strong influence on high school baseball. Well, Blackie Blackburn is one of those legendary people concerning the baseball world.

Starting in 1947, coach Blackburn became the Head baseball coach at Abilene High School. During the next 24 years he put together one of the greatest baseball programs in the history of Texas high school baseball.

During this time period, his teams won 14 district championships leading to a record of 409-205. His teams were state finalist five times then he won back to back state championships in the UIL state high school baseball championships in 1956-1957.

Blackie Blackburn was one of the real first legendary coaches where twice he won the "Texas Coach of the Year award." Later, in his life, his dream came true as they named the baseball field after him in honor of his life as the Head Baseball coach at Abilene High School.

ANDY MALONE-ABILENE COOPER HIGH SCHOOL

Andy Malone was one of the true legends of high school baseball not only in the Panhandle/Plains region but in other parts of Texas. He had success at every stop that he coached which included Abilene Cooper, New Diana, Beckville, Fort Worth Western Hills, Texarkana Texas high school, Jefferson, Hallsville and Longview. Coach Malone guided New Diana and Beckville to the state baseball tournament.

Overall, Coach Malone had an 861-345 record in 41 years of coaching high school baseball. At Abilene Cooper he had a 220-52 won lost record. Cooper won two state championships, 1987 and 1988, under Coach Malone's guidance.

His 1987 team with a record of 33-3 was considered the co-national champions by Collegiate Baseball. Abilene Cooper enjoyed six district titles and advanced to the state baseball playoffs seven consecutive baseball seasons.

Andy Malone was inducted into the "Big County Athletic Hall of Fame" in 2013 and the Texas High School Baseball Association "Hall of Fame" in 2012.

JOHN DUDLEY-CORONADO HIGH SCHOOL

If anyone who knows John Dudley knows that he belongs in whatever positive legendary category you want to place him. He has done more for the Panhandle/Plains region than any coach you can name that is still alive. And guess what, I'm not talking baseball. His commitment to Coaches outreach is far and above the normal calling but what is most impressive is that he walks the walk as well as he talks the talk.

What is most impressive about Coach Dudley is that he started his career at Atkins Junior High in 1966. Since John played for Coach Moegle, Legendary baseball coach at Monterey it would be normal for him to coach at Monterey where he was named assistant football coach and assistant baseball coach coming from Atkins Junior High School. Then in 1973, Coronado High School hired John as their head baseball coach where he would stay until he retired.

During his career at Coronado his teams advanced to the playoffs thirteen times with his 1995 team advancing to the Texas UIL State baseball tournament finals. Although they finished as the runner up, that baseball team will long be remembered in this region.

John Dudley was a member of the Board of Directors of the Texas High School Baseball Coaches Association, served as the Director of

Region I for two years, and the Secretary-Treasury from 1980-82. He was selected to coach the North All-Stars in the THSBCA All Star game in 1994.

Many awards have come across John Dudley's life. He was inducted into the Texas High School Baseball Coaches Association "Hall of Fame" in 1999, he was named as a "Coach That Makes a Difference" by Fox Sports Southwest Network, High School Xtra Division in 2002, and he was award the Kal Segrist Lifetime Achievement Award for contribution to West Texas Baseball in 2003. Not only that, John was the district "Coach of the Year" eight times. Dudley was selected as a "Teacher You Can Count On" by KCBD-TV in 2002, and as the "Secondary Social Studies Teacher of the Year" by the Staked Plains Council for the Social Studies in 2003.

ALBERT LEWIS-SNYDER HIGH SCHOOL

One of the greatest comments someone could say about a person came from one of the teachers at Snyder when Albert Lewis first became a part of the baseball program as Speedy Moffett assistant baseball coach. It was a tough time at Snyder like so many other schools in Texas when all school integrated causing many problems for educators everywhere. Simply put some teachers just didn't know how to handle the different cultures, black students. The comment, "He was the best thing to ever happen at Snyder High School" referring to Albert Lewis as a teacher, not a coach. He knew how to handle black students with discipline problems showing us the way and paving the way for all teachers at our school.

Coach Lewis became the head baseball coach at Snyder High School in 1977 after being an assistant for twelve years. In the seventeen years through his guidance Snyder advanced to the high school playoffs fourteen times with eleven district championships, and three regional titles. Coach Lewis took his team to the UIL Baseball State Tournament three times winning the gold in 1983.

Albert Lewis was inducted into the Snyder Athletic Hall of Honor. Later, this Lubbock Dunbar graduate was selected into the Texas High School Baseball Coaches Association "Hall of Fame" in 2003.

JOE RAY HALSEY-ANDREWS HIGH SCHOOL

When a coach builds a program from the ground up that program becomes like marriage. Joe Ray Halsey did just that, building the Andrews baseball program from the ground up and he was responsible for everything that happened for the Andrews high school baseball program.

He was known as tough intense coach on the field but off the field a true gentleman in all regards. He coached baseball at Andrews for 28 years guiding the Mustangs into the UIL Texas State baseball tournament three times. But more important was the fact that when he gave up the baseball program, he didn't want all his work to go for nothing, so he looked hard for a replacement. When he finally handed the baton to Rodney Gardner, Coach Halsey felt complete for he knew his work was going to continue for a long time under Coach Gardner's leadership. Sure enough, the baseball program at Andrews has continued its success with their new coach.

Joe Ray Halsey is now the President of the Retired Texas High School Baseball Coaches Association and currently he was selected in 2007 by the THSBCA into the "Hall of Fame."

FRED OLIVER-PLAINVIEW/MONTEREY

For sure we don't want to forget to appreciate Coach Oliver for his achievement in high school baseball in the Panhandle/Plains region making coaching stops at Plainview and Monterey.

While coaching at Monterey he led them to the UIL Baseball State Tournament in 1996.

He also took Lufkin to the baseball state tournament in 1992 and ended his baseball career at Highland Park where he retired. His overall coaching record at Highland Park was 101-43-2 and his total coaching record was 587-321 as a head baseball coach.

Coach Oliver was inducted into the National High School Baseball Coaches Association and the Texas High School Baseball Coaches Association "Hall of Fame."

On his retirement, Coach Oliver made this statement, "I was always able to pick where I wanted to be, and I was blessed to be in the right place at the right time."

ROD GARDNER-ESTACADO/ABERNATHY/ANDREWS/OTHERS IN NEW MEXICO

Winning baseball games was second nature to Coach Gardner because he did it time after time regardless of where he was coaching. Rod started his baseball coaching career in New Mexico at Elida, class "A", then to Aztec, class "AAA" and to Alamogordo, class "AAAA". Finally, Coach Gardner took the Head Baseball position at Lubbock Estacado and for 13 years he started building his reputation as an outstanding baseball coach. Then he traveled to Abernathy for 6 years and on to Andrews for 14 years with a grand total of 40 years of being a head baseball coach, 33 in Texas and 7 in New Mexico.

During this period his teams won 21 district championships and advanced to the play-offs 31 years. Twice he directed his team to the State Boys Baseball championship once in Texas at Andrews, 2009, and once in New Mexico at Aztec, 1978.

Also, he stayed busy because he was the Regional Director of the Texas High School Coaching Association in 1992-1993. In 1998, he was selected to coach the North/South baseball all-star game [small school division] of the Texas High School Coaching Association.

Rod Gardner became a household name when it comes to high school baseball as he compiled a won lost record of 725-440. His son, Matt is the pitching coach at Texas Tech but most important, Rod is known as a teacher of the game and has helped many young people achieve in the classroom and on the baseball diamond.

KELLY HARGROVE-WICHITA FALLS RIDER

Who is a coach that is one of the greatest coaches in the Wichita Falls Independent School District, especially Rider High School? If you guessed Kelly Hargrove, you got it right.

Coach Hargrove was the Assistant Baseball coach at Wichita Falls Rider high school from 1994- 1997. From 1998-2006 he was the head baseball coach becoming the leader in games won as the baseball coach at Rider High School and Wichita Falls Independent School district history. Kelly Hargrove was 216-99-2 at Rider leading Rider to 5 district championships, the play-offs 8 of 9 years, which included 3 straight regional finalist [2004-2006] Coach Hargrove has coached in 60 playoff games winning 38 playoff contest which is more than any other baseball coach in the WFISD history.

Kelly Hargrove was the "District coach of the year" 5 times. The 2008 baseball team presented him a plague in the 3rd base dugout at Pride Field honoring his strong accomplishments to the Rider Baseball program.

STEVE STONE-WICHITA FALLS RIDER

The problem with recognizing Legends especially for winning games, someone before them usually broke the ice and set the tone to win games. However, the truth is very few of those coaches are mentioned when we talk of legends. Steve Stone is one of those coaches.

He was the 10th Head Baseball coach at Rider High taking over a program that hadn't won a district championship or in 20 years. In 1995 Rider won its first district championship since 1975. He was the first baseball coach to win 100 games at Rider High School.

Coach Stone set the tone for positive winning baseball then Coach Hargrove took the baton from Coach Stone carrying the baton further than any baseball coach has in the history of WFISD.

LEGENDARY SCHOOLS IN BASEBALL- [NO COACH WAS NOMINATED]

It takes a family to have a constant tradition of winning and that means sacrifice and dedication from not only the coach and players but the administration, teachers, students and community. To keep a tradition from one year to the next is very difficult to maintain and it can only happen if everyone [family] commits to the success of the high school program.

The following schools are legends and should be recognized as such.

- Abilene Wylie- made 9 appearances at the UIL State Baseball Tournament
- Stamford-made 5 appearances at the UIL State Baseball Tournament
- New Deal-made 5 appearances at the UIL State Baseball Tournament

NOTE: BASEBALL COACHES FROM THIS AUTHOR

[IF I MISSED SOME BASEBALL COACHING LEGENDS I WANT TO SAY I AM SORRY FOR NOT MENTIONING YOU] IT WAS JUST SOMETHING THAT COULDN'T BE HELPED BECAUSE VERY FEW BASEBALL COACHES WERE NOMINATED AND PRESS COVERAGE WAS LIMITED BECAUSE MOST OF THE PRESS COVERAGE WAS ABOUT LEGENDARY BASEBALL PLAYERS FROM OUR REGION, NOT COACHES.

Track And Field

Just like basketball, just like volleyball and just like baseball certain specific schools had track success in the Panhandle/Plains region.

Track is another sport that takes a beating in the spring because of weather conditions which can determine success of failure in Track. Track is a timed sport for most part so when an athlete competes in a wind storm of 25-30 miles with the temperature around 40 degrees their performance will be altered by the environment and compared with performance in the East, South, and West Texas athletes where the wind and cold can create an uneven playing field

Boys track started in 1911 while girls track started in 1972. In the larger schools, most teams have a girl's coach and a boy's coach. But in many schools one person coaches both so we are going to keep them together.

Here are the schools that have had success at the state level in Track from the Panhandle/Plains region. The UIL record inventory goes back to 1911. At that time, only the state champion winner is mentioned.

[None] means that no schools from the Panhandle/Plains region qualified for the State Championship.

Format: [Year-Winner] only winners from the Panhandle/Plains region will be listed

1911	None
1912	None
1913	None

1914	UIL went to two divisions of public schools. Class 1A and Class B were added	
1921	1A	None
	B	None
1922	1A	None
	B	None
1923	1A	Electra
	B	La Grange
1924	1A	Wichita Falls
	B	None

1925	The UIL dropped all classifications and just had one winner
1925	Abilene
1926	None
1927	Electra
1928	None
1929	San Angelo
1930	None

The first twenty years of completion at the State Level of the UIL was slow at best as far as Track and Field is concerned in the Panhandle/Plains region. Electra won 3 State Championships in this period taking top honors. LaGrange, Wichita Falls, Abilene, San Angelo, and Indian Gap each won one state championship during the first twenty years of UIL Track and Field.

1932	None
1933	None
1934	None
1935	None
1936	None
1937	None
1938	None
1939	Brady
1940	None
1941	None
1942	None
1943	None
1944	None
1945	None

```
1946      None
1947      None
```

1948 UIL went to 3 Classifications: 1A, 2A, B, City

```
1948    1A      Seminole
        2A      None
        B       None
        City    None
1949    1A      None
        2A      None
        B       None
        City    None
1950    1A      Brady
        2A      None
        B       Rising Star
        City    none
```

```
1951    UIL went to three classifications, 1A, 2A, B
1951    1A      None
        2A      None
        B       None
1952    1A      None
        2A      None
        B       None
```

The second twenty years of UIL State Track and Field championships were limited to 3 schools each winning one state championship. Those schools were Seminole, Brady and Rising Star. It is very clear at this point that the Panhandle/Plains region takes a beating from the weather making it most difficult to excel at Track with the other regions in Texas.

```
1953    1A      None
        2A      None
        B       None
1954    1A      Andrews
        2A      Abilene
        B       None
1955    1A      None
        2A      None
        B       None
1956    1A      None
        2A      None
        B       None
1957    1A      Stamford
        2A      None
        B       None
1958    1A      None
```

	2A	Andrews
	B	None
1959	UIL went to 5 classifications: 1A, 2A, 3A, 4A, and B	
1959	1A	None
	2A	None
	3A	Andrews
	4A	Abilene
	B	None
1960	1A	None
	2A	None
	3A	Andrews
	4A	Abilene
	B	None
1961	1A	None
	2A	None
	3A	Andrews
	4A	Abilene
	B	Lazbuddie
1962	1A	None
	2A	None
	3A	None
	4A	None
	B	None
1963	1A	None
	2A	None
	3A	None
	4A	Amarillo Tascosa
	B	None
1964	1A	None
	2A	None
	3A	Kermit
	4A	Abilene Cooper
	B	Booker
1965	1A	None
	2A	None
	3A	None
	4A	None
	B	Booker
1966	1A	None
	2A	None
	3A	None
	4A	None
	B	None
1967	1A	None
	2A	None
	3A	None
	4A	None
	B	Vernon Lockett
1968	1A	None

	Class	Champion
	2A	None
	3A	Lubbock Dunbar
	4A	None
	B	Vernon Lockett
1969	1A	Lubbock Cooper
	2A	None
	3A	None
	4A	None
	B	None
1970	1A	None
	2A	None
	3A	Lubbock Estacado
	4A	None
	B	None
1971	1A	Crowell
	2A	None
	3A	None
4A	None	UIL started Girls track in the spring of 1972: 1A and B
	B	Rule

The next era in track that changed the picture of track was the addition of girls track in the UIL. In 1972, Girls Track was inserted into the State UIL Track/Field championships. The Panhandle/Plains region had lots of success in this period. Andrews was the dominant track and field team in this period with 5 state championship placed in the trophy case. Right on the heels of Andrews was Abilene High School winning 4 UIL State Track/Field championships. Vernon Lockett and Booker both won 2 UIL State Track/Field championships during this period. Those schools with one track/field championship in this period belonged to, Stamford, Lasbuddie, Amarillo Tascosa, Kermit, Abilene Cooper, Crowell, Rule, Lubbock Dunbar, Lubbock Cooper and Lubbock Estacado. All together now Abilene has 5 state championships

Boys Track			**Girls Track**		
1972	1A	None	1972	1A	None
	2A	None		B	Gruver
	3A	None			
	4A	None			
	B	Wall			
1973	1A	None	1973	1A	None
	2A	None		B	None
	3A	None			
	4A	None	UIL added 2A to girls' track and field in 1974		
	B	Rule			
1974	1A	None	1974	1A	None

Year	Class	Name	Year	Class	Name
	2A	None		2A	None
	3A	None		B	None
	4A	None		UIL added 3A, 4A to the track and field classifications in 1975	
	B	Rule			
1975	1A	None	1975	1A	None
	2A	None		2A	Olton
	3A	None		3A	None
	4A	None		4A	None
	B	None		B	None
1976	1A	Memphis	1976	1A	Paducah
	2A	None		2A	None
	3A	None		3A	Canyon
	4A	Abilene		4A	None
	B	None		B	Meadow
1977	1A	None	1977	1A	Paducah
	2A	None		2A	None
	3A	None		3A	Canyon
	4A	None		4A	None
	B	None		B	None
1978	1A	None	1978	1A	Bovina
	2A	None		2A	None
	3A	None		3A	Canyon
	4A	None		4A	None
	B	None		B	None
1979	1A	None	1979	1A	Sunray
	2A	None		2A	None
	3A	None		3A	None
	4A	None		4A	None
	B	None		B	Miami
1980	1A	None	1980	1A	None
	2A	None		2A	Clyde
	3A	None		3A	None
	4A	None		4A	None
	B	None		B	Miami

1981   **Uil went to 5 classification: 1A, 2A,3A,4A, and 5A in girls and boys track and field**

Year	Class	Name	Year	Class	Name
1981	1A	None	1981	1A	None
	2A	None		2A	None
	3A	None		3A	None
	4A	Andrews		4A	None
	5A	None		5A	None
1982	1A	None	1982	1A	None
	2A	None		2A	None
	3A	None		3A	Slaton
	4A	Lubbock Estacado		4A	None
	5A	None		5A	None
1983	1A	None	1983	1A	None

Year	Class		Year	Class	
	2A	None		2A	None
	3A	None		3A	None
	4A	Lubbock Estacado		4A	None
	5A	None		5A	None
1984	1A	None	1984	1A	None
	2A	Panhandle		2A	None
	3A	None		3A	None
	4A	None		4A	Sweetwater
	5A	None		5A	None
1985	1A	Munday	1985	1A	None
	2A	None		2A	Hamlin
	3A	None		3A	None
	4A	None		4A	None
	5A	None		5A	None
1986	1A	Gruver	1986	1A	
	2A	None		2A	Hamlin
	3A	None		3A	None
	4A	Lubbock Estacado		4A	Pampa
	5A	None		5A	None
1987	1A	None	1987	1A	None
	2A	None		2A	None
	3A	None		3A	None
	4A	None		4A	None
	5A	None		5A	None
1988	1A	Munday	1988	1A	Munday
	2A	Haskell		2A	None
	3A	None		3A	None
	4A	None		4A	Pampa
	5A	None		5A	None
1989	1A	Rotan	1989	1A	Munday
	2A	None		2A	None
	3A	None		3A	None
	4A	None		4A	None
	5A	None		5A	None
1990	1A	Munday	1990	1A	Munday
	2A	None		2A	None
	3A	None		3A	None
	4A	None		4A	None
	5A	None		5A	None
1991	1A	Munday	1991	1A	Munday
	2A	Albany		2A	None
	3A	None		3A	None
	4A	None		4A	None
	5A	None		5A	None

SUMMARY: BOYS STATE CHAMPIONSHIPS IN THIS 20-YEAR PERIOD

The next twenty years of the UIL boys Track/Field state championship saw two schools come to the top. Munday had 4 state championships in this period while Lubbock Estacado had 3 state championships. Of course, that will give Lubbock Estacado a total of 4 state championships in track/field of the UIL. Not to be outdone, Rule won 2 gold trophies in that period which will give Rule a total of 3 championships. Winning one state championship during this period was Haskell, Albany, Rotan, Memphis, Wall, Gruver, and Panhandle. Also, Andrews won 1 championship bringing their total to 6, and Abilene won one bringing their total to 5.

SUMMARY: GIRLS STATE CHAMPIONSHIP IN THIS 20-YEAR PERIOD.

Munday must have been waiting for UIL girls track for a long time because they dominated girls track with 4 State UIL Girls Track//Field Championships. The boys' team and the girl's team from Munday won 7 state championships during this 20-year period. Behind Munday, Canyon had 3 state championships showing that they can win in another sport besides basketball. Next Hamlin, Miami, and Paducah won two gold championships during this period. Winning 1 state championship was Bovina Sweetwater, Olton, Sunray, Clyde, Slaton, Gruver and Pampa.

1992	1A	None	1992	1A	None
	2A	None		2A	None
	3A	None		3A	None
	4A	None		4A	None
	5A	None		5A	None
1993	1A	None	1993	1A	None
	2A	None		2A	None
	3A	None		3A	None
	4A	San Angelo Lakeview		4A	None
	5A	None		5A	None
1994	1A	Sudan	1994	1A	Cross Plains
	2A	None		2A	None
	3A	None		3A	None
	4A	None		4A	None
	5A	None		5A	None

1995	1A	Roscoe	1995	1A	None
	2A	None		2A	None
	3A	None		3A	None
	4A	None		4A	None
	5A	None		5A	None
1996	1A	Paducah	1996	1A	N
	2A	N		2A	N
	3A	N		3A	N
	4A	N		4A	N
	5A	N		5A	N
1997	1A		1997	1A	N
	2A	Stamford		2A	Canadian
	3A	N		3A	N
	4A	N		4A	N
	5A	N		5A	N
1998	1A	N	1998	1A	N
	2A	N		2A	N
	3A	Vernon		3A	N
	4A	N		4A	N
	5A	N		5A	N
1999	1A	N	1999	1A	Munday
	2A	N		2A	N
	3A	N		3A	N
	4A	N		4A	N
	5A	N		5A	N
2000	1A	N	2000	1A	N
	2A	N		2A	Spearman
	3A	N		3A	N
	4A	N		4A	N
	5A	N		5A	N
2001	1A	Trent/Iraan	2001	1A	N
	2A	N		2A	Cisco
	3A	Abilene Wylie		3A	N
	4A	N		4A	N
	5A	Abilene		5A	N
2002	1A	N	2002	1A	Shamrock
	2A	N		2A	N
	3A	N		3A	N
	4A	N		4A	N
	5A	N		5A	N
2003	1A	N	2003	1A	N
	2A	N		2A	N
	3A	N		3A	N
	4A	N		4A	N
	5A	N		5A	N
2004	1A	N	2004	1A	N
	2A	N		2A	Crane
	3A	N		3A	N
	4A	N		4A	N
	5A	N		5A	N

Year	Class		Year	Class	
2005	1A	N	2005	1A	N
	2A	N		2A	N
	3A	N		3A	Canyon
	4A	Crowley		4A	N
	5A	N		5A	N
2006	1A	Rotan	2006	1A	N
	2A	Crane		2A	N
	3A	N		3A	N
	4A	N		4A	N
	5A	N		5A	N
2007	1A	Rule	2007	1A	N
	2A	N		2A	N
	3A	N		3A	N
	4A	N		4A	N
	5A	N		5A	N
2008	1A	Rule	2008	1A	Rochelle
	2A	N		2A	N
	3A	N		3A	N
	4A	N		4A	N
	5A	N		5A	N
2009	1A	Canadian	2009	1A	N
	2A	N		2A	N
	3A	N		3A	N
	4A	N		4A	N
	5A	N		5A	N
2010	1A	N	2010	1A	N
	2A	N		2A	N
	3A	N		3A	N
	4A	N		4A	N
	5A	N		5A	N
2011	1A	Munday	2011	1A	N
	2A	N		2A	N
	3A	N		3A	N
	4A	N		4A	N
	5A	N		5A	N
2012	1A	Munday	2012	1A	N
	2A	N		2A	N
	3A	N		3A	N
	4A	N		4A	N
	5A	N		5A	N

2013 UII created a division I and II in Class A

Year	Class		Year	Class	
2013	1A-I	Munday	2013	1A-I	N
	1A-II	Lenorah Grady		1A-II	Gail Borden
	2A	N		2A	N
	3A	N		3A	N
	4A	N		4A	N
	5A	N		5A	N
2014	1A-I	N	2014	1A-I	N
	1A-II	Bronte		1A-II	Cross Plains

	2A	N		2A	N
	3A	N		3A	N
	4A	N		4A	N
	5A	N		5A	N

2015 **UIL went to six divisions: 1A, 2A, 3A, 4A, 5A, 6A**

2015	1A	Water Valley	2015	1A	Cross Plains
	2A	New Deal		2A	N
	3A	N		3A	N
	4A	N		4A	N
	5A	N		5A	N
	6A	N		6A	N
2016	1A	Water Valley	2016	1A	N
	2A	New Deal		2A	N
	3A	N		3A	N
	4A	N		4A	N
	5A	N		5A	N
	6A	N		6A	N
2017	1A	Turkey Valley	2017	1A	N
	2A	New Deal		2A	N
	3A	N		3A	N
	4A	N		4A	N
	5A	N		5A	N
	6A	N		6A	N
2018	1A	Turkey Valley	2018	1A	N
	2A	N		2A	N
	3A	N		3A	N
	4A	N		4A	N
	5A	N		5A	N
	6A	N		6A	N

SUMMARY: BOYS TRACK/FIELD THE LAST 27 YEARS

Munday and New Deal each had 3 UIL State Track/Field championships during this last period. Over- all, that would give Munday 7 championships since the start of track/field. Next, Rule, Water Valley and Turkey Valley had 2 gold championships during this period. That would give Rule 5 state championships total. Those schools with 1 state championship during this period of time were San Angelo Lakeview, Sudan, Crane, Roscoe, Paducah, Canadian, Stamford [2 gold trophies], Vernon, Lenorah Grady, Trent, Iraan, Bronte, Abilene Wylie, Abilene [6 gold trophies], Crowley, and Rotan [2 gold trophies]

Ron Mayberry

SUMMARY: GIRLS TRACK/FIELD THE LAST 27 YEARS.

Cross Plains with 3 state UIL track/field championships finished first in this period. The teams with 1 UIL State Championship during this period was, Canadian, Spearman, Cisco, Shamrock, Crane, Rochelle, and Gail Borden County. Also, with 1 state championship were Munday which gave them a total of 5, and Canyon which gives them a total of 4.

UIL
Boys Track/Field teams [started in 1911]   Girls Track/Field teams [started 1972]

STATE CHAMPIONS Small Schools		STATE CHAMPIONS Small Schools	
Munday	7	Munday	4
Rule	5	Cross Plains	3
Electra	3	Paducah	2
Rotan	3	Shamrock	2
New Deal	3	Cisco	2
Booker	2	Gruver	1
Turkey Valley	2	Olton	1
Water Valley	2	Meadow	1
Stamford	2	Bovina	1
Brady	2	Sunray	1
Clyde	1	Clyde	1
Iowa Park	1	Slaton	1
Lazbuddie	1	Albany	1
Kermit	1	Canadian	1
Clyde	1	Spearman	1
Wall	1	Gail Borden County	1
Panhandle	1		
Gruver	1		
Haskell	1		
Sudan	1		
Roscoe	1		
Paducah	1		
Iraan	1		
Canadian	1		
Lenorah Grady	1		
Bronte	1		
LaGrange	1		

Boys State Champions Large schools		Girls State Championship Large schools	
Abilene	6	Canyon	5
Andrews	6	Pampa	2
Lubbock Estacado	4	Sweetwater	1
Vernon	2		
Abilene Wylie	1		
Wichita Falls	1		
San Angelo Central	1		
Seminole	1		
Amarillo Tascosa	1		
Abilene Cooper	1		
Lubbock Cooper	1		
San Angelo Lakeview	1		
Wichita Falls	1		

UIL CROSS COUNTRY STARTED IN 1972

The following schools were state champs in Cross Country starting in 1972

Boys			Girls		
1988	4A	Canyon Randall	1976	4A	Amarillo
90	2A	Sundown	77	4A	Amarillo [2]
92	2A	Sundown [2]	79	B	Clyde
93	1A	Plains	80	3A	Tulia
93	3A	Canyon	83	3A	Nazareth
94	2A	Sundown [3]	84	3A	Dalhart
94	4A	Canyon [2]	85	2A	Nazareth [2]
95	2A	Sundown [4]	86	2A	Nazareth [3]
95	4A	Canyon [3]	87	2A	Nazareth [4]
01	1A	Iraan	88	1A	Munday
02	1A	Iraan [2]	88	2A	Spearman
02	4A	Frenship /Wolfforth	88	3A	Perryton
03	1A	Iraan [3]	89	1A	Munday [2]
04	1A	Plains [2]	89	3A	Canyon
05	1A	Sundown [5]	90	1A	Gruver
06	1A	Hart	90	3A	Canyon [2]
06	2A	Wall	91	1A	Claude
06	4A	Big Spring	91	3A	Canyon [3]
07	1A	Sundown [6]	92	1A	Booker
08	1A	Sundown [7]	93	3A	Canyon [4]
08	2A	Wall [2]	94	3A	Sanford-Fritch
09	1A	Plains [3]	96	4A	Pampa
10	1A	Sundown [8]	98	3A	Brownfield
12	1A	Forsan	98	5A	Amarillo [3]
16	2A	Sundown [9]	01	3A	Ballinger
17	2A	Sundown [10]	02	1A	Iraan

03	3A	Canyon [5]
04	3A	Canyon [6]
05	1A	Sundown
05	4A	Hereford
06	1A	Sundown [2]
06	2A	Shallowater
06	3A	Canyon [7]
06	4A	Hereford [2]
07	2A	Wall
07	4A	Hereford [3]
08	1A	Sundown [3]
08	2A	Spearman [2]
09	1A	Gruver [2]
09	2A	Spearman [2]
10	1A	Gruver [3]
10	2A	Spearman [3]
11	1A	Gruver [4]
11	2A	Spearman [4]
12	2A	Bushland
13	4A	Canyon Randall
14	1A	Hartley
14	2A	Sundown [4]
16	1A	Hartley [2]
16	2A	Sundown [5]
16	5A	Canyon Randall [2]
17	1A	Nazareth [5]
17	2A	Sundown [5]
18	1A	Happy
18	3A	Tulia [2]
18	4A	Canyon [8]

SUMMARY BOYS CROSS COUNTRY:

Sundown was clearly the dominate boys' team winning 10 UIL State Championship in Cross Country. Plains, Canyon, and Iraan with three gold championship appearances finished second. Wall with two state champion trophies was third but Sundown, Plains Canyon, Iraan, and Wall consisted of 21 of 25 state championships in Boy's Cross Country.

SUMMARY GIRLS CROSS COUNTRY:

Canyon girls winning 8 UIL State Cross Country Championships was the leader in this UIL sport. Sundown and Nazareth with 5 State Championships was second in cross country running. Next, with 4 UIL

State Championships, was Gruver but Spearman, Amarillo and Hereford were close behind with 3 state championships. Tulia, Canyon Randall, Hartley, and Munday had 2 state cross country championships

Track and Field/ Cross Country running takes a beating when it comes to comparing the Panhandle/Plains region to other regions particularly in regions where the weather is not a factor in events and training. I tip my hat to the coaches that coach track in the Panhandle area because I have been there myself. I have been a head track/field-cross country coach giving me some experience of the advantages and disadvantages coaching in the Panhandle/Plains region. Those schools and coaches that have won state championships in Track/Field from the Panhandle/Plains region are very special because it is so difficult to win a state championship in track/field from that region. Their mental toughness is never a question mark because that is what their athletes must have in order to compete.

There are so many coaching legends that coach Track/Field/Cross Country that it is almost impossible to just mention a few. UIL Boys Track/Field started in 1911 while UIL Girls Track/Field started in 1972. Most small schools have just one coach that coaches both genders, but the larger schools usually have a coach for both genders. Also, many track/field coaches don't get much press time which means information about them is limited, which means they get limited recognition for the job they do. Also, track/field is often considered an individual sport more so than a team sport which means coaches don't get as much credit as in other sports.

Coaching Legends of Track, Field and Cross Country in the Panhandle/Plains region that was nominated from their peers.

JOHN WHINNERY SR-DUMAS/ AMARILLO HIGH

Coach Whinnery could be known as a coach that could coach many sports, including Football and Wrestling. Whinnery was inducted into the Fort Dodge Sports "Hall of Fame" in 1962 in the sport of wrestling.

Coach Whinnery started the Amarillo Relays in 1949-50 track season. At Amarillo High he coached Amarillo High School to five consecutive district championships. During that same time, he produced three individual state champions in Track/Field between 1945 and 1950.

Whinnery went to the University of Iowa where he participated in Football, Wrestling and Track/Field. John transferred to Northeastern University, Oklahoma where he established the Oklahoma collegiate record in the discus. Coach Whinnery graduated from Northeastern University and received his master's degree from West Texas State University.

Coach Whinnery was selected as the outstanding track coach in the first half of the century. He took a position at West Texas State in 1957 as an assistant professor of education and intramural sports. At West Texas State, John created the first full time intramural program.

Coach John C. Whinnery Sr was inducted into the Panhandle Sports "Hall of Fame." John retired from West Texas State University in 1974. Later, he won three gold medals in the Georgia Senior Games. Coach Whinnery died in 1985.

PHIL SWENSON-IRAAN/WINK/GARDEN CITY/HAMLIN/ BROWNWOOD/ ROSCOE

Coach Phil Swenson went to high school at Avoca, Texas, then college at McMurry University, Abilene, Texas. He is known as a track/basketball coach. In track/field coaching girls his teams won three state championships. Not to be outdone, he was part of another state championship in Track but wasn't the head coach.

His mark on Texas sports scene was when he was selected to the Texas Girls Coaches Association "Hall of Fame." His basketball coaching led to 447 wins, making several regional appearances.

Phil claim to fame came when he was selected to the Big County Athletic "Hall of Fame".

JOE BAIN-STINNETT/MEMPHIS/AMARILLO HIGH SCHOOL

Coach Bain coaching career came up the hard way straight out of Crockett Junior High School but not before he spent ten years coaching in Stinnett and Memphis. Being a native of his hometowns, Stinnett and Memphis, he was called to coach many sports and do many things for the good of the students at both schools.

Then Amarillo High finally hired him, and it was 1979 before Coach Bain became the Head Track/Field coach at Amarillo High School. Then suddenly, coach Bain became a household name when it came to track/field. Amarillo High School became a track/field powerhouse for the next twenty-seven years. His track team won the Region 1-5A title which was the first by an Amarillo School in 27 years.

His track teams won fifteen district titles in twenty-one years and he is responsible for twenty- five individual and three relay teams qualifying for the UIL State Track/Field meet. Twelve of the sixteen school records were set by athletes under Coach Bain.

Joe was a graduate of West Texas State University.

E.J. "JEEP" WEBB-CANYON/BORGER

How many track coaches have awards named after them? Well, Jeep Webb does at Borger High School. Borger created the "E.J. Webb" award that happens to be awarded to a senior female athlete.

At Borger I met Jeep during my many coaching stops. I had heard so much about him that I became big eyed being around him but after a while, I realized why his reputation is outstanding from a coaching standpoint. He was everything I would want in a coach. He cared about his athletes, he cared about the coaches that he worked with, he cared about the students at Borger, and he cared about the city of Borger. He was an example for all to be around.

Coach Webb had a career coaching football, girls' and boys' basketball, and track/cross country which lasted forty-five years. Two things that everyone remembers about coach Webb is his leadership abilities especially when he was so instrumental in started girls' sports in Canyon and Borger. In Borger Webb started girls' basketball, track and cross country and in Canyon he was directly involved with starting the girls' basketball program.

Jeep has been inducted into the Texas Girls Coaches Association "Hall of Fame" and the Panhandle Sports "Hall of Fame." His cross-country teams at Borger were the runner-up girl's cross- country champion in 1991 and 1992.

JOHNNY ALLEN-AMARILLO CARVER HIGH SCHOOL

Not many coaches can say that they coached at a high school when it first opened and then when it closed. Johnny Allen was there when Amarillo Carver, Amarillo opened and was there when it closed.

Coach Allen believed he could get his players to be better than they thought they could. He was a strong motivator by his work ethic, his discipline, and his belief that they could do more than they were doing. He pushed his athletes by his coaching work ethic then finally getting their work ethic to where he wanted it to be, so they could be as good as they wanted to be.

He was responsible for three state track/field championships in a row and then he won a state football championship, their only football state championship.

I met Coach Allen when he was the swimming pool manager of the North Heights Swimming Pool, Amarillo, Texas. I was swimming director at Thompson Park swimming pool, Amarillo, Texas and often traveled to North Heights to help in teaching swimming lessons. I remember that I was so intimidated by him that I had to build up my courage just to go there.

Amarillo Carver closed after being open for nineteen years. Coach Allen moved to Horace Mann Middle School and then finished his career teaching at Amarillo High School.

FONTZ MYATT-AMARILLO PALO DURO

What legendary track coach entered the Army when he was 17 years old, fought in World War II, and was wounded twice in the battle of Okinawa? Frontz Myatt who spent twenty-four years coaching track at Palo Duro, Amarillo, Texas was that guy.

After Myatt was discharged from the Army, he attended McMurry University, Abiliene, Texas participating is football and track. He had a time of 9.7 in the 100-yard dash, 21.3 in the 220 dash, and 47.5 in the 440. In 1969 his 440-relay team set a national high school record of 41.2. Of course, those records have been broken in our day, but it says he was an outstanding athletic runner and he has the proof in the record books.

When Coach Myatt came to Palo Duro as the Head Track coach, Palo Duro, was the floor matt in the District. They didn't even score a point in the district meet the year before. In his first year, Palo Duro lost the District Championship by ¼ of a point. After that it was all history as Palo Duro became force to deal with in the Panhandle of Texas concerning track.

Coach Myatt was the coach at Palo Duro for the next twenty-four years where they won sixteen district championships and established themselves as the frontrunner in track concerning the district championship.

PERCY HINES-ESTACADO HIGH SCHOOL

Track during the 80's, one name was dominant during that period concerning track and field. Percy Hines who was the head track coach at Estacado was a household name if you were involved in Track/Field. In that period, the track team at Estacado has been described as powerful, dominant, and even "dynasty."

Coach Hines was the master behind Estacado track in that period. In 1983 Estacado boys track team won their second consecutive Texas State UIL Track/Field championship. Because of their dominance Coach Hines and the entire team were honored with the induction into the

Lubbock Independent School District "Hall of Fame." Estacado also won the UIL State Track/Field championship in 1982 and then won it again in 1986.

What really made the 1983 championship so special was that Coach Hines added some talent to his already talented team by the name of Percy Hines III. His son was attending Coronado High School but decided to transfer to Estacado his senior year so his dad could coach him.

Coach Hines was named the "Track/Field News 4A "Coach of the Year" in 1983. What was so special about this track team was that they didn't win one gold metal but instead had enough points to win the state track meet in 1983. What that means is that everyone contributed to the state championship which brings pride to the Lubbock ISD.

CAYLENE CADDEL-ESTACADO HIGH SCHOOL

Caylene Caddel had many hats that she wore at Estacado High School before winning championships in Track and Field. She started in 1977 at Estacado and spent many years on the hardwood coaching basketball as an assistant coach, and even was the head volleyball coach for one year. Coach Caddel was the Head Track/Field coach for Girls track for twenty-four years winning the ten district championships and many state qualifiers over that twenty-four- year period

Coach Caddel was a strong member of the Texas High School Girls Coaching Association from 1983-2011. She was a member of the board of directors of this association for four years, serving one year as vice president and one year as president. She was always trying to promote girls track and field and was a tireless worker.

Caylene was a strong personality in the teaching arena also teaching biology, health, and physical education. She was always involved with the FCA at Estacado as a huddle leader. Coach Caddel was selected as an All-Star Coach for the 4A-5A three times. Then in 2005 she was selected as the "Coach of the Year" by the Texas High School Girls Coaches Association in Girls track and field.

NATE SAWYER-LAKE VIEW, SAN ANGELO

When you think of Track at Lake View you think of Nate Sawyer. Coaching at Lake View for thirty-four years, he saw the transformation of track and field in the early 1980's to what it is now. The biggest change was created by adding Cross County to track programs and then cross country became the backbone of a successful track program. If you were involved with cross country coaching your job would start in August just like football or volleyball. Coach Sawyer saw this addition as a tool for recruitment and a tool for conditioning. Soon girls' basketball

coaches would recommend cross country for their players during this time of the year giving them extra conditioning in the early months of preparation. It was a win-win deal for all involved.

Coach Sawyer was a two-time Lake View "Hall of Honor" induction, and he was inducted for winning the UIL State Track and Field Championship in 1993. Then in 2014 he was inducted again for achievements in Track/Field from 1983 until 2014. He coached 18 college scholarship track athletes, seven division 1 athletes, five Division 2 athletes, five Junior College athletes, and one NAIA athlete. Overall, he made twenty-five state meet track appearances and forty- three with a top 2 finish in cross country and track for 1983-2015.

Coach Sawyer is a big believer in staying healthy by running. He says, "Running is a positive life skill that needs to be taught to all kinds of kids." "For one thing running leads to discipline and more important how to succeed in life." "Also running leads to a healthy lifestyle and better health. Of course, Nate Sawyer life was saved by his conditioning by running because he went through two brain surgeries for cancer. All doctors agreed that Coach Sawyers excellent physical shape was the reason he survive.

Legendary coaches that made a difference in high school track then went into the college arena of track.

BARBARA CROUSEN-ABILENE COOPER HIGH SCHOOL

Barbara Crousen holds the honor of knowing that she stands beside her Big Country "Hall of Fame" husband Joe Crousen because she was also selected to the Big Country "Hall of Fame." Barbara was selected in Track and Field and Joe in football. They were the very first husband and wife combination to be selected into the Big Country Hall of Fame.

After thirty-two years of coaching high school track, including Abilene Cooper, she was hired at McMurry University as the men's and women's coach in Track and Field. While at Cooper she had a wonderful career coaching track. In 1995 she was named the Texas High School Girls Coaching Association "Track coach of the Year" then she was selected by the Abilene Independent School district as the "Physical Education Instructor of the year."

In 1993, she served as the President of the Texas High School Girls Coaching Association. She had many awards and outstanding achievements at McMurry University but the one that stands out for most people is the fact that Coach Crousen became the first woman to coach a men's team to the NCAA Championship in any sport when McMurry won the NCAA Division III outdoor track championship. Oh, by the way, she repeated another championship in 2012.

BOB GROSECLOSE-ABILENE EAGLES

Coach Groseclose went to high school in Breckenridge when they were winning almost everything that matter in sports. He must have learned how to win because that is just what he did at Abilene High School as the Head Track and Field coach.

Abilene High School was a dominant force in track and field during his coaching days winning The UIL State High School Championships in track and field. His first championship was in 1954 and everyone was surprised but then when he won two in a row, 1959 and 1960, everyone expected it. It's the price you pay as a coach when you win championships.

Bob was known as a track coach that knew something about every event that track offers athletes to compete. Often you would hear comments about how much knowledge Bob had about track, especially all the events. One time on the way back from the Red Raider Relays the Abilene Bus broke down. The bus was in a dangerous position on the road, so the entire track team got out of the bus and attempted to move it into another a safer place. While the track team was pushing the bus, a sports photographer was traveling on the same highway. When he saw what was happening, he stopped and took several pictures of the bus with the track athletes pushing the bus. The next day the front page of the Abilene Newspaper said, "The Eagles finally ran out of gas."

Bob was inducted into the Big Country "Hall of Fame" in 2013. Very few track coaches can say that two track facilites at two different schools were named after the coach. Coach Groseclose left Abilene to become a college track coach at Northeast Louisiana, now known as Louisiana-Monroe. After winning 19 conference championships at Northeast Louisiana the track field was named after Coach Groseclose. Also, Abilene High School track is named after Bob Groseclose. I would say if you had two tracks named after you it should declare you as a legend.

FRANK BARKER-LEVELLAND / BORGER

Coach Barker is the perfect example of coaching legend in all sports but particularly Track. Most people don't know who he is but if you ever have contact with him, you will get the feeling that he is special human being. Guess what, Frank graduated from Texas Tech, participating discuss, shot and javelin. Often, he would fill in the 440-yard dash. He became hooked on coaching helping underclassmen in the field events when he was at Tech.

In 1969 he moved to Levelland, and accepted a position with the Levelland Independent School district. In 1976, Coach Barker started the first cross country team at LISD. Later in 1979 girls were added to the cross country UIL event. Soon Levelland became a very successful cross- country team, one where other athletes would come to coach Barker for help, particularly those from small schools. Over all his boys' team won 5 district championships while his girls' team won 6 district championships his teams qualified for Regional 31 years and went to state 13 years. When he became the Head, girls track coach his girls track team won 8 district championships. During that same period, he coached many athletes that were state champions,

All-Americans and even set state records and 1 national record in track. One of his athletes refers to him as "a walking encyclopedia of track."

This is a quote from a former Principal at Levelland, Virdie Montgomery who made Frank a "Lobo Legend" in 2005. It is a clear statement of why he is considered a Legend in the Track world.

In 1969, Frank Barker tolled into Levelland, Texas. His mark has been left on that community and school district in the most positive manner ever since. He is a consummate professional and a man of character, spirit, integrity, and talent. He has captured the hearts and minds of students throughout his career and on top of all those qualities he has generated a success in his career that has been able to accrue on behalf of Levelland High School with his knack for winning and above all his love for kids and the impact he has had on their lives

He has taught at every grade level from fist grade to seniors. He has coached football, track, volleyball, cross country and basketball. In 1976, Coach Barker pioneered the cross-country program. Coach Barker was instrumental in bringing girls into the program. His tenure at LHS has seen incredible success. His legacy lives on in the man that kids call, "Coach." He epitomizes all that is good in his profession and is truly an ambassador, confidant, and a teacher to the hundreds of kids and colleagues that have crossed his path. It is truly a pleasure and honor to include Coach Frank Barker in the "Logo Legend wall of honor" at Levelland High School.

Since his retirement from the public schools, he has coached at Lubbock Christian University and South Plains College.

BILL CARTER-TASCOSA

Coach Carter won a state championship in Track at Tascosa and was selected into the "Hall of Fame" at Abilene Christian University. Also, he was selected into the Texas Senior Games "Hall of Fame" in 2003. I apologize that I don't have more to say about this great coach, but this is all the information I could find. Coach Carter was nominated by two people, so I worked hard to find information about him, but all the information was limited.

JAMES MORRIS-BROWNFIELD

Coach Morris was a legendary track coach that was a household name when it came to track and field + cross country. He served as the Brownfield Head Track coach from 1959-1980 winning several awards. But what most people remember about Coach Morris is his willingness to officiate track meets and soon he was expected at almost all track meets. He became the Head Track Coach at South Plains College and track history at SPC followed him each year in both cross country and track and field. Overall, he was a factor in the track world for over 50 years.

OTHER TRACK COACHES THAT MADE A HUGE DIFFERENCE ON THE HIGH SCHOOL LEVEL

- **Don Black-Post, Frenship, Roosevelt Don Carper-Amarillo Caprock**
- **Kengle [Doc] Pearson-Spearman, Perryton James Gandy-Lubbock Coronado**
- **Bruce Land-Dumas**

LEGENDARY SCHOOLS IN TRACK AND FIELD:

We should never forget those who dedicated great effort to track/field in order to accomplish the success of the following schools. Winning a state team championship just doesn't happen by accident. But more to the point, it takes a family of people to have tremendous success of winning a team state championship.

- *Munday is a powerhouse track program that produced 7 Boys UIL State Track and Field championships and then produced 4 Girls UIL State Track/Field championships. All total that is 11 state gold trophies in Track/Field.*
- *Abilene and Andrews – when you associate success and track for boys - Abilene and Andrews are always at the top of your list. Both schools had 6 state championships.*
- *Girls track in Canyon is awesome. The Canyon Girls track program has produced 5 UIL State Track Championships.*
- *Rule Boys track and field has produced 5 UIL State Track/Field Championships.*
- *Lubbock Estacado boys' track and field has produced 4 UIL Championships.*

Team Tennis

UIL TEAM TENNIS STARTED IN 1983. Individual tennis started in 1919 for the boys and 1920 for the girls. The events were Boys Singles, Boys Doubles, Girls Singles, and Girls Doubles. Then in 2006 UIL added Mixed Doubles. So, Tennis was considered an individual sport for many years until 1983, when Team Tennis was introduced.

Tennis is another sport that takes a beating with the weather in the Panhandle/Plains region especially small schools where they don't have indoor facilities available.

However, the UIL allows only 4A, 5A, and now 6A to participate in Team Tennis. Word is that they are going to allow 3A this coming year. When you live in a small school, most everyone participates in all the sports that they can. That being the case, Tennis usually doesn't draw that many athletes to participate mainly because of facilities, lack of experienced coaching, and mostly other conflicting sports. Most coaches in small schools coach many sports and most of the time a coach will be assigned to coach Tennis that has limited knowledge of the sport.

Because of those problems in smaller schools, Tennis is considered an individual sport because of the conflicts I just mentioned.

NOTE: The UIL added Team Tennis in 1983. Tennis was the word before 1983 and in the UIL, and they have all the individual championships from the start to the finish but there is no mention of which schools won the state championship especially in the lower school classifications.

The following Tennis teams have played for the UIL State Championship in Team Tennis:

Year	School	Classification	Result [S-Semi-Finals/ R-Runner up/W-Winner]
1983	Lubbock Cooper	4A	S
1984	Abilene	5A	S
1985	Abilene Cooper	5A	S
1986	Abilene Cooper	5A	R
1987	Abilene Cooper	5A	R
1988	Lubbock Coronado	5A	R
1989	Big Spring	4A	S
1989	Abilene Cooper	5A	S
1990	Wichita Falls	4A	S
1991	Wichita Falls	4A	R
1991	Abilene	5A	W
1992	Wichita Falls	4A	R
1992	Abilene Cooper	5A	S
1993	Wichita Falls	4A	S
1993	Abilene Cooper	5A	W
1994	Wichita Falls	4A	S
1994	Abilene Cooper	5A	W
1995	Abilene Cooper	5A	W
1995	Wichita Falls	4A	R
1996	Amarillo Tascosa	5A	W
1997	Wichita Falls	4A	S
1998	Lubbock Coronado	5A	R
1998	Wichita Falls	4A	S
1999	Wichita Falls	4A	R
1999	Abilene	5A	W
2000	Wichita Falls	4A	S
2001	Wichita Falls	4A	S
2002	Wichita Falls	4A	S
2003	Lubbock Coronado	5A	W
2003	Wichita Falls	4A	S
2004	Wichita Falls	4A	R
2005	Wichita Falls	4A	S
2006	Wichita Falls	4A	S
2007	Wichita Falls	4A	S
2008	Wichita Falls	4A	S
2009	Wichita Falls	4A	S
2010	Wichita Falls	4A	S
2010	Lubbock Coronado	5A	S
2011	Wichita Falls	4A	S
2012	Wichita Falls Rider	4A	S
2013	Wichita Falls Rider	4A	S
2014	Lubbock	4A	S
2015	Abilene Wylie	4A	W
2016	Abilene Wylie	4A	R
2017	Abilene Wylie	4A	W
2018	Abilene Wylie	4A	W
2018	Amarillo	5A	R

2019	Abilene Wylie	5A	R
2019	Amarillo Tascosa	6A	S
2019	Canyon	4A	R

Summary of Team Tennis at the State Tennis tournament since 1983

SUMMARY OF TEAM TENNIS AT THE STATE TENNIS TOURNAMENT SINCE 1983

You don't have to be a rocket scientist to know that Wichita Falls dominated Team Tennis from the standpoint of qualifying. Wichita Falls made 21 appearances at the State UIL Team Tennis Championships. Wichita Falls played for the state championship 5 times and finished with 5 runners up trophies.

Abilene Cooper made 8 State UIL Team Tennis appearances playing for the State Championship 5 times winning 3 State Championships. They also had 3 state semifinal appearances.

Abilene Wylie started late but once that started, playing for the State UIL Team Tennis it was automatic playing for the state championship 5 times and winning the title 3 times.

Lubbock Coronado made 4 state tournament appearances playing for the championship 3 times and wining 1 gold metal championship finishing runner up 2 times and 1 semifinal appearance. Abilene made 3 state tournament appearances winning the UIL State Team Tennis championship 2 times. They also had 1 semi-final appearance. Amarillo Tascosa had 2 state tournament appearances winning the championship once and finishing as a semifinalist once.

Those with one state tournament appearances are Canyon [R], Big Spring [S], and Lubbock [S]. **Wichita Falls and Abilene dominated the Team Tennis State Tournament with 37 state tournament appearances**

Legendary coaches in Tennis are more like Individual coaches instead of team coaches especially in small schools. Since this book is about team coaches, instead of individual coaches, Legends in the high school programs of tennis will be limited.

HIGH SCHOOL COACHING LEGENDS FROM THE PANHANDLE/ PLAINS REGION LEANNE SCOTT-ABILENE COOPER HIGH SCHOOL

Coach Scott coached Abilene Cooper in Tennis for 20 years setting a mark so high not many can follow. She led Abilene Cooper to 3 straight UIL State Team Tennis [5A] championships. She was a high school coach that made a difference on the high school level. Many high school tennis players seek outside help with their game such as Tennis Pros or College Coaches.

She backed up those state championships with 14 district championships in 17 years as a head coach. Coach Scott was a household name when it comes to Tennis on the state level of play. Here teams were ranked #1 for three years in a row and #2 in the state for 3 other years. She used her coaching skills as a coach in Tennis with an overall record 430-48 won/lost record in dual matches. That included 57 consecutive wins from 1993-1995.

Leanne Scott was named to the Big Country Athletic "Hall of Fame" in 2015. In 1993 she was named the 5A Team Tennis Coaches Association "Coach of the Year." In 1996 Coach Scott was named "Coach of the Year" by Texas, New Mexico, and Arizona National Federation Interscholastic Coaches Association. In 1997 she was named "National Coach of the Year" by the same organization.

DAVID KENT-AMARILLO HIGH SCHOOL

David Kent story is a good one for sure. What makes him unique is that after retirement, he went into politics as the Republican Party Chairman for Brazos County. There may be another Tennis coach that went into politics but now, he is the only one that I know about.

Coach Kent is well known throughout the tennis world and particularly in the Panhandle/Plains region. He played his high school tennis at Amarillo High School then went to Texas Tech where he helped the Red Raider Tennis team finish 2nd in the Southwest Conference.

After graduating from Texas Tech, he started his coaching career at Amarillo High School and Midland High School. Coach Kent was an outstanding Tennis Player but where he gained his fame was coaching Tennis which he did for 38 years both in high school and college. Coach Kent was a very successful college coach and most of the time, we would not mention a college coach but his influence on the High School level was awesome. To be honest, it was a no brainer. He has been selected 5 times for the "Hall of Fame" and he said, "All of my hall of fame selections was outstanding and I don't have a favorite one to talk about but being selected into the Tennis Association's Collegiate Men's "Hall of Fame" in Athens, GA was special because Jerry Simmons [Also from Amarillo] was selected the same year.

BRANDON CLARK-SAN ANGELO LAKEVIEW HIGH SCHOOL

Brandon Clark started the Lakeview Tennis program from the bottom pits to the top. He had a small wooden hut he used to store his stuff and at the same time, a place to hang his head when he wasn't coaching. Brandon Clark passed away from stomach esophageal cancer but his efforts concerning tennis will never be forgotten.

How many coaches get a building named after them that is located on the high school campus. Well the Brandon Clark Tennis Complex at Lakeview High School was named after him. Not only that but the San Angelo Independent School District administrators, faculty and staff helped dedicate the tennis complex by having a ceremony outside the Brandon Clark Complex.

Speaking on Brandon's behalf, San Angelo's Superintendent Dr. Carl Dethloff said, "It is a privilege to be here this afternoon as we honor and dedicate this state-of-the-art athletic facility as the Brandon Clark Tennis Center." He continued, "At Lakeview, it was not even a question who would be the namesake on this building." For sure Brandon Clark made a dent in San Angelo and particularly at Lakeview High School.

JOHNNY SIMMONS-TENNIS PRO IN THE WICHITA FALLS AREA

Going away from high school coaches being named, we had to mention Johnny Simmons in the same vein as Wichita Falls tennis. Team Tennis started in 1982 and by 2019, Wichita Falls High School made 21 state tournament appearances. Not only that, Wichita Falls Rider High School made 2 trips to the UIL State Team Tennis Championship. So, with 23 appearances at the state championship, someone somewhere made a huge impact on high school tennis. During that time, Rider alone had 18 coaching changes in Tennis, not including the coaching changes at Wichita Falls High School.

Wichita Falls Tennis Association reached new heights in the 1970's and the early 1980's. Johnny Simmons, a teaching pro at this association was one of the reasons the high schools at Wichita Falls has so much success. He stated, "We still have parents who turn to us to teach their kids the game but not as many as we once had." He continued "I've met some great Kids and their parents. I've watched young boys and girls grow in the sport, even get married, become parents and then eventually I would get the chance to work with their kids."

IKE GRACE-ABILENE/LUBBOCK/BROWNWOOD

The TTCA, named Team Tennis Coaches Association has a Hall of Fame that lists all the outstanding coaches in that association. What is special is this association has a special award called the "Vision Award" given to the coach that has a vision for his team, players and program. But what is important is that the coach that is recognized is a coach that has a vision for life also.

This award goes to a coach that knows where their program is going and knows how to motivate his players around him to get the job done. Ike Grace received this award this year. Coach Grace was the head woman tennis coach at Brownwood, Abilene, and Lubbock. His attitude and work ethic put him in a different category and soon people started noticing, particularly Oklahoma State University where he later became the head women's tennis coach.

What made this award so special is that his daughter Cari Grace, ex tennis coach at Texas Tech accepted the award for him because Ike Grace died in December of 1985

JIM CARTER-LUBBOCK CORONADO/LUBBOCK MONTEREY

When trying to gain information concerning Tennis one name came to the top many times. Coach Carter coached at Lubbock Coronado 3 different times. At Coronado he coached from 1969-1980, then 1984-1990 and 1998-2005. All you must do is walk into the tennis facility and you can see history that was made at Coronado, many from Coach Carters 24 years.

During that period his teams won 427 matches and lost 54. Add 3 regional championships, 3 regional runner-up's, 2 state team runner-up's and 1 state UIL team championship to his resume and you can see why he was a household name in Tennis. Add to that, his teams were ranked #10 in the state for 13 consecutive years.

His teams won 21 District championships and were ranked #2 in the state of Texas in 1998 and 2000. His team was ranked #3 in 1999 and #4 in 2000. In 1999 the girl's tennis team was ranked #3 and #5 by the National High School Tennis Coaches Association.

Jim Carter was named Texas Tennis Association "Coach of the Year" in 1988, 2000, and 2004. He was also selected into the Texas Tennis "Hall of Fame" in 1992. In 2011 Coach Carter was inducted into the Lubbock Independent School District "Hall of Fame."

DALTON HILL-SWEETWATER/EL PASO IRVING

Coach Hill has the star put on his name because he started his coaching career in football in the 50's of which he was very successful then became a legend in Tennis. Not many tennis coaches can claim that statement.

What is even more impressive is that he had never played the sport but soon his name was a household name in Tennis in the Panhandle/

Plains region. Then coach Dalton accepted a good tennis program in El Paso Irving and from that point on, Dalton Hill became a legend for all tennis coaches to learn from and follow.

He was president of the Texas Tennis Coaching Association and was inducted into the Hall of Fame in 1981

PAUL BROTHERTON-WICHITA FALLS RIDER

Who starts their career as a professional baseball athlete playing in a minor league then decides to go another direction toward a different sport then becomes a legend in that sport? Yes, Paul Brotherton did just that and became known especially in Wichita Falls as a legend in tennis coaching at Rider High School.

Coach Brotherton was known as a person that loves kids and his players competed hard for him as a coach. They enjoyed playing tennis for coach Brotherton. He also ran a sporting goods store in Wichita Falls giving him the opportunity to promote the sport of tennis in the Wichita Falls area.

Because of his success at Wichita Falls Rider, Paul Brotherton was inducted into the Texas Tennis Coaching Association "Hall of Fame in 1988. "

FRED, JOHN, NOVICE, AND DAVE KNIFFEN-CLYDE, TEXAS

Although this book is about legends of coaching the Kniffen family should be at the top of the list. This is a family of tennis players that had a huge impact on tennis in the Plains region located in Clyde, Texas.

John played tennis at Texas Tech University and Fred who was the oldest coached in Abilene then went to gain some fame coaching tennis at Tyler Junior College. Also, John and Novice coached at Sweetwater and Andrews. Finally, they retired and bought some land at Menard and started working to build a tennis program at Menard. Soon Menard won the state championship 4 years in a row.

All four have been a huge factor in tennis and all four have been officers in the Texas Tennis Coaches Association making a difference in the sport of tennis. All four have made a huge difference in young tennis players trying to learn the sport of tennis.

Soft Ball

UIL SOFTBALL DIDN'T START TILL 1993 and didn't have all the classifications until 2000. Not everyone played softball at the start in 1993 but soon, especially by the year 2000, the UIL had enough teams to create five different divisions of play. Then in 2015, the UIL added 6A which meant soft ball had six divisions of competition.

UIL HAD ONE DIVISION AND CALLED IT 5A

None means that no school from the Panhandle/Plains region qualified for the State Championship in softball

93	5A	None	

UIL added 3A

94	5A	None	
	3A	Clyde	S
95	5A	None	
	3A	None	

UIL added 2A, 4A and 5A

96	5A	None	
	4A	None	
	3A	Abilene Wylie	S
	2A	Coahoma	R
97	5A	None	
	4A	Andrews	S
	3A	Breckenridge	R
	2A	None	
98	5A	None	
	4A	None	
	3A	None	
	2A	Coahoma [2]	W
99	5A	None	
	4A	None	

	3A	None	
	2A	Coahoma	

UIL added 1A

2000	5A	None	
	4A	None	
	3A	None	
	2A	None	
	1A	None	
2001	5A	None	
	4A	Wichita Falls Rider	S
	3A	None	
	2A	Archer City	W
	1A	None	
2002	1A	None	
	2A	Coahoma [4]	S
	3A	None	
	4A	None	
	5A	None	
2003	1A	Windthorst	R
	2A	Coahoma [5]	R
	3A	None	
	4A	None	
	5A	None	
2004	1A	Windthorst [2]	W
	2A	Clyde Eula	S
	3A	None	
	4A	None	
	5A	None	
2005	2A	Coahoma [6]	S
	3A	None	
	4A	Andrews [2]	S
	5A	None	

UIL added 1A

2006	1A	Clyde Eula [2]	W
	2A	Coahoma [7]	S
	3A	Clyde	S
	4A	None	
	5A	None	
2007	1A	Seymour	S
	2A	Coahoma	S
	3A	Burkburnett	R
	4A	None	
	5A	None	
2008	1A	Clyde Eula	S
	2A	Coahoma	R

	3A	Burkburnett	S
	4A	None	
	5A	None	
2009	1A	Forsan	W
	2A	None	
	3A	None	
	4A	None	
	5A	None	
2010	1A	Forsan	W
	2A	None	
	3A	None	
	4A	None	
	5A	None	
2011	1A	Albany	S
	2A	Wall	S
	3A	None	
	4A	None	
	5A	None	
2012	1A	None	
	2A	None	
	3A	None	
	4A	None	
	5A	None	
2013	1A	Albany [2]	S
	2A	Hawley	S
	3A	Burburnnet	S
	4A	None	
	5A	None	
2014	1A	None	
	2A	Hawley [2]	S
	3A	Snyder	S
	4A	None	
	5A	Lubbock Coronado	S

UIL dropped 1A and added 6A

2015	2A	Hawley [3]	S
	3A	None	
	4A	Snyder [2]	S
	5A	None	
	6A	None	
2016	2A	Windthorst [3]	R
	3A	Colorado City	R
	4A	None	
	5A	None	
	6A	None	

UIL added 1A

2017	1A	Hermleigh	S

Year	Class	School	Result
	2A	Archer City [2]	S
	3A	None	
	4A	Vernon	S
	5A	Canyon	S
	6A	None	
2018	1A	Borden County	S
	2A	Albany [2]	S
	3A	None	
	4A	Vernon [2]	R
	5A	None	
	6A	None	

State Tournaments Appearances		State Tournament Championships		State Tournament Runner-ups	
Coahoma	11	Forsan	2	Coahoma	4
Windthorst	4	Clyde Eula	2	Windthorst	2
Clyde Eula	4	Archer City	1	Burkburnett	1
Hawley	3	Windthorst	1		
Andrews	3	Coahoma	1		
Archer City	2				
Albany	2				
Snyder	2				
Vernon	2				
Clyde	2				
Burkburnett	2				
Forsan	2				
Canyon	1				
Hermleigh	1				
Colorado City	1				
Wall	1				
Lubbock Coronado	1				
Wichita Falls Rider	1				
Abilene Wylie	1				
Breckenridge	1				
Borden County	1				
Seymour	1				

Least We Forget-High School Coaching Legends from the Panhandle/Plains region is a book about coaching legends of the past, coaching legends that we should never forget. The sport Softball is a relatively young sport, therefore coaching legends are limited. However, what I have found out is there are many outstanding coaches that are coaching at the present time. Most likely some will be called legends after they retire from softball, but when you consider softball has only participated in the UIL 26 years, most of the legendary softball coaches are still coaching.

JIMMY "JJ" JOHNSON-LUBBOCK CORONADO

Who wins district championships 19 of 20 years, 1998-2017? WOW! Jimmy JJ Johnson the Head Softball coach at Lubbock Coronado and the ladies that represented Lubbock Coronado softball accomplished that feat. You just don't do that without a family of people to support your program and all coaches appreciate that accomplishment.

Coach Johnson softball team advanced to the class 6A regional semifinals before his last season as the softball coach at Coronado High School. His 2014 team finished in the State Championship Softball tournament in the semifinals with a 36-4 record. Overall, his coaching record is 557-122-4, and his impressive district coaching record of 221-9-1.

When you put it all together, Coach Johnson ended his coaching career with 19 Bi-District Championships, 14 Area Championships, 9 Regional Quarterfinal Championships, 1 Regional Semi-Finalist, 1 Regional Final Champion, and 1 State Semifinalist.

When you put his accomplishments together you end up with 13 District "Coach of the Year" awards. If you investigate his resume, it doesn't take a rocket scientist to understand why Coach Jimmy "JJ" Johnson was moved into athletic administration as the Assistant Athletic Director for Facilities and Operations in the Lubbock Independent School District.

LEGENDARY SOFTBALL SCHOOLS IN THE PANHANDLE PLAINS REGION

COAHOMA

Since I coached at Howard College of Big Spring, Texas I know about the Coahoma Softball tradition. It was something that I enjoyed reading about but what I respected was the dedication and sacrifice everyone associated with the softball team gave for the good of the softball program. Coahoma made 11 UIL State Tournament appearances, playing for the state championship 5 times and winning once. From my point of view that deserves a salute from all coaches coaching any sport. It is not easy to get to the state tournament and to do it 11 times is awesome.

WINDTHORST AND CLYDE EULA EACH HAD 4 STATE TOURNAMENT APPEARANCES TO COME IN SECOND.

Golf

BOY'S GOLF BECAME A UIL sport during the school year of 1948-1949. Girl's golf officially started in 1972-73 season. Golf is another sport that takes a beating from the weather particularly in the Panhandle. Another factor for success in golf is whether the city has a golf course. It is a huge advantage for high school golf when the city maintains a 9 hole or an 18-hole golf-course, and this so true in small schools where a golf course is just too expensive to maintain. Also, the weather is a factor in maintaining a golf course, so the weather is a huge factor for success in golf. With that said, let's look at the state champs from the Panhandle/Plains region in golf starting in 1949 for boy's golf and 1973 in girl's golf. Only the state champs are listed, and none are listed if another school outside the Panhandle/Plains region happens to win the state championship.

[N-None] Means that no from the Panhandle/Plains region won the state championship. [Year Classification School]

The first year in golf the UIL had one classification called City.

1949	City	None

In 1950 the UIL added 2A classification

1950	City	N
	2A	N

In 1951 the UIL dropped City and added 1A, and B classification

1951	1A	N	1952	1A	N	1953	1A	N
	2A	N		2A	N		2A	N
	B	N		B	N		B	N
1954	1A	Stamford
	2A	Amarillo
	B	N
1955	1A	N
	2A	N
	B	N

1956	1A	N
	2A	N
	B	Ranger
1957	1A	N
	2A	N
	B	N
1958	1A	Shamrock
	2A	N
	B	N

In 1959 the UIL added 3A and 4A

1959	1A	N
	2A	N
	3A	N
	4A	N
	B	N
1960	1A	N
	2A	N
	3A	N
	4A	Andrews
	B	N

1961	1A	N	1962	1A	N	1963	1A	N	1964	1A	N
	2A	N		2A	N		2A	N		2A	N
	3A	N		3A	N		3A	N		3A	N
	4A	N		4A	N		4A	N		4A	N
	B	N		B	N		B	N		B	N

1965	1A	Memphis	1966	1A	N
	2A	N		2A	N
	3A	N		3A	N
	4A	N		4A	N
	B	Shallowater		B	N
1967	1A	Albany			
	2A	N			
	3A	N			
	4A	N			
	B	N			
1968	1A	McLean			
	2A	N			
	3A	N			
	4A	N			
	B	N			
1969	1A	N	1970	1A	N
	2A	N		2A	N
	3A	N		3A	N
	4A	N		4A	N
	B	Bronte		B	N
1971	1A	N			
	2A	N			
	3A	N			
	4A	N			

	B	Anton
1972	1A	N
	2A	N
	3A	Sweetwater
	4A	N
	B	Forsan

In 1973 the UIL added Girl's golf

Girls golf started with two divisions A and B

Boys			Girls		
1973	1A	N	1973	A	N
	2A	N		B	N
	3A	Sweetwater [2]			
	4A	N			
	B	N			
1974	1A	N	1974	A	N
	2A	N		B	N
	3A	N			
	4A	N			
	B	Booker			

In 1975 the UIL added 1A, 2A, 3A, 4A to the girl's classification

Boys			Girls		
1975	1A	N	1975	1A	Farwell
	2A	N		2A	Spearman
	3A	N		A	N
	4A	San Angelo Central		4A	N
	B	Booker [2]		B	Booker
1976	1A	N	1976	1A	Farwell [2]
	2A	N		2A	N
	3A	N		3A	N
	4A	N		4A	N
	B	N		B	Booker [2]
1977	1A	N	1977	1A	Farwell [3]
	2A	N		2A	N
	3A	N		3A	N
	4A	N		4A	N
	B	N		B	Booker [3]
1978	1A	N	1978	1A	N
	2A	N		2A	N
	3A	N		3A	N
	4A	N		4A	N
	B	N		B	N
1979	1A	N	1979	1A	N
	2A	N		2A	N
	3A	N		3A	N
	4A	N		4A	N
	B	N		B	N
1980	1A	N	1980	1A	Farwell [4]
	2A	N		2A	N
	3A	N		3A	N
	4A	N		4A	N
	B	N		B	Booker [4]

In 1981 the UIL dropped class B and added Class 5A

Year	Class	School	Year	Class	School
1981	1A	N	1981	1A	N
	2A	N		2A	N
	3A	N		3A	N
	4A	N		4A	N
	5A	N		5A	N
1982	1A	N	1982	1A	N
	2A	N		2A	N
	3A	N		3A	N
	4A	N		4A	N
	5A	Abilene Cooper		5A	N
1983	1A	N	1983	1A	Sundown
	2A	N		2A	N
	3A	N		3A	N
	4A	N		4A	N
	5A	Abilene Cooper [2]		5A	N
1984	1A	N	1984	1A	N
	2A	N		2A	N
	3A	N		3A	N
	4A	Pampa		4A	Mineral Wells
1985	1A	N	1985	1A	N
	2A	N		2A	N
	3A	N		3A	N
	4A	N		4A	N
	5A	N		5A	N
1986	1A	N	1986	1A	Booker [5]
	2A	Stanton		2A	N
	3A	N		3A	N
	4A	N		4A	Snyder
	5A	N		5A	N
1987	1A	N	1987	1A	Booker [6]
	2A	N		2A	N
	3A	Abilene Wylie		3A	N
	4A	Andrews [2]		4A	Andrews
	5A	N		5A	N
1988	1A	Baird	1988	1A	Booker [7]
	2A	N		2A	N
	3A	N		3A	N
	4A	N		4A	N
	5A	N		5A	N
1989	1A	Baird [2]	1989	1A	Booker [8]
	2A	N		2A	N
	3A	N		3A	N
	4A	N		4A	Andrews [2]
	5A	N		5A	N
1990	1A	Robert Lee	1990	1A	Booker [9]
	2A	N		2A	N
	3A	N		3A	N
	4A	N		4A	Andrews [3]

	5A	N		5A	N
1991	1A	Robert Lee [2]	1991	1A	Booker [10]
	2A	N		2A	N
	3A	N		3A	N
	4A	N		4A	Andrews [4]
	5A	N		5A	N
1992	1A	Robert Lee 3]	1992	1A	Booker [11]
	2A	N		2A	N
	3A	Abilene Wylie [2[		3A	N
	4A	N		4A	N
	5A	N		5A	N
1993	1A	Booker [3]	1993	1A	Booker [12]
	2A	Cisco		2A	N
	3A	Graham		3A	N
	4A	N		4A	N
	5A	N		5A	N
1994	1A	Baird [3]	1994	1A	Robert Lee
	2A	N		2A	N
	3A	N		3A	N
	4A	N		4A	N
	5A	N		5A	San Angelo Central
1995	1A	Booker [4]	1995	1A	Wheeler
	2A	Memphis [2]		2A	N
	3A	N		3A	N
	4A	N		4A	N
	5A	N		5A	N
1996	1A	Booker [5]	1996	1A	Wheeler [2]
	2A	Baird [4]		2A	Post
	3A	N		3A	N
	4A	N		4A	Andrews [5]
	5A	N		5A	N
1997	1A	N	1997	1A	Baird
	2A	N		2A	N
	3A	N		3A	N
	4A	N		4A	Snyder [2]
	5A	N		5A	N
1998	1A	Shamrock [2]	1998	1A	Baird [2]
	2A	N		2A	N
	3A	N		3A	N
	4A	N		4A	N
	5A	N		5A	N
1999	1A	Sterling City	1999	1A	Baird [3]
	2A	N		2A	N
	3A	N		3A	Lamesa
	4A	Andrews [4]		4A	N
	5A	N		5A	N
2000	1A	Wheeler 2000		1A	Baird [4]
	2A	N		2A	N
	3A	N		3A	Breckenridge
	4A	N		4A	N

		Left			Right
	5A	Lubbock Coronado		5A	N
2001	1A	Wheeler [2]	2001	1A	Baird [5]
	2A	N		2A	N
	3A	Sweetwater [2]		3A	N
	4A	N		4A	N
	5A			5A	N
2002	1A	N	2002	1A	Baird [6]
	2A	N		2A	N
	3A	N		3A	Breckenridge [6]
	4A	N		4A	N
	5A	N		5A	N
2003	1A	Memphis [3]	2003	1A	N
	2A	N		2A	N
	3A	Snyder		3A	Snyder [3]
	4A	N		4A	N
	5A	N		5A	N
2004	1A	N	2004	1A	Baird [7]
	2A	N		2A	N
	3A	Slaton		3A	N
	4A	N		4A	N
	5A	N		5A	N
2005	1A	N	2005	1A	Baird [8]
	2A	N		2A	N
	3A	N		3A	Snyder [4]
	4A	N		4A	N
	5A	N		5A	N
2006	1A	N	2006	1A	Shamrock
	2A	N		2A	N
	3A	N		3A	Snyder [5]
	4A	N		4A	N
	5A	N		5A	N
2007	1A	N	2007	1A	Memphis
	2A	N		2A	Wall
	3A	N		3A	Andrews [6]
	4A	N		4A	N
	5A	N		5A	N
2008	1A	Robert Lee [4]	2008	1A	N
	2A	N		2A	Wall [2]
	3A	Graham [2]		3A	Andrews [7]
	4A	N		4A	N
	5A	N		5A	N
2009	1A	Robert Lee [5]	2009	1A	Baird [9]
	2A	N		2A	Wall [3]
	3A	N		3A	N
	4A	N		4A	N
	5A	N		4A	N
2010	1A	Robert Lee [6]	2010	1A	Baird [10]
	2A	N		2A	N
	3A	N		3A	N
	4A	N		4A	N

Year	Class	Champion	Year	Class	Champion
	5A	N		5A	N
2011	1A	Robert Lee [7]	2011	1A	Baird [11]
	2A	Wall		2A	Tuscola Jim Ned
	3A	N		3A	Andrews [8]
	4A	N		4A	N
	5A	N		5A	N
2012	1A	N	2012	1A	Memphis [2]
	2A	N		2A	N
	3A	N		3A	Andrews [9]
	4A	N		4A	N
	5A	N		5A	N
2013	1A	N	2013	1A	Memphis [3]
	2A	N		2A	N
	3A	Andrews [5]			
	3A	Andrews [10]			
	4A	N		4A	N
	5A	N		5A	N
2014	1A	N	2014	1A	N
	2A	N		2A	N
	3A	Andrews [6]		3A	Andrews [11]
	4A	N		4A	N
	5A	N		5A	N

In 2015 the UIL added 6A classification

Year	Class	Champion	Year	Class	Champion
	1A	N		1A	N
	2A	N		2A	Memphis [4]
	3A	N		3A	N
	4A	N		4A	Andrews [12]
	5A	N		5A	N
	6A	N		6A	N
2016	1A	N	2016	1A	N
	2A	N		2A	Wellington
	3A	N		3A	N
	4A	N		4A	N
	5A	N		5A	N
	6A	N		6A	N
2017	1A	Happy	2017	1A	N
	2A	N		2A	Memphis [5]
	3A	N		3A	N
	4A	N		4A	Andrews [13]
	5A	N		5A	N
	6A	N		6A	N
2018	1A	Garden City	2018	1A	N
	2A	N		2A	N
	3A	N		3A	N
	4A	N		4A	Andrews [14]
	5A	N		5A	N
	6A	N		6A	N

Summary of Boys golf [State Champs] for the last 69 years from the Panhandle/Plains region.

Large Schools		Small Schools	
Andrews	6	Robert Lee	7
Sweetwater	1	Booker	5
Lubbock Coronado	1	Baird	4
Amarillo	1	Memphis	3
Snyder	1	Shamrock	2
San Angelo Central	1	Wheeler	2
Abilene Cooper	1	Stamford	1
Pampa	1	Ranger	1
Abilene Wylie	1	Shallowater	1
Graham	1	Mclean	1
		Bronte	1
		Anton	1
		Forsan	1
		Stanton	1
		Cisco	1
		Sterling City	1
		Garden City	1
		Slaton	1
		Wall	1
		Happy	1

Summary of Girl's golf [State Champs] the last 45 years in the Panhandle/Plains region

Large Schools		Small Schools	
Andrews	6	Robert Lee	7
Andrews	14	Booker	12
Snyder	5	Baird	11
Breckenridge	2	Memphis	5
Mineral Wells	1	Farwell	4
Lamesa	1		
San Angelo Central	1	Wheeler	2
		Spearman	1
		Sundown	1
		Robert Lee	1
		Tuscola Jim Ned	1
		Shamrock	1
		Post	1
		Wellington	1

LEGENDARY SCHOOLS THAT HAVE WON STATE GOLF CHAMPIONSHIPS

NOTE:

Since the beginning of UIL Girl's golf the Panhandle/Plains region has won 45 state championships in Girl's golf. But what is most impressive is that Girls golf in this region has won the state championship in the lowest classification 31 of 45 years. That means that since the beginning of girls' golf a school from the Panhandle/Plains region has won the State Champions 69% of the time. Any way you look at that statistic it is awesome.

Also, Andrews has won 20 UIL State Golf Championships when you combine both girls and boys golf. Booker has won 17 UIL State Golf Championships and Baird 15 when you combine both girls and boys golf teams. Memphis and Robert Lee each have 8 state championships when you combine both teams.

Somewhere, within these schools someone had a tremendous influence on these golf programs. It just doesn't happen that often without a championship type of influence. I want to recognize these schools, cities, and all the supporters that helped with the tradition that these schools represent every year.

RICKY GUY-CLAUDE/MEMPHIS/RIVER ROAD

Ricky Guy, presently retiring from coaching at River Road is a coach that everyone notices even if they don't know him. He has a huge body about 6'7", and he usually is riding on the back of a golf cart with his players. That is my image of him since I have watched his golf teams compete at the Regional Golf Tournament and the State UIL Golf Championship.

The truth of the matter is that coach Guy was an outstanding basketball player that played at Texas Tech University. After college, he started his coaching career at All Saints, Lubbock, Texas, quickly moved to Lakeview, then to Claude. While at Claude, he was the head Boys' basketball coach but following success there, he took a coaching position at his hometown Memphis, Texas. He was the named the Head Boys basketball coach and head golf coach.

Ricky Guy was an excellent coach and was a strong addition to the staff at Memphis but his ability to relate and build the golf program at Memphis was what divided him from other coaches. His golf teams won 3 state championships at Memphis, 2 on the boy's side and one on the girls' side. But what most people don't know is the fact that his teams were the state runner up 6 times in his career at Memphis.

He was then was named "Coach of the Year" from the Texas Panhandle Sports Hall of Fame in 2004, 2008 and 2011.

Then his career took a nosedive as he discovered he needed a heart transplant. After waiting for two years he finally received a donor for his heart, and he recovered by becoming the Head Basketball coach [517 wins] /Head Golf coach at River Road High School. After 36 years he is retiring from the education world that he has known but not without sadness from himself and others. The Assistant Superintendent at River Road ISD said this about Ricky Guy, "Coach Guy is an inspiration to us all and he will be deeply missed. Educators like Ricky Guy only come around once in a lifetime."

JOHNNY AUSTIN-TASCOSA COUNTY CLUB

High School golf is a sport that requires much training and skill before an athlete can perform any skills in the sport golf. That is why most high school golf athletes spent most of their training time with a professional golf coach. Without a golf course to play regularly and a golf professional to guide and direct high school golf would not be very competitive with good golfers anywhere in the world. Many high school golf coaches do an outstanding job of coaching and working their players to maximize their skill level. But many golf coaches are assigned to coach golf. Although those coaches do everything they can, the golf pro is the expert and high school golfers need that kind of coaching.

Johnny Austin was the professional golf pro at Tascosa Country Club located in Amarillo, Texas. In 1955, Tascosa Country Club opened and hired him and for the next 28 years Johnny Austin made a difference in many young people in the golf arena.

He was a great teacher of the game of golf and his influence on young high school golfers was a blessing to the high school golf coaches in that area.

Also, golf is a game that early participation is critical to success, especially experiencing learning from a professional golf instructor. Another way golf is experienced is by learning from another young college golfer/turned pro using that kind of success as an example to follow. The following are young golfers that had a huge impact on high school golf simply by being who they were on the golf course and by their success on the playing golf.

The following young professional golfers made a huge impact on high school golf

- John Paul Cain-Sweetwater
- Charles Coody-Stamford
- Judy Casey-Abilene
- Bob Estes-Abilene Cooper
- Rex Baxter-Amarillo
- John Farquhar-Amarillo

HIGH SCHOOL GOLF COACHES THAT WILL BE MISSED AND SHOULD NEVER BE FORGOTTEN FOR THEIR CONTRIBUTION TO HIGH SCHOOL GOLF.

Dan McDonald	Wichita Falls
Barry Minke	San Angelo Central
Laverne Weinette	Booker
Ron Pichard	Booker
Mark Burgen	Andrews
Rick Harvey	San Angelo Central
Wade Walker	Amarillo
Todd Handley	Andrews
Ken Hicks	Tascosa

Wrestling

WRESTLING HAS BEEN A PART of the sports program in Panhandle for many years all the way back to 50's but it is a sport that has limited schools that participate in the UIL, particularly schools 3A, 2A, and 1A. With that in mind, we have limited information to write about.

The record books of the UIL State Wrestling schools in 4A, 5A, and 6A are in the UIL web site wrestling archives starting in 1998.

[None] No one from the Panhandle/Plains region qualified

UIL State Wrestling champions from 1998-2017

Boys   **Girls**

UIL Wrestling had only one classification

Year	Boys School	Boys Place	Year	Girls School	Girls Place
1998	Amarillo Tascosa	Champion	1998	Amarillo Caprock Hereford	Runner up 4th
1999	Canyon Randall	3rd	1999	Amarillo Caprock Amarillo Palo Duro	Champion Runner up
2000	Canyon Randall	3rd	2000	Amarillo Caprock Amarillo Palo Duro	Champion Runner up
2001	Canyon Randall	3rd	2001	Amarillo Palo Duro Amarillo Caprock	Champion 4th
2002	Amarillo Tascosa	4th	2002	Amarillo Caprock	Champion
2003	None		2003	Amarillo Caprock	Champion
2004	None Amarillo		2004	Amarillo Caprock Palo Duro	Champion Runner up
2005	Canyon Randall Dumas	Runner up 4th	2005	Amarillo Caprock Amarillo High	Champion 4th
2006	None		2006	Amarillo Caprock	Champion
2007	Canyon Randall	Runner up	2007	Amarillo Caprock	Champion
2008	Canyon Randall	Champion	2008	Amarillo Caprock Amarillo Tascosa	Champion 3rd
2009	Canyon Randall	Champion	2009	Amarillo Caprock Amarillo Tascosa	Champion 3rd
2010	None		2010	Amarillo Caprock	Champion
2011	None		2011	Amarillo Caprock	Champion

2012	None		2012	Amarillo Caprock	Champion
2013	**UIL added 4A and 5A**				
2013	Canyon Randall	4A Champion	2013	None	
2014	None		2014	Amarillo Tascosa	5A Champion
2015	None		2015	None	
2016	None		2016	None	
2017	Dumas	5A Champion	2017	None	

Summary: In the girl's division, Amarillo Caprock dominated the UIL State Wrestling Championships with 13 state winners in 21 years. That means that Caprock girls won the state championship 62% in the 21 years that was recorded in the UIL website for wrestling. No other school in the Panhandle/Plains region can claim that kind of dynasty in any sport. On the boys' side of Wrestling, Canyon Randall made 7 appearances and won the gold twice. Not only that, the city of Amarillo and the schools in Amarillo won 15 of 21 state championships in UIL wrestling. There is no other comparison when it comes to winning state championship city to city or school to school. 71.4% of the time, a school from Amarillo won the state UIL girls wrestling championship. Awesome is the word.

LEGENDS IN WRESTLING THAT WE SHOULD NEVER FORGET

JAMES KILE/JOHNNY COBB-TASCOSA HIGH SCHOOL JAMES KILE

Very few coaches that coach wrestling get much press coverage, but James Kile was different. The main reason is that he was a football and basketball official for 40 years working many colleges and high schools throughout the Panhandle/Plains region. At one time he was the state President of officials for both football and basketball.

James worked the summers as the manager of the Amarillo Country Club swimming pool which led to his being popular with kids and parents. No one would know that he was the state AAU Diving Champion. What made that so impressive was that James had polio in the fifth grade.

Another fact of his importance and his influence he had on the sports world in wrestling was his involvement with the Boys Club of Amarillo.

Coach Kile was an original member of the Maverick Boys Club when it opened in 1936. Then to top that, he was a board member for 28 years. His influence was instrumental in many young boys coming up through the Maverick Boys Club.

He coached wrestling and taught school at Amarillo Tascosa for 35 years. He was the guy everyone leaned on when it came to coaching and teaching wrestling in the Panhandle/Plains region.

James Kile was inducted into the Panhandle Sports "Hall of Fame" and retired from teaching and coaching in 1994.

JOHNNY COBB

Coach Cobb was an outstanding wrestling coach and he became the first ever wrestling coach at Wayland Baptist University. As a wrestling athlete he was a three-time district champion at Tascosa High School in the 60's. As a high school wrestler, he only lost one high school match in the 3 years at Tascosa.

In 1988, Johnny Cobb started his high school coaching the girls' and boys' team at Tascosa. He was at Tascosa from 1990-2008 where he led Tascosa to 3 UIL State Wrestling Championships. If you look at Wrestling in the State of Texas you will see that wrestling in Amarillo was very successful winning several state championships. During Coach Cobb's stay at Tascosa High his wrestlers won 21 individual state titles. One of those went on to the 2000 Olympics and won a gold trophy.

For his successes Johnny was selected twice as the Texas High School "Coach of the Year". He was a member of the Texas Wrestling "Ring of Honor" and the Texas chapter of the National Wrestling "Hall of Fame" in Stillwater, Oklahoma. He was the founding father of the first kid's wrestling program in the Texas Panhandle of Texas at the Maverick Boys Club in 1971. He is a member of the Panhandle Sports "Hall of Fame."

Soccer

HIGH SCHOOL SOCCER WAS ONCE considered a sport that they played in large cities like Dallas, Ft. Worth, Houston, El Paso. That was until the UIL adopted Soccer as a team sport in 1982-83. Soon many schools started high school soccer. The State UIL Soccer championship started in 1982-83 but it wasn't until 1996-97 that a team from the Panhandle/Plains region made the final four at the soccer state tournament.

1996-97	Wichita Falls Rider	4A	Semi-finals

In 1998/99 the UIL added two boy's divisions, 4A and 5A

1999-200	Wichita Falls Rider	5A	Winner
2000-2001	San Angelo Central	5A	Runner up
2002-2003	Wichita Falls Rider	4A	Semi-finals
2005-2006	Wichita Falls Rider	4A	Runner up
2006-2007	Wichita Falls Rider	4A	Winner
2011-2012	Wichita Falls Rider	4A	Runner up

In 2014/15 the UIL added 6A

2016-2017	Wichita Falls High	5A	Semi-finals

It doesn't take a rocket scientist to figure that in soccer Wichita Falls Rider was the dominate soccer team in the Panhandle/Plains region. Also, on the same note, it is very clear that the Panhandle/Plains region was limited in the schools that had success in soccer during the first 20 years that soccer was part of the UIL.

Girls' soccer during the first 20 years in the UIL was very similar to the boys in terms of state tournament appearances.

2007-2008	Wichita Falls Rider	4A	Runner up
2008-2009	Wichita Falls Rider	4A	Semi-finals

WICHITA FALLS RIDER HIGH SCHOOL - LEGENDARY SOCCER PROGRAM

KENNY CATNEY

Coach Catney went to work at Wichita Rider in 1986 as the Head Soccer coach. He is one of five soccer coaches that have over 400 wins in the state of Texas. Kenny Catney was promoted to Athletic Director at the Wichita Falls Rider and is currently the Athletic Director at Frenship Independent School District.

At Wichita Rider he had a won lost record of 402-53-31 along with 17 district championships. His teams qualified for the UIL State Soccer Tournament three times and won the Class 4A championship trophy in 2000.

On November 20, at the annual conference meeting, he was inducted into the Texas Association of Soccer Coaches "Hall of Honor."

Short note:

Nominations for legendary soccer coaches received little attention except Kenny Catney and it is clear to me that he had a strong positive influence in the Wichita Fall Rider soccer program.

Somewhere along the path of coaching someone made a huge difference in soccer at Rider. Winning six UIL State Boys soccer championships and making two state tournament appearances on the girl's side tells you that many people made huge sacrifices in the soccer program at Rider. You don't advance to the state tournament championships without a huge commitment from administration, athletes, students and community support. Personally, I salute **Wichita Falls Rider High School on your accomplishments in the sport of high school soccer.**

Swimming and Diving

IF IT WAS LEFT UP to me, the UIL would have added swimming and diving many years ago because that was my favorite sport. Swimming and Diving is the only UIL sport that the Panhandle/Plains region hasn't won a state championship in both boys and girls.

The UIL started Swimming and Diving in the 1969-1970 school year. Then in 1998-1999 the UIL established two classifications in swimming, 4A and 5A. In the year 2014-2015 the UIL dropped 4A and added 6A.

Since most of the powerhouse swimming teams are from other regions the Panhandle/Plains region is somewhat overlooked by sport writers but there are close to 19 schools from this area that participate in the UIL swimming and diving sport.

At this present time, no school from the Panhandle/Plains region has won the UIL State Team Swimming Championship.

However, two names are mentioned in the same vein as Legends in other sports because of the impact and influence they had on Swimming and Diving.

LEGENDARY COACHES IN SWIMMING/DIVING

BEVERLY BALL-ABILENE HIGH/ COOPER HIGH

If there was ever someone that deserves to be named a legend in a sport, Beverly Ball is at the top of the list. Beverly coached swimming and diving in and around Texas for more than 60 years. She was the swimming/ diving coach at Abilene High School and Abilene Cooper High School for 42 years [1951-1999].

Coach Ball was involved with swimming and promoting swimming from the time she was hired until the time she retired. She was involved in the TISCA organization for 42 years being a part of this organization in every possible way. For her efforts she received the first ever service award for the TISCA. On that same note, she was inducted into the Texas Swimming and Diving "Hall of Fame."

In 1952 she started an age group swimming program and before it was all over, she was inducted into the Big Country "Hall of Fame."

Coach Ball was one of a kind. After retirement from the high school environment, she started the McMurry University Swim team and had success from the start with three division 3 conference championships. She has had success wherever she coached and was the first person to receive the Chuck Moser "Coach of the Year" award. Beverly was born and grew up in Throckmorton, Texas.

DAVID HAGUE-SAN ANGELO CENTRAL

After 41 years of coaching swimming and diving, David Hague is retiring from San Angelo Central High School located in San Angelo, Texas. As the executive director of the National High School Coaches Association said, "David Hague exhibits a strong dedication to supporting and developing his high school student athletes in the classroom and outside of it." He also said, "He has established San Angelo Central as one of the consistent swim programs in Texas."

With that said, David Hague, boy's and girl's swimming and diving coach at San Angelo Central High School was selected by the National High School Coaches Association as its "National High School Boys Swimming Coach of the year."

Coach Hague went out with a bang as both his teams won the district 2-6A championships this year. Winning the district championship with the boy's team was the ninth straight title, giving them a district championship 13 times.

Not to be outdone, the girls swimming and diving team won the district title 10 times out of 13 years. All together David Hague teams won 33 combined district championships and 2 regional championships. He was selected "Coach of the Year" in district 43 combined times. Eight combined times he was selected "Regional Coach of the Year", and in 2016 Coach Hague was named the Texas Class 6A State Boys "Coach of the Year."

Coach Hague has been retired from the coaching duties only one year so my guess he will reap the awards as he enjoys his retirement in his later years.

References

[Allen "bones" simpson]. [2015]. [Obituary concerning legendary basketball coach "bones" simpson]. Texas/Amarillo. Amarillo Globe news

[All-time coaching records]. [2006]. [Football coaching records in Texas ending in 2006]. Texas. TXSWA-all time coaching records

[An unforgettable coach: AHS' jan barker headed to state hall of fame]. [2017] [Information Concerning legendary volleyball coach jan barker]. n/a

[Attending wayland was wilson's best decision]. [Information concerning basketball coach Kathy Wilson and wayland Baptist university]. Texas/Plainview. Wayland Baptist University Website.

Berryman, C.J. [2014]. [Hereford coach's profile: Brenda kitten]. [Information concerning legendary volleyball coach, brenda kitten]. Texas/Hereford. Hereford Brand

[Big country athletic hall of fame]. [2015] [Athletic induction to the big country area for outstanding achievement in athletics]. Texas/Abilene. n/a

[Bobby davis file]. [2002]. [History of bobby davis football coach]. Texas/Lubbock. Lubbock online] ascoallstarclassic.com Lubbock avalanche journal.

Byrd, R. [2011]. Mike Lee: coach: no regrets, save four costly wink losses] Texas/San Angelo. San Angelo Standard Times.

[Bobcat athletic hall of fame]. [2012-2018]. [San Angelo Central High School athletic hall of fame] Texas/San Angelo. n/a

Brown, T. [[2011]. [Lakeview's tony mauldin retires after 37 years]. [Information concerning legendary basketball coach tony mauldin]. ESPNDallas.com

Bryce, C. [2017]. Bobcat athletic hall of fame. [Inductees 2018]. Texas/San Angelo. San Angelo Standard times

Campbell, D. (2017-18). Texas football. [Texas high school football record book]. [Coaching archieves, wins, play-offs, state championships]. Texas. n/a

Carson, P. [Dunbar high school]. [A salute to the old Lubbock dunbar high school, teaches, coaches, and administration]. Texas/Lubbock. Caprock Chronicles.

[Ceremony honors blaine]. [2006]. [Information concerning legendary coach john blaine]. Texas/Dimmitt. The Castro County News.

Clarkson, R. [2006]. [Amarillo national bank coach of the year: eddie Metcalf, Stratford football]. Texas/Amarillo. Amarillo Globe News

[Clifton mcneely]. [2003]. [Obituary about the legendary coach clifton mcneely]. Texas/Dallas Dallas morning news.

[Coach Nita Vannoy]. [2018]. [Information concerning legendary volleyball coach nita vannoy].

Texas/San Angelo. n/a. Web site of Central high school, San Angelo, Texas.

Cox, C. [[2013]. [Scots baseball coach oliver also announces retirement] [Information concerning Legendary baseball coach fred oliver] Texas/Dallas. Park Cities People

[Find a grave]. [2015]. [Obituary of James Marvin "jim" wilcoxson]. Texas/Amarillo. Boxwell Brothers funeral directors.

[Find a grave]. [1993]. [Obituary of kenneth wayne cleveland]. Texas/Wellington. The wellington leader.

[Four coaches leave their mark on mustang football] [Town talk radio 'the voice of west Texas" providing Information about four coaches that coached football at Denver city, Texas]. Texas/Brownfield. Towntalk Media productions.

[Girls' basketball league]. [n.d.]. [Short history about girls' basketball before the uil starting in 1938]. Heartoftexas tales.com.

Giles, L. [1999] [2017]. [Walker never had a losing year.] [Winningest football coach in Texas]. Texas/Amarillo. Amarillo Globe news.

Gove, C. [1999] [Four area teams rise above the crowd-combination of good players, coaches is the Key]. Texas/Amarillo. Amarillo.com-Amarillo Globe-News.

Gove, C. [1999]. [Hamrick resigns at canyon to take Athens coaching post]. Texas/ Amarillo. Amarillo Globe news

Haynes, M., Wohlfarth, D. [2008] Pride of the Plains. [50 years of the Panhandle Sports Hal of Fame] Copywrite 2018, Texas/Amarillo. Cenveo printing.

Hofeditz, J. [2017]. [Larry Wartes coached more than football]. [Larry Wartes]. Texas/ Abilene/Amarillo. Abilene reporter news. Amarillo globe news.

[Former borger coach to be inducted into texas high school basketball hall of fame]. [2017. Texas/Borger. Borger News-Herald

[Jerry Joe Blakely]. [2014]. [obituary for Jerry don blakely]. Texas/Amarillo. Lubbock avalanche journal. [Johnny Simmons, tennis teaching pro]. [2017]. [Wichita falls teaching pro makes a difference in young players coming up to the high school level]. Texas/Wichita Falls. Times record news

Jones, T. [2017]. [Former vista ridge coach mike martin to be posthumously inducted into the Texas girls coaches association]. Texas/Austin. Statesman.

Keegan, T. [2015]. [Brandon's father is coach schneider]. [Information concerning brandon schneider and his legendary father bob schneider]. Kansas/ KUsports. com.

Lahnert, L. [2013]. [Ex-wt standout, ahs coach dale blaut headed to sports shrine] [Information concerning legendary basketball player and coach, dale blaut]. Texas/Amarillo. Amarillo Globe news.

Lahnert, L. [1999]. [Hale resigns pampa basketball job, takes post in weatherford]. Texas/Amarillo. Amarillo Globe News.

LeRoy, O. [2015]. [Coaches surprised at warren's retirement announcement]. [Information about Football coach Steve Warren]. Texas/Midland. Midland Reporter News

[LG Wilson] [2001] [Obituary Search] Texas/Lubbock. Lubbock online.com

Lindrren, S. [2016]. [Lake view tennis complex dedicated to legend brandon clark]. Texas/San Angelo. [sangengelolive.com]

[Local sports briefly]. [2014]. [Memorial tribute to legendary basketball coach ted whillock].

Lubbock/Texas. Lubbock Avalanche-Journal [lubbockonline.com]

[Lubbock Independent School District hall of fame]. [2011-2018] [Athletes from Lubbock isd selected to Lubbock hall of fame from 2011-2018]. Texas/Lubbock. n/a

[O.W. Follis]. [2009]. [Obituary concerning legendary basketball coach o.w. follis] Texas/Lubbock. Lubbock.online.com

[Panhandle sports hall of fame]. 1959-2019. [Texas sports hall of fame members that impacted sports in the panhandle]. Texas/Amarillo. n/a

[P.E. Shotwell]. [Historical information about pete shotwell]. Wikipedia, the free encyclopedia [Rider raiders baseball hall of fame]. [2018]. Texas/Wichita Falls. n/a

Rosetta, R. [2000]. [Ritchey enters hall of honor]. Texas/Lubbock. [Information concerning tom ritchey entering the hall of honor]. [Lubbock online] Lubbock Avalanche Journal.

[Sherwood award winner]. [2017]. [West Texas football classic coaching information about don cumpton]. Texas/Lubbock. 2017 all-star classic.

[Sherwood award winner]. [2016] [West Texas football classic coaching information about butch Henderson]. Texas/Lubbock. Ascocallstarclassic.com

Silva, C.J. [2017]. [Sports] [Coronado's dean lived dream before retiring from coaching, teaching]. Texas/Lubbock. Lubbock Avalanche-Journal [lubbockonline.com]

Simmons, B. [2009]. [Coaching great Charlie johnson among southeastern university athletic hall of fame]. Oklahoma/Durant. Durant Daily Democrat.

[Snyder athletic hall of honor]. 2004-2018. [Snyder high school athletic hall of honor inductees from 1910-2019]. Texas/Snyder. n/a

Springer, B. [2017-18]. [Texas basketball magazine]. Texas coaching records. Texas/ Houston n/a

Terrigno, P. [Q&A with members of levelland's 1952 state semifinal boys' basketball team]. Texas/Lubbock. Avalanche Journal [lubbockonline.com]

[Texas association of basketball coaches web site.] [2018-19] [Texas association of basketball past president's bio's and pictures]. Texas. n/a

[Texas association of soccer coaches web site.] [2018-19]. [Texas association of soccer coach's hall of honor]. n/a

[Texas high school baseball coaches' association]. [2018-2019]. [Hall of fame] n/a

[Texas high school coaches association]. [2018-2019] [Texas high school coaches hall of honor.] List of Hall of honor members. Texas/San Marcos. n/a

[Texas girls coaches association]. [2018-19] [Texas girls coaches hall of fame]. Texas. n/a

[The old coach network]. [2017]. [Information concerning Leo Brittian, legendary football coach]. Texas/nd. www.theoldcoach.net. www.timesrecord.com. thscabuyersguide.com. www.zoominfo.ccom.

[Uil, athletic state champions archives]. [1910-2019] [The university interscholastic league web site]. University of Texas at Austin. Texas/Austin. n/a

[Uil basketball state championship magazine]. [2017-18-19]. [Coaching wins, boys' basketball state champions, team information, most state tournament appearances, most state champions, state championships records, winning percentages]. Texas/San Antonio. n/a

[Wayland Baptist university web site]. [2018]. [Athletic sports hall of honor]. n/a

[Wayland Baptist university web site. [Melynn hunt, assistant athletic director at Lubbock isd, assistant women's basketball coach] n/a

Walker, J. [2000]. [Warbird's churck moser was more than winning coach]. [Information about Chuck walker as a football coach]. Texas/Abilene. Reporter - News

Watson, G. [[2005]. [Sam tipton sees bright future for girls' athletics] [Information concerning Legendary coach wayne tipton is provided in this story]. Texas/Lubbock. Lubbock Avalanche Journal [lubbockonline.com]

Welps. [2019]. [Retiring coach Guy will be deeply missed by River Road community]. Texas/Amarillo. Amarillo globe news

[Whatever happened to coach dean weese?]. [2002-updated 2004]. [Information concerning the Legendary girls' basketball coach dean weese]. n/a

Wilbanks, B. Dr. [update: 2013] [Texas high school basketball state champions]. [[review of the uil state boys' basketball tournament starting in 1921]. Texas/Austin.

Williams, D. [2006]. [Coaches gather to honor Sherwood]. [Information about greg Sherwood being Inducted into the Texas high school hall of fame]. Texas/Lubbock. [Lubbock Online]. Lubbock Avalanche journal.

Williams, D. [2018]. [Don black, defensive architect of frenship playoff teams, dies unexpectedly].

Texas/Lubbock. Lubbock avalanche journal. [lubbockonline]

Winkle, I. [2017]. [Beloved basketball coach dies] [Obituary and information concerning legendary basketball coach jim reid]. Texas/Ingram. West Kerr Current News.

Zuvanich. A. [2005]. [Eddins taking things easy after long coaching career]. Texas/ Lubbock [Lubbockonline.com] Lubbock Avalanche Journal.

Zuvanich, A. [2011]. [Taylor to coach one last game] [Information concerning johnny taylor, football coach at Idalou, Texas]. Texas/Lubbock. [lubbockonline.com] Lubbock Avalanche Journal.

Zuvanich, A. [[2006]. [After some delays, irlbeck coaches his 1,000 victory]. [Information about legendary basketball coach carl irlbeck]. Texas/Lubbock. Lubbock Avalanche-Journal.

www.ingramcontent.com/pod-product-compliance
Lightning Source LLC
Chambersburg PA
CBHW020719130726
47899CB00011B/535